Goodbye, Goodness

Goodbye, Goodness

a novel by

Sam Brumbaugh

 OPEN CITY BOOKS

New York

Printed in the United States of America

Excerpt from "I Know a Man" by Robert Creeley, from *Collected Poems, 1945-1975*,
copyright © 1983 The Regents of the University of California. Lyrics from "St. Stephen"
by Robert Hunter, copyright © Ice Nine Publishing Company. Used with permission.
Lyrics from "Noble Englishman" by Michael Hurley, copyright © Snocko Music, BMI.

The author wishes to thank the Garst Museum in Greenville, Ohio, for
providing excerpts of "The Story of My Life" by Annie Oakley, 1926.

Portions of this book previously appeared in *The Southwest Review*.

Design by Nick Stone.
Cover art by Jeremy Blake, courtesy of Feigen Contemporary.

Library of Congress Cataloging-in-Publication Data
Brumbaugh, Sam, 1966-
Goodbye, goodness : a novel / by Sam Brumbaugh.

p. cm.

ISBN 1-890447-39-0 (pbk.)

1. Fugitives from justice—Fiction. 2. Motion picture producers and directors—Fiction.
3. Oakley, Annie, 1860-1926—Fiction. 4. Traffic accidents—Fiction. 5. Malibu (Calif.)—
Fiction. 6. Seaside resorts—Fiction. 7. Drug traffic—Fiction. 8. Friendship—Fiction. I.
Title.

PS3602.R837G66 2005
813'.6—dc22   2004027002

OPEN CITY BOOKS
270 Lafayette Street, Suite 1412
New York, NY 10012
www.opencity.org

First Edition
05 06 07 08 09   10 9 8 7 6 5 4 3 2 1

For Galaxy and Rowan

. . . the darkness, I sd, sur-
rounds us, what

can we do against
it, or else, shall we &
why not, buy a goddam big car,

drive, he sd, for
christ's sake, look
out where yr going.

—Robert Creeley

1

I picked myself up off the dirt shoulder and stood in the safety lane of the highway. Glass and pebbles dropped off the underside of my arms. Cars rushed by, a steady whoosh tailed by moans. My head felt heavy, my body a draft of air as I took a step and moved slowly out into the traffic. A sedan screeched to a halt at my hips. I turned, held my hands out, my fingers touching the hood.

I crossed headlights, horns and shouting. A chain-link fence ran along the opposite side of the highway. I climbed the fence, made my way through a ditch full of trash, and up a slope to a concrete path. I crossed the path, stepped over a low wall, and my feet sunk into sand. A moonscape of sand lay ahead, and city lights splashed across the ocean's surface. Dark ridges hooked inward on either side of the ocean, and I could not understand which way was Malibu. There was a lifeguard stand with a yellow sign, and I went up for a closer look, thinking it might be a map. But it was only an ad for a pickup truck. I heard screaming and looked up. The Ferris wheel on the pier had blinked on and was spinning.

I headed the opposite way, up the dark arc of beach. Ahead, like the glowing front of a train I was riding, was Malibu. The air off the water had a salty, gelatinous coolness, and when the wind whipped a certain way there was a faint tang of DDT. The waves rumbled up, crashed, and hissed back through the rocks as the rocks knocked each other around. I walked along the water's edge. The sand was hard. I could walk forever; my legs were like pistons and numbness separated my body from my brain. I did not feel fatigue, only an odd momentum inside. I understood my life had just broken off, and only a few bright miles lay ahead. Squelches came from somewhere out on the water. I could not tell if they were animal or electronic.

The beach narrowed. Ended. I stopped at a chain-link fence. Sailboat masts in rusty disuse poked out above the green mesh. I walked along the fence, up steps to the highway, and continued north along the emergency lane. A steady hum of cars hemmed me in on the right, bathing me in the glow of oncoming headlights. Red lights tore out from behind the cars, and I kept averting my eyes. The ocean and the highway each had their own white noise, blending into one another's like distant rain. The cliffs were dark and bare and loomed close. Occasionally they sloped away into mountains, dotted teasingly with the sparkling lights of houses.

The beach resumed. Ended again at a pier of tumbled boulders.

I climbed the boulders and came back onto the highway. I walked for hours through the night, crisscrossing from highway to beach until light began to shoot out high and pale over the mountains. The day was breaking. My shoes were wet. I stopped, and without sitting down, took them off. I was on a long stretch of wide beach, a small creek cutting across the sand to the sea where a few surfers were already out bobbing in the water. I crossed the creek and came to a fence with a sign:

PRIVATE
NO TRESPASSING

The fence extended out over the surf, but the bottom half had been cut away. I ducked under and came onto

Malibu Colony. The beach houses were hunched closely together on the dunes, their various colors coming to light in the brightening dawn.

Down the beach, two women were speed-walking toward me in tracksuits. I saw the house, the big black windows. The women were getting closer. I had to hurry. With a last burst of energy, I scrambled up the dune toward the house's sea wall. I stepped over the gate and slipped into a patch of palm foliage. I took a last look behind me. White air sifted through the beach's rising darkness, pressing the sand with a pale glow. The speed walkers passed, hips swiveling, awkwardly pumping their arms, and staring at their feet.

I turned and made my way down the narrow, sandy alley beside the house. At the second support pole, I slipped under the house. The sand was cold, and there was the smell of wet wood. I crawled, feeling upward with my hands in the blackness. I found the outline of the panel, pressed hard with both hands, and the wood gave.

I pulled myself up and swung the panel back down into the floorboard. I stood, nearly falling over the pairs of sneakers in the dark closet.

I slid open the closet door and in the gray light I could see the teenager's room was still undisturbed. The thick green rug, the Norwegian black-metal posters mixed up with the glass-framed pictures of Tuscany. The chipped white desk and shelf. The single bed. I was so tired now with the bed right there. I stepped into the room, stood for a moment, and listened. The air was stale and undisturbed. A gray mist filled out the skylight above. My feet were leaden, my legs ached, and up through the rest of my body, I felt nothing. But my head was hardening like a cinder block around my eyes, a diving, roller-coaster pain.

I went into the bathroom, splashed water on my face, cupped my hands, and drank. I looked at myself in the mirror. One eye was black and there was a long, red gash down the side of my neck. The blood had pooled and crusted thickly on my collar. I looked down. In the cracks of the blue counter, there was a white residue, and a clear cellophane top unwound from Leonard's pack of cigarettes rested on the tile. No one had been here. No one had even come to clean. My head throbbed. I took off my shirt. The scab on my neck tore and a line of blood swept down my chest. I brushed it off with tissue and pressed more tissue into the cut. I rinsed my hands and feet in the bath.

I dropped naked into the bed, halfheartedly prettified with thick pillows and a floral quilt. I suspected I had a concussion, but fell immediately into a long and dreamless sleep.

2

I took off from the Raleigh ward early one morning with a mug of coffee and a bag in the backseat. I cut across to Wilmington, and headed down the southern coast's giant swath of asphalt, the endless, ever broadening seam of concrete. Driving through the day and into the night, it began to feel as if the earth underneath would break apart without the highways, as if they were the groundwork, the promise for some new, better landscape not yet materialized.

I passed through clumps of sprawl and lights and malls, through the stillness of the old cities, through soft, fenced hills and flat farmland. At night the darkness was malleable in my eyes, and time on the highway melted away without incident. No one seemed to be in the cars passing by, only the occasional, flickering blue glow of a television screen. No one was under the glow on the side of the road, and when I'd catch a glimpse of the big black Atlantic, there were never lights. People, it seemed, had been swept away.

Driving became long hours of pure aloneness, the stillness inside the car falling into silence. Humming along at seventy miles per hour, there was nothing; a frontier through glass and nothing but maybe an accident to break the natural momentum toward nothing. The road flew by, but inside the car was frozen as a still life, a still life with dashboard, coffee cup, and the arc of the wheel. A still life with passing scenery. But the scenery went by so fast it wasn't noticeable. It might as well have all been the same. The roads were.

The next afternoon I crossed a bridge in Louisiana. I came down off the bridge and stopped at a small town. I walked until I found a restaurant. I ordered a crab-cake sandwich. It was like a wet gray mop. The bayou crab did not have the milkiness, the suppleness of the Chesapeake crab. As a boy, one of the first things I'd learned how to make was crab cakes. My father and I would go to his friend Ray's farm near Centerville. We'd trap dozens of crabs, steam them pink, and pick the meat—long, intricate work with little reward—then mix the crabmeat up with dry mustard, Old Bay, egg, and breadcrumbs. We'd fry them in butter and eat them with lemon and cut up tomatoes. After dinner my father and Ray and their friends would sit around drinking beer and talking in the fading light of the long summer night. There was a minibike, and I would ride for amazing stretches along cornfields, sneaky tributaries, and chain-linked woods; insects snapping off my skin.

I paid, got up, and walked along the old slave cabins backing the big old houses. The alley road was sand, and buckled in disarray where the sand met concrete. A few cabins faced the bay. One had been converted into a market selling newspapers, gum, and trinkets. I bought a postcard and a newspaper. The back of the postcard said the town, at the turn of the century, had been the center of the world for oysters. I crossed the road and sat down to read in the empty square overlooking the bay. The bay smelled of rotting shellfish. The seagulls shrieked and played in the sun.

I drove across Texas. East Texas was like the South with its red dirt and pine trees and sprawl. After I passed through the long suburbs of Fort Worth, the prairie opened up, and the heat in the distance turned the road to water.

The sun set ahead of me. I drove into the night. The moon was in the road, and I drifted down it like a cloud.

On the empty highway near Abilene, an old Roadmaster ripped by, a gray bearded biker in a sleeveless jean jacket, a chunky girl behind him in a red thong bikini. She was passed out, her head flopping backward, her arms loose at her sides. The biker's leather jacket—wrapped around her and tied at the biker's waist—was the only thing keeping her on.

I stayed outside Lubbock in a brand-new Holiday Inn. Chlorine vapors from the indoor pool floated through the halls, and the windows were not openable. The bartender, weary with headaches from the fumes, had propped open the doors of the empty bar with big stones. I had bad dreams and felt sick in the morning.

I came into Tucson a day early. I found a cheap hotel, drank a cup of coffee, and walked the blinding white, empty downtown. There were a few people around from before. In doorways, just standing there. Deeply creased, tan faces, round broken noses, and pinched straw cowboy hats. You could see something in their eyes, a haunted sense of lost authenticity. A few probably did well leading rides on the new dude ranches. Most sat in the old Greyhound station, putting quarters in the little televisions attached to the chairs, and slept a block away at the SRO. The sun they'd spent their lives under was poison now, and you could see the red heat rising from the distant rows of new houses.

I drove out of town to a river. The sky was powder blue and draining to white at the edges. I parked among Winnebagos and colorfully decaled Subarus and Volkswagens shimmering in the desert heat. I made my way down a red canyon. The valley floor was scattered with bent-over clover, sagebrush, and cactus. There was a clearing of soft yellow sand where the river pooled. Young hippies—thin straggly boys and moon-faced girls with beaded Rasta bags—lay out on giant rocks. A few elderly tourists sat on folding chairs at the river's edge. Festive black dogs ran along the water's edge, through blue flowers rising out of the sand. One dog swam against the tide crinkling at the river's center. He was going nowhere. I could not decide whether to sit down, swim, or walk around. I did not want to be with anyone, but I wanted to shake myself. I stood there. The desert was immobilizing. Only the sky moved.

The next evening I drove over to the club. There were flyers with Kimmel's face pasted on the front doors, but the doors were locked. I went around the side of the building, walked up a loading ramp into the main room. A bearded man in a black T-shirt was rolling an amplifier across the stage. Another man moved dials in the sound booth. The room smelled of stale beer and bleach and was dark and empty. Video-game machines blinked and blipped in a corner by the bar. A back door was propped open. There was a small, weed-strewn parking lot. I noticed a large, familiar figure out there, sitting on the hood of a car, hunched over a cigarette. The sun was setting flamboyantly, squeezing its juiced light through the mountain crevices. The fading sunlight met the light from the parking-lot lights overhead, and pressed his skin with a sandy, orange glow. I tried to fit the figure into Kimmel's form. I expected it to be Kimmel. But it wasn't. It was Will.

Will heard my footsteps on the gravel and turned and stared. His eyes had a vandal's glint, and as he smoked, his long face was full of movement, as if it had been broken and then reconstructed. He ran a hand through his roughly parted brown hair and smiled as I came up to him, an easygoing, athletic sort of smile, as if he couldn't wait to hit me on the back and tell a joke. But his mouth was open and trembled slightly, as if withholding a dark reserve, as if he couldn't quite remember how the joke went.

"Hayward," he leaned forward and gave me a hug. He smelled faintly of licorice, and I could feel his heart pounding under his shirt.

I smiled and stepped back. He was dressed in khakis and a surf-shop T-shirt under a browning seersucker jacket. "Where's Kimmel?" I asked.

"Inside. But the bar's not open yet," he said. His face was flush and he was sipping from a plastic cup.

"What's that, then?" I asked.

"Absinthe," he said. "Kimmel has a bottle. He smuggled it back from England inside a rolled-up *Paris Match*." He looked down into the drink. "It must have really cost him. He drizzled a few drops into my cup like it was balsamic vinegar."

"Isn't that stuff legal now?" I asked.

"Not this kind, I don't think."

"How's Kimmel doing?"

Will gave me a long look, as if he hadn't thought about it until I'd asked. "He's all right. His record is doing well in England. And it's doing well here in certain, rarefied urban circles that, unfortunately for Kimmel, don't like to let go of what they know."

"I haven't seen his record anywhere."

"Have you looked?"

"Not really," I said.

"You should buy it," he said, still looking at me.

"You know, Will, last week he left a message about these shows. Before that, I hadn't heard from him in over a year."

"Kimmel can sit quietly for an awfully long time."

"He builds barricades when there's bad news."

"He's a musician," Will said. "He probably believes that's a primary tenet."

"What's that?"

"They don't get back to people. That's just their deal."

"That's not a belief," I said. "It's just a way he's decided to be."

Will flicked his cigarette onto the gravel. He put his cup down on the car hood and lit another. He took a drag and shrugged. "You're on your way to LA?"

I nodded.

"You have a place to stay out there?"

"The production rented me a place."

"I'll be there tomorrow," he said. "There's a conceptual-dance producer I'm doing a thing on. He's staging a ballet based on the life of Charlie Manson." Will shook his head and smiled. "Apparently, he was just trying to put over some obscure little act of theater, but then all these big LA write-ups came in calling the show 'groundbreaking' and a 'genre indictment,' you know, because the ballerinas had armpit hair or whatever . . ."

The last carnival streaks of light were fading over the dark mountains. Will's voice slowed as he looked up at the sky. "But I don't know," he said, his voice trailing away, "it sounds sort of hopeful—all those greasy-haired chicks doing anything for his incarcerated love . . ."

I laughed for the first time in weeks. "Will," I said, "I don't think the ballerinas are actually Manson acolytes."

His eyes had frozen on the sky and he seemed to have lost his train of thought. For a moment, he seemed genuinely mistakenly transfixed. There was something ungainly about Will. Sensually pained, the cracked face of a man with a strained heart. But his body was lean, and he had a lanky enthusiasm. After years of ricocheting freelance through various weeklies and tabloids, he had just recently begun to establish himself with profile pieces for the *New York Times* magazine and a few of the more adventurous monthlies. Back in New York, when Helen and I were still together, Will and I would meet occasionally for a beer. But after a few minutes his pager would usually buzz, and he'd get right up and be gone, leaving everything we were drinking and everything we were talking about half finished. Will had a big, klutzy spirit, worked hard, and seemed on his way to bigger and better things. He didn't know what things he wanted to connect to yet—he was still freelance, whatever that means in terms of connecting, but I always felt a kind of desperate ambition emanating from him.

"I told Kimmel about the ballet," Will said. "He said he hoped they were using some of Manson's music. He said Manson actually wrote good songs, but then all those groupie sluts Manson gave to the Beach Boys and all the other showbiz types, well, they were just raging with venereal diseases. So, you know . . . he never got offered a record deal."

"That's Kimmel's big take on Manson? As a songwriter?"

"Manson would never have bothered to kill all those people if he had an album to turn in to Warner Brothers. Cat Stevens would never have killed all those people."

"Cat Stevens?"

"I'm just saying, singer-songwriters don't kill people, okay?"

"Didn't Cat Stevens want to kill Salman Rushdie?"

"Not directly," Will said. "Anyway, look, the point is about Manson, and Manson's become sort of pointless. It's like Che, or Frida Kahlo. There's very little left to say about those people. That's why they are always on postcards."

"So why write about him?"

"Because this producer has finally—although probably inadvertently—found a way of dispensing with Manson,"

Will said. "You reduce him down to a ballet? It kind of drains the menace."

Will slid off the hood and stood up. He looked around. The sky had grayed and the air was suddenly cool. He gave me a long look. "You sure you're okay for LA? You can stay at my hotel. I got a suite."

"I'm okay."

"All expensed . . . "

"It's okay."

"So you finally left Helen?"

I nodded.

"Last time I saw her, her eyes were like a girls' school."

"What do you mean?"

He picked up his drink off the car hood. He took a last sip and gave a little wince. Then his chest seemed to relax. "I mean small dark windows surrounded by heavy stone. There was a pressure of silence behind them. Like a girls' school."

We went inside, into the main room and back around the little stage. There was equipment—drum cases, amps, and lights—lined up against the wall. A door behind the stage led to steps. We went down the steps. A woman yelled, and Will, behind me, turned around and stopped.

I continued down a cement-floor hallway. There was a small room at the end. I stopped, and stood at the door.

Kimmel was sitting in an office chair, alone in what looked like a janitor's office. His guitar case was propped against a rusty, broken boiler taking up half the floor.

"How are you, Kimmel?" I said.

He looked up, raised his eyebrows—seemed about to say something, but then just gave me a smile. He was leaning back in the chair with his legs crossed, staring at me with a glassine-like curiosity as if I'd just been dropped out of the blue by a helicopter. His eyes looked tired, and did not get up. He had gotten so thin, and with his thinness his features had sharpened and there was a bruised handsomeness under his cheekbones.

"It's not really a very loaded question," I said.

"No," he said, "no, it's not." He wore Top-Siders, jeans, and a chocolate-brown sweater over a green shirt. His black hair was a motley and thick bowl, and there was coolness to his face, a kind of deadpan silence difficult to bridge.

I stepped in and looked around the room. Band stickers and graffiti covered the wall. *Arizona rules no one.* A bowl of ice, bottles of water, and a stack of plastic cups rested on a folding table. There was a burnt, dry languorous odor, and underneath a pressing smell of mildew. "Nice room," I said.

"Will couldn't take it down here. He went off hours ago to demand a better room," Kimmel said with a shrug. He had a slightly bent, aquiline nose and his voice seemed to take its time getting across the small room. "I've been sitting here since. You're the first person to come in."

"You don't seem surprised."

"To see you?" His coal eyes jumped back with a hint of mockery, but he was smiling. "I've seen enough of you over the years so that it's never a surprise."

"I'm not here to surprise you."

"It's good that you never do. It's a compliment."

He stood and crossed the room to the table. He walked by me so slowly, with a slightly rigor mortis stoop, as if his whole body had begun to slacken, as if his insides, his desires, were slowly constricting. He'd lost much of the youthful hardness in his chest and arms. There was still hardness there, but it was only like a coating. He took a bottle of water and sat back down. He looked worn out. I had a feeling something had gone wrong with a woman. But he never talked about women. Except once in college, he'd told me he wanted a wife who would cook and sit with him at night by the fire while he read his history texts or played his guitar. Knit, poke the embers, bring him tea or whiskey, tobacco for his pipe. It was the easiest desire—his boarding school, Anglophobic sort of ever-removed love. But his desires that way were never really understandable to me.

Voices and footsteps came echoing down the hall. Kimmel and I both looked to the door as Will appeared, followed by a pretty half-Mexican girl holding a clipboard. She was short, in a wool miniskirt and black stockings and boots. She was young—in college probably—with a serious and unreadable mask of a brown face. In contrast, her hair was in pigtails and she was wearing a green and white Newport cigarette T-shirt. *Alive With Pleasure*.

Will glanced quickly around the dank room. "Wait," he said, staring at her, "I need a pass for *this*?"

"All the upstairs rooms are taken," she said. "The headliners have a horn section."

"You really couldn't find anything better?"

She gestured with her clipboard toward Will, but she was looking at Kimmel—her bright black eyes set deeply in her round face. "Okay?"

Kimmel looked sharply at her. "What do you mean, 'okay'?"

"I'm hospitality."

"How did you get past the checkpoint?"

"Checkpoint?" she said, looking around. "There's no checkpoint. What are you talking about? I work here. I'm the checkpoint. I'm hospitality."

"Then you should leave."

"Why would you want me to leave?" she said, unruffled. "I'm here to ask you if you need anything."

"We need beer," Will answered.

"You need passes," she said to Will. "Like I told you before you barged past me, Kimmel needs to put you down for passes."

"Okay," Will nodded slowly, "we'll agree to passes."

"Wait," she looked at Kimmel, "is he your manager or something?"

Kimmel shook his head. "Look at this room, does it look like I have a manager?"

"But if you want a good solid show," Will went on, still nodding, "Kimmel needs beer, and a bottle of top-shelf Russian vodka."

She stared at Will for a moment, looked back at Kimmel. "You don't draw well enough for top shelf."

"You should leave," Kimmel said to her, "because this room you've put me in is completely inhospitable and a disgrace."

"But you came right into this room and sat down and haven't left," she said. "You've been here since you got here."

He stared at her. "And nobody has offered me anything. Not a thing. I have a rider, you know."

"I have not seen a rider."

"Well, it should have been forwarded. One thermos of coffee—real milk, no packets. One cheese sandwich. One bag of sour balls."

"Sour balls?"

"For my throat. Now, please, fulfill the rider."

She shook her head. "I'll see what's around. Are you soundchecking?"

"You'll have to ask Burt," Kimmel said.

"Who is Burt?" she said, glancing at me.

"Burt's my drummer."

"Where is he?"

"He's not here."

"So," she said, "you're not checking?"

"You'll have to ask Burt."

She shook her head. "Is there anything else I don't need to hear?"

"Please," Will said, "we'd like some vodka."

She hesitated at the door. "We'll see," she said as she left.

Will turned abruptly around to face Kimmel. "She's in charge of the alcohol, you idiot."

"Go get it somewhere else then."

"Open up that bottle of absinthe," Will said impatiently. "I know you've squirreled it away somewhere."

"It's not really for you, Will," Kimmel said without inflection, glancing at me. "You already have too much of whatever you have in you for that stuff to be worth it."

Will, in an instant, was standing over Kimmel. "You are always this clever little fucker who seems right about everything you say. At least when you say it. But anybody could easily be more right about anything you say, if they really thought about it."

He hung over Kimmel for a long moment, then he turned and walked over to the door. He looked down the hallway. "She's not coming back," he shook his head. "No way."

He looked back at Kimmel, his eyes narrowing. "You know what your problem is?"

Kimmel shrugged.

"With a stranger, you have no instinct of loyalty." Will said. "I mean, you just don't know how to greet people."

"I didn't greet her."

"But you should have."

"It's not complicated like that, Will."

"What is it then?"

"I get nervous before I play and people, in places where I'm playing, expect conversations I don't want to give them."

"What? A polite exchange?" Will said, leaning over Kimmel again. "I really feel for you. I mean, there's so much work to a greeting—why should you have to master the obligation of a cliché or two?"

Will turned and looked around the room, shifting uncomfortably, as if aggravated by some forever bobbing, internal discord. He seemed to swallow against it. His gaze settled back on Kimmel. His eyes hardened and his jaw jerked out slightly, as if he suddenly sensed vulnerability. Against his own momentum, he turned and walked out of the room.

Kimmel, after a long moment, swiveled in the office chair and stood up. He looked at me. "Let's have a drink," he said with a nervous brightness.

He went over to his bag and dug out the absinthe. He set up the bottle and the plastic cups on the table and with a quick acuity, his hands rising and falling as if attached to strings, mixed in ice and sugar and water. His fingers were long, stiff, and delicate like wineglass stems.

He handed me a cup and tipped his toward me. "You made it," he said, gripping and holding onto my hand with sudden, genuine relief at my company.

The sugar was grainy on the ice and the liquor had gone from green to white. It was good—a quick warming sensation—and I found myself staring at Kimmel. Sharing this absinthe with Kimmel, Kimmel excluding Will—it was a boarding-school level maneuver, as if there had to be exclusion for anything to have any meaning. No wonder Will had walked out. But I could never understand what there was between them; a faith in an incident, or a blood-vow silence over some mishap. There was a secret there. Highly regarded or shameful, I could not tell. Kimmel and I had been room-mates in college. But Kimmel and Will had been roommates at boarding school, and that meant more, and that also meant there were places I would never go with either of them. Smooth, well-carved places they were silent about. A place where they hid, a place they idealized but that stalled them, and where I did not want to go. I'd always assumed it was about boarding school. (They still—almost accidentally, but not quite—dropped corny old nicknames for each other from back then, and their first names seemed expendable and their last names, or Will's at least, often hung for a moment at introductions. Kimmel's last name was French, his first name a mystery, and the name he went by was a boarding-school abbreviation of his mother's last name.) Whenever their boarding school came up, even after all this time, a casual, smirking gloss would flash across their faces. And I'd sense the briefest moment of confusion, of linger-ing regret. A moment when they actually believed life would never be better. *The Glide of the Scull, The Speed Across the Water, The Perfect Rhythm*, these were the phrases on the back of the crew T-shirts Will had won way back then. He jogged in those shirts now, but they were wearing thin and his shoulders were cutting through the backs. Will had been a great rower, and at their school, with a self-aware, hyper snobbery, it had been the rowers, and not the football play-ers, who had been seen as the heroes. And they were told their heroes there would be the heroes everywhere. The world—or the East Coast at least, would unfold itself for them to walk on. Presidents had come through there row-ing. But the world was no longer bothering to accommo-date. They came out and no one they knew was in charge anymore. They came out and no one cared. If anybody had heard of the school, it was usually for reasons assigned to a previous century. And it became a time in Will and

Kimmel's life they carried around behind them like a dead weight. Like a debt. The more they went without being able to let it go, to just simply let their time there exist like every other part of their past, the more a drag it became, and the more the antagonism rose up between them.

But most of Will's crew T-shirts were long ago covered with stains and loaned out or lost. He had an unself-conscious air of reckless disregard about him, and he *was* loyal. He would go anywhere with Kimmel because they'd once been roommates in the red brick and snow. But Kimmel seemed caught between going too far, drolly flattening his vowels at people, or becoming painfully rutted and not talking at all. Will had learned a conversational ease in most walks of life, and while he could get extremely agitated extremely quickly, he also had some deeply ingrained sense of last-second limits. He had shaken off much of the stiff sanctity of his privileged youth. Kimmel had only converted it into a musician's icy disdain.

Kimmel was shorter than Will. He'd played on the same junior-varsity hockey line with Will at their boarding school. He had a low, sinewy center of gravity and a fluid drive that must have got him down the ice. But Will had moved on to a varsity line and by the time I'd met Kimmel in college, he'd already turned his graceful hands to the guitar, studied all the time, and ceased to compete or even exercise.

When Kimmel was still a teenager, his stepmother and her new husband had taken over the Beacon Street house he'd grown up in. He was only allowed to stay there when she was there. Consequently, he never did. He took a few of his father's things, and never went back. In the immediate years after college, he tried and failed at a number of small time office jobs. And service jobs—with his unique inability to fake politeness—were out of the question. He mostly traveled about with his guitar and without any money, Will often having to pay his way. One year he wound up having to live with Will in Baltimore. Will was working at the *Sun*, and didn't mind in the least. But the dependency seemed to strain and embarrass Kimmel. And as he moved through his twenties, playing his guitar and not really doing much of anything, he'd taken on an increasingly groundless and brittle encumbrance, and seemed to be falling further behind Will, struggling through a dark frustration to keep up. And now, even though Kimmel was finally having some success, I worried for him. When Will and I were kids, before Will had gone off to boarding school and met Kimmel, Will and I had briefly known each other. Will's best friend at the time had been a kid named Wendell Blow, and their disastrous relationship had an astonishingly similar tension to Will's friendship with Kimmel.

In the fall of 1980, Will, Wendell Blow, and I all arrived at the same middle school. A private Episcopalian school in Washington, D.C. Its address was a mountain, disputably the highest spot in the city (it was still the Cold War and the new Russian consulate across the street made the same claim). Nuclear air-strike sirens would go off every other Friday at noon, and there was a cathedral between our school and the girls' school. One morning in chapel, our prematurely gray chaplain—he'd got his feet wet in the sixties and still looked concerned about it—brought up with a cautious reverence the surprising fact that our school was named after a saint who had been de-sainted.

"Well, what is he," Will yelled out, "now that he's not a saint on earth?"

"Yeah, what is he then?" Wendell Blow, sitting next to him, yelled accusingly.

"A saint of air?" Will persisted. "I mean, was he ever even a person?"

The chaplain pressed down the air with his hands like he was closing a box.

After chapel, as I pulled books out of my little green locker, Will came up and poked a finger in my chest (I'd got up my nerve that morning, and stuck my "The Jam" pin on the lapel of my blue blazer). Will ripped off the pin and handed it to Wendell Blow. Wendell threw it the trash.

"Do you believe in God?" Will asked.

I looked at him.

"Fuck," he glanced at Wendell, and then back at me. "He doesn't even know."

"I know," I said.

"Can you play guitar?"

"Yes," I lied without hesitating.

Will turned and looked at Wendell. Wendell gave me long, scornful look. He announced I was going to play rhythm guitar in S.O.A, and he ordered me to throw away my Jam records and whatever crucifixes I had lying around.

Will was apparently also in S.O.A. Will was one of the biggest guys in our class, and the best wrestler. A "Special Beat Service" pin was on the lapel of his black blazer (this seemed unfair when I considered my Jam pin in the trash), and there was breakfast food in his thick braces and all over his tie.

"What's S.O.A?" I asked.

"S.O.A," Wendell stated dramatically, "stands for Stiff on Arrival."

Wendell wore a cheap black blazer and had stiff white hair like Billy Idol. He wore a Dead Kennedys pin. No punk slouching there, as there was a Kennedy kid in the class ahead of us.

Will poked me in the chest again. "How'd your mother die?" He asked with marked skepticism.

"Oh man, she drowned," Wendell said.

"She fell into the river," Will added hopefully.

I just shook my head. It was embarrassing at that age to have a dead parent, especially when it had been such a mundane occurrence as a car accident. And I was embarrassed it had happened before I had any memory of her.

"You know," Wendell said, stepping up to me.

"He doesn't say much," Will said, "but he knows."

Will and Wendell turned and walked away down the hallway, both doing their best Sid Vicious bob. They were a hard duo to crack. They both had parents that had died too, and rumor was they sniffed glue. Wendell had famously written a poem about it in English class called "To the Bottle I Bow."

But even at that young age, they both had a dismissive, slapdash elegance, a rangy allure, and a sure-handed sense of wealth underneath the punk shabbiness, years beyond everybody else. Their sort of look and attitude at that school usually meant a quick humiliation and a social free fall. But they were already squirming under the pressures of expectation the rest of us were just beginning to sense, and nobody touched them.

I joined the band.

We practiced two or three times in the drawing room of Will's brick town house on P Street. Nobody was ever around except for a Jamaican maid who'd bring us iced tea and foil-wrapped triangles of English Tiger Milk cheese. Will was a terrible bassist and the only thing I could play were the three intro chords to "Polythene Pam." I'd lean against the wall and strum the chords in different sequences while Will and Wendell leaped around and kicked each other, and Wendell spewed about barricades and cunts. Will was bigger, and really knocked Wendell around. They were best friends, and like good young punk wannabes, they hated each other for it.

Then, out of the blue, Will moved to New York City. His sudden midterm departure was glamorously mysterious. There was a rumor his mom was marrying a famous newspaper reporter and they were moving into John Lennon's building.

After Will had moved, Wendell and I tried once to practice in Wendell's cramped cellar. I came down the musty, cement stairs and before I'd even uncased my guitar, Wendell greeted me by banging out a ramshackle, speed-freak take of "Imagine." The ceiling was so low he'd had to play bent over, but he had an intentionally jerky, clipped way of strumming, and it sounded sort of strange.

He finished, looked up at me. "Hayward," he said politely, "I've written a new song. Want to hear it?"

He bent his scrawny frame back over his guitar, hit the same chord hard about five times and blurted out:

You're out of the band,
You're out of the band,
You're out of the band . . .

I didn't care. It was funny—his first decent song. It was obvious with Will gone we no longer had a place to practice, and anyway, there was no room for a rhythm guitarist in a band called Stiff on Arrival.

In December of that year John Lennon got shot. There was furious television coverage. I watched the television, stunned, as Will emerged from the crowded candlelight vigil outside the Dakota. He crossed behind the on-camera reporter, ducked under the yellow tape, and without a look back at the camera or at the candle-laden faces, walked into the dark mouth entrance of the Dakota. He walked right across where Lennon had just gotten shot, a hockey bag over his shoulder and a big hockey stick wagging in the air behind him.

Wendell was kicked out soon after Will left. He went to a school-without-walls and found a job at Commander Salamander. He got more ragged out and menacing in ripped T-shirts and big black boots, and began to hang out with the other punks in front of the Georgetown Roy Rogers. Occasionally I'd walk by their corner, but he wouldn't acknowledge me.

Except for once. Never looking at me, saying my name while staring down at my Tretorn tennis shoes, Wendell told me S.O.A. were playing that night at an all-ages place off Dupont Circle.

My father was away.

I got my bike and went.

Everybody had big black boots on, and I looked down at my tennis shoes and immediately understood Wendell's invitation. I stood against a brick wall in back of the tiny club because a lot of people had noticed my Tretorns. Wendell stood onstage with a bolt of white hair across his eyes and the sides of his head shaved. He was looking out over the halfhearted, flailing mosh, open-mouthed and glitter-eyed. His arms were spread and his mouth set in a hard pout like a hawk's beak. He saw me in the back—I was sure he did—and his icy, ethereal blue eyes held back an impossible frustration. It made my heart jump with an uneasy flicker of adulthood. I was struck by Wendell at that moment, his porcelain coolness, and underneath, a skewed, youthful rage and a gulping conviction I could never get out. I proceeded to run my high school years into the ground, sitting spaced out in Battery Kimball Park in a faded green army jacket, drinking beer with my black-haired zombie of a girlfriend. She was a bulimic, new-wave sad sack who subsisted on

Dexedrine and Cheetos and occasionally threw them up on me.

Wendell spun so furiously through his next few years, he actually seemed to combust. He quit school, quit S.O.A. (to be replaced by Henry Rollins), and went to London. In London, he disappeared into thin air.

The few times I'd asked, Will had claimed Wendell was running a soft jazz label based in San Francisco. But one night in New York in the mid-nineties, I ran into Wendell's red-haired, stockbroker brother Edward. He was sitting alone, drinking a martini at the Gramercy Park Hotel bar. He said, with a touchingly durable, sad mystification, they'd never found a trace of Wendell.

I was sitting at the table, holding my empty cup of absinthe as if it were screwed into the table's surface. It felt as if hours had passed. Kimmel was looking at me as if he knew I was thinking about him. There was a movement at the door and I looked up. The girl stood at the door, holding her clipboard. Her oval face was placid and she was looking curiously at us. "Half hour," she said, with a wave of her clipboard.

Kimmel turned to the door but she was gone before he could respond. She hadn't brought a thing.

Kimmel kept staring at the door. "I have to go up now," he finally said.

He got up slowly, as if unwinding himself out of the chair. He got his pick and strap, slid the absinthe bottle up into the neck, and closed the case.

I followed him upstairs and out the loading doors. It had gotten dark out, the desert air dry and cool. We came around to the front of the club. There were a lot of young people milling around the entrance. Some were dressed mock prep-pie like Kimmel. I wondered if Kimmel was simply dressing in the hand-me-down preppie way he'd been taught to dress, or if he was subtly mocking himself by dressing as he'd been taught. I noticed eyes following Kimmel as we walked up to Burt, his drummer. Burt was just outside the front doors, shaking everybody in the ticket line's hand, telling people to enjoy the show. Burt looked older, in his late forties. He had a pointy face, blond straggly hair coming out from under a Bruins cap, and a thick blond mustache. He was drinking a beer and reeked of pot.

Kimmel grudgingly introduced me.

Burt greeted me, "Hi Jack," then grabbed me around the neck, and held the beer bottle to my throat like a knife.

He released me, looked at me, and laughed.

I laughed. It was such a dumb joke, and he'd done it in such a believing way, it was actually funny.

"C'mon," Kimmel said with an embarrassed smile, "I want to make sure you get to your booth all right."

A crowd had tightened into a ring around us, but Kimmel put his head down and took my hand and led us right though the throng and into the club. He made a motion toward us to the door person. She stamped my hand as I hung on behind him. The crowd was divided by a floor to ceiling net. Kimmel led me to a roped off booth in the back of the section marked, OF AGE.

We sat down. In the booth next to us, three men sat drinking salt-rimmed martini glasses of tequila. A white RESERVED placard rested in the middle of the table. Two of them wore leather jackets and had thick black hair. The other was fair-haired, and wore a thin white fur coat. They all wore expensive white sneakers. The guy in the fur coat leaned over the booth and effeminately introduced himself to Kimmel.

Kimmel nodded, and turned back to me without saying anything to the guy. He raised his eyebrows with an amused smile.

"What?" I leaned forward.

"Your guess," he smiled, "dealers or A&R?"

"Wait," I glanced over at them and then back at Kimmel. "For you?"

"Which do you think would be more assimilable?" he said, and then turned and stared as Burt loped up onstage and began gimmicking around with his drums.

"Where did you find Burt?" I asked.

"Believe it or not, he found me. He has a studio in Jamaica Plain. He let me stay there on the floor when I was first starting to work things out," Kimmel said, watching him plug in the amps and tap the microphones. "He's actually pretty smart, in a spontaneous sort of way. But he doesn't know when he's saying something smart—he can't tell—so he's always on edge that way. Because he can also be very stupid. And because he's on edge he's always pacing around getting stoned. He's always stoned. And always pacing. Every waking minute, pacing and stoned. He's almost fifty. It's pretty unbelievable."

Burt, beer in hand, gave the okay sign to the sound guy and walked off. The piped music was lowered and the house lights were dimmed. The stage was empty. Kimmel sunk down into the booth. "You know, Hayward," he said, "so many people are just horrified by boredom . . . " He stared at the table. "Why is that? I mean, what's the big deal, because I really don't mind it at all."

Before I could answer, the clipboard club girl walked by our table, paused, and gave Kimmel a glance as she checked her watch.

Kimmel saw her, but did not look up until after she'd left. "I have to go," he said, sliding out of the booth and standing up. "Still the opening act."

He headed off through the milling crowd. I could not tell if he was following her or going to get ready to play. Kimmel's opinions of women had always been never-never land, especially in terms of consummation. In college, when I'd first met Kimmel, he wore a tailored gabardine English suit everywhere he went and was impossibly pursuing our beautiful history professor, Lulu Smith. Lulu was fresh out of Oxford and all first-year enthusiasm with her red cheeks, big breasts, slender arms, and round pale face. She wore wool skirts even in the hottest weather, and day after day you could see the black hair matted under her tan stockings.

Kimmel first came up to me after one of Lulu's lectures. He was more animated then. He poked a finger in my chest. "You are late with the Disraeli paper."

"How do you know that?"

"Lulu sends me out to deal with truants like you."

"You're the T.A.?"

"I, on occasion, sit with Lulu in the teachers' conference room drinking Cokes and eating cookies. She tells me these things."

He nodded as if he had my assent.

I made a move to step around him.

"You," he said, "are wearing a white T-shirt."

"So."

"Plain white. It's doesn't seem like enough. Are you sure you haven't forgotten something?"

I looked him up and down. With his neat suit and round Bostonian accent, he had a purposefully exaggerated skin of collegiateness. With Kimmel, I soon learned, there was always at least one layer of faking. I noticed a book sticking out of his shoulder bag: *Memoirs of a Fox Hunting Man*.

I grabbed the book, opened it up, and began to read out loud: "Aquamarine and celestial were the shoals of sunset as I hacked pensively home from Dumbridge . . . "

He reached over and snatched it back.

"You can't," I said, pointing to the book, "be serious about that stuff."

"Recommended by Lulu," he said. "Now, I have to go. She's asked to see me after class."

I stared at him. "You know," I said, "forget about Lulu. What you need is to sleep with a whore. You're like a mawk-ish British schoolboy."

"What? What did you just say?"

"Why don't you read Sherwood Anderson, or someone like that?"

"Sherwood Anderson?" He said with disbelief, his thick hair quivering.

Kimmel and I became friends and the next year we were roommates. He had his corner with his neatly made bed and guitar and stacks of books and papers. He worked hard and was usually at class or in the library. He kept weird hours, and we didn't see each other much except when Will would occasionally visit, or in the mornings. Mornings he'd put on his suit, comb his hair down, comb it down and comb it down, and step outside. His hair would immediately begin to fray, and in a matter of minutes would splay out like a run over black umbrella. His hair, completely contradicting his tidy attire, gave Kimmel a slightly disheveled air of aching possibility, as if he were holding on to something holding him back. But every single day I'd known him in college, he'd worn all or part of one of his gabardine suits, tight in the chest and always with the same nonplussed archness. I could never tell if Kimmel, by wearing the suits, was mocking the idea of a New England education, mocking an English education, or if he took it seriously as a self-imposed uniform because he took his academics so seriously. Probably both. But I had no idea at the time that the suits had been his father's. They fit him perfectly.

Surprisingly, Kimmel was never beaten up. It was a small, conservative, athletic college, and any smart-ass boy (in a suit no less) incessantly cozying up to a professor would normally have been instantly and repeatedly pulverized by the hockey players. But Kimmel was from Boston and had grown up playing hockey and he wasn't afraid of any of those townies. Eventually, they began seeking him out for last-ditch, pretest tutorials. A few—under their pinched baseball caps and slouched and dull-eyed exterior—were extremely bright but embarrassed about it. They'd buy him beer as payment—he'd demand Guinness, and sit around the student lounge after night lectures, drinking— and with a sweetly hesitant earnestness, try out their thesis ideas on him.

Will slid into the booth with cups of beer just as the house lights went completely dark. The stage glowed like a shell and the chatter softened to murmurs. Kimmel walked out, bent over with his hands in his pockets, as if occupying himself under a spotlight couldn't have been more mundane. A crowd had pushed up tightly against the stage, and Will and I had to stand up on the back booth to see.

Burt drummed and Kimmel played his G's and E's and sang. Burt at one point—obviously drunk, got up from his drums in the middle of a song to go get a beer, asking someone, anyone, to fill in. A few songs later, he was drumming and at the same time talking loudly over Kimmel's singing to a pretty girl up front. But he couldn't hear what she was saying because they were in the middle of the song. So he got up, tried to step over his kit to hear her better. He tripped, falling hard as his snare drum crumbled noisily underneath him. The crowd cheered. Kimmel strummed along, bent morosely over like a little boy, saying nothing and pretending not to notice.

. . . the negative reggae
on the silver exchange . . .

I didn't understand what he was talking about, and couldn't believe how haphazard the whole thing was. It was sort of charming. And the songs were good. Simple and pretty, some were off-the-cuff nonsense, others had either a cryptic yearning or a quick humor.

Time waits for no one,
lord,
why did I ever move on.

The song initially came across as a second guess at a breakup. But I'd never actually seen Kimmel in a real relationship, and as the song ended, it was unclear what he was getting at. He had a songwriter's knack for taking a cliché line—the hokey country "time waits for no one, lord"—and adding a second line and turning the cliché on its head, making it completely ambiguous. The "lord" was its own line, but also part of the first line, as well as the second. Each way meant something slightly different every time he sang it. When the "lord" was attached to the second line, he's just realizing time waits for no one. When it is attached to the first line, he has known it all along. When the lord is in the middle, he'll never understand.

It was also a joke. And it also wasn't.

Kimmel talk-sang through the next song. It seemed to be about a kid coming home from college transformed into a Deadhead. His dad is a buzz-cut cop who still holds hippies responsible for everything. The kid wants to take a hippie girl to the Worcester Dead show, but the dad won't lend him the car unless he vows not to do drugs. The chorus is the kid sanctimoniously refusing to do so by quoting the Dead (there was a gleeful banality in Kimmel's voice when he sang the chorus):

Can you answer? Yes I can
But what would be the answer
To the answer man.

The song ends with the dad meeting a sad, discombobulated fate. He mistakes the kid's acid tabs, left behind hidden in a Band-Aid tin, for corn-removal tabs.

"That's my favorite one," Will said in the slow clapping after the song. "You know," he said, "none of these songs wish anybody well."

"He doesn't wish himself well."

Will gave me a long mocking look. "Wait, you didn't know Kimmel was once a Deadhead?" There was a slight turn of malice in his voice.

"You're kidding. He despised that band. He despised Deadheads."

Will stared at me with a fixed smile.

"Don't be territorial about it, Will. Christ."

He laughed. "Well, it wasn't so much tie-dyes—he never wore those. But bare feet, a loose-limbed, inane smile— most of the usual accoutrements of that kind of surrender."

He shook his head, looking up at Kimmel winding his guitar back into tune. "But you know, that's not fair. For most of those kinds of kids at our school, the Dead were everything. For Kimmel they were just one thing. He'd learned a lot of their songs on his guitar—he got the music sheets from some mail-order place. He was into it by himself, not in a sociable way, which was unusual . . ."

Will stopped talking as Kimmel started in on another song. Kimmel hadn't looked back at Burt or counted off, and Burt looked caught between finishing his beer and coming in on time. When Burt didn't come in, Kimmel stopped playing. He dropped his arms and stood there staring at the stage carpet as if completely unaware of Burt, of the crowd.

"Okay, man," Burt said into his microphone, putting his beer down. "Ready steady back here . . . "

"Can we turn off the drummer's microphone?" Kimmel said into his microphone, squinting through the stage lights toward the sound booth.

"I mean," Will said in the lingering silence, "Kimmel had his Dead records and all that Jonathan Edwards kind of crap. But he also started playing my records—Joe Pop-O-Pie and the Dogmatics. He couldn't believe these stupid bands I liked were from Boston and he didn't know about them. He was, at the time, sort of defensive and territorial about Boston . . . I think by then he was losing the house . . ."

Kimmel slowly began to play again. Red light beat down upon his face. Burt gingerly tapped the drum skin with his knuckles, trying to figure out what song Kimmel was starting up.

"That's when he got all those suits," Will said over the music, slowly nodding as he watched Kimmel. "Those gabardine suits were all he kept."

There were a few more songs. Will began to lose interest in the show. He went and got us more beer, slipped back into the booth, and sat there drinking and looking bored.

The last song began with a fast, catchy tempo, quickly broke down into a snareless drum cacophony, came back together, and ended with a slow chorus:

Every sunrise
falls to lead,
every time I dream,
I just go to bed.

Will glanced up at me as Kimmel sang these lines, and we both burst out laughing.

The girl with the clipboard was watching nearby. She overheard us. "That's sad," she said.

The headlining band played.

Will and I waited in the booth for Kimmel. He came back up onto the stage. He sat on the edge as it was being cleared, a thick semicircle of people reaching up with CDs for him to sign, or with money to buy the record. But then they didn't leave. They stayed, some just staring and some asking questions. They were all young and they all wanted something from Kimmel. But they looked like they didn't even know what it was. Kimmel's green alligator shirt was dry of sweat, and he seemed cheerful, gently animated by the attention. God knows what those kids were saying, but Kimmel exuded patience nothing like before the show. But now he was on a stage.

The club began to clear out, and eventually Kimmel stood while a last small gaggle of kids hung on at the stage's edge. He turned to leave, only to turn back to answer a last question. He knelt down and nodded and began again to talk to one of the kids.

Will stood up. He shook his head.

"What?" I said.

He was watching Kimmel. "All that stagy listlessness, it's finally paying off."

"Maybe it's not so stagy. Those kids don't seem to be too into poses."

"When all you have is one pose, it doesn't seem like a pose."

"I don't know, Will," I said. "He looks pretty sincerely not so good."

They'd announced last call and Will, ignoring me, turned and walked over to the bar.

We eventually found Kimmel in the cramped basement room. The man in the fur coat was coming out when we came in. Plastic cups lay across the sticky, concrete floor. On a table, cold cuts glistened and there were a few stray grapes. Kimmel sat alone on a metal folding chair. His back was slumped against the wall, and he eyed us without expectation and with a little antagonism. He gestured toward a full bucket of beers floating in ice water.

"You can really go up there and do that," I said to Kimmel.

"I don't know," he shrugged.

The girl came in and stared down at her clipboard. "Burt told me to tell you," she said, "he got his half of the money from me."

Kimmel smiled thinly, rocked his head back and forth in a kind of singsong rhythm, as if silently mocking what she had just said.

She looked at him. "He says he'll see you in Phoenix. And he wants to know about your guitar?"

"I'll take it," Kimmel said.

"And your half?" she said, holding out a small brick of bills wrapped up in a settlement sheet.

"Just give it to Burt," he said.

"Kimmel," I said as she left, "that's a pretty girl."

"Yes," Will enthused, "let's bring her out."

"Let's just go," he said, standing up and looking at me. "Let's get out of here."

He turned his back to us and pulled his sweater on.

Will hurried out after the girl.

Kimmel packed his things into the guitar case. He turned with the case in hand. Will and the girl stood at the door.

Kimmel stared at them for a moment, announced he was leaving.

She held up the stack of bills again. "Why do you want to go already?"

"Because," he said, looking from Will to her and back again, "I just don't have the tolerance for nonsense that the man you're bound to go home with tonight is going to have."

He took the bills out of her hand and walked out the door.

Out in the dry, cool night, Kimmel seemed restless as we walked, both loosened up and depressed by performing. "Sorry about that in there," he said. "I get so uncomfortable in these clubs. I don't know why. And then Will starts pressing me."

"He just wanted more of that absinthe."

"With that stuff, you just need a little bit," Kimmel shook his head. "He wouldn't have stopped . . . "

We walked for a while in silence. "That man in the white fur coat," he finally said, "he flew in from LA. He wants to give me a hundred thousand dollars."

"That's good."

"But, you know, I don't care. I don't care about this kind of world."

"What world?"

"Playing around. That's all it is, am I correct? Playing around."

"It's a livelihood. You've just started."

"No, I've been at it longer than you realize."

We walked along a block of low, red brick buildings, blackened air conditioners bulging out of the windows. "I write a few songs," he said. "They just come. And then they are gone. Finished. I really don't have to do anything. They just come through me. But even when they come through me, I don't *feel* anything."

"What do you want to feel?" I asked.

"I'm not sure," he said. "Useful, maybe."

"You don't know?"

"How could I know? I don't even really know what any of them mean."

We came to an intersection: a palm tree slanted out of a trellised hole. Across the street, cubes of light rose up a pre-fab apartment complex, and above us stars speckled the Arizona sky like confetti. "And then everything else, I dislike," Kimmel said, shaking his head. "I don't like playing with other musicians. I don't like jamming. I don't like recording, and I don't like people looking at me. But it's not just that. The people, the real musicians I'm always opening for, they've got something figured. I don't know what yet. But there's this coy obliquity. This determination to stay underwhelmed."

"But Kimmel, you are sort of that way."

"Maybe. But I get so bothered. And I'm not really a musician, you understand, mentally."

"How so?"

"I cannot get lost in it."

We continued on in silence. At the next light, a black sedan brushed by our knees. We stepped back and watched it surge into the avenue's scattered traffic.

I looked around, up at the street sign. Will had given me the address of a bar. "Oh," I said. "Wait, wrong way."

We'd walked five blocks in the wrong direction. I took Kimmel's guitar for him, and we doubled back against a desert breeze, walking against the gleaming cars rushing up the main old drag of Tucson. Ahead, sitting at a bus stop, was the pretty girl from the club. We had just walked right by her.

She was sitting alone, her hands crossed over a canvas bag on her lap. The professional serenity was gone from her face and she looked tired, upset.

We stopped.

Kimmel looked at me. He seemed confused. He hesitated, went up to her. "What's wrong?" he said.

"I just missed my bus," she said without looking up at him.

"I thought you'd be going out," he said.

"I don't go out," she said, staring straight ahead across the avenue. "I work, and then I go home and wake up and go to class. And then I work."

"What are you studying?"

"Photography."

"That's what people your age do when they have no idea what they are doing."

"I thought maybe," she said wearily, "we were through with that kind of talk."

Kimmel looked over at me, back at her. He looked down the avenue for a bus.

"Nothing's coming," she said. "Believe me."

"We'll wait with you, if you like," he said.

"Don't you have to meet your friend? He's down the road with a couple of the girls from the club."

"We're in no rush," Kimmel said.

"Suit yourself," she shrugged. "The next bus is in an hour and a half."

Kimmel stared at her. "But it's so late already. What are you going to do?"

"Sit here," she said. "Miss a night's sleep."

"What are you going to do for breakfast?"

"Oh no," she said, glancing up at him with a cautious laugh, "none of that stuff."

"No, I mean, just come with us for a second."

"Why?"

"Just come on, just for a second."

"I have Mace."

"No, just, let's go in that little mart over there and get you some things for the morning."

She was staring up at him.

"You have time," he said.

"I don't have any money."

"I'm buying. You paid me."

Kimmel took her hand and she stood up. She was wearing a shiny blue windbreaker and there were runs in her black stockings down where they met her boots.

"What's your name?" he said.

"Angela," she said.

We crossed the avenue and went into a shabby, brightly lit, all-night market. Kimmel walked with her to the back refrigerator and filled his arms up with eggs, tortillas, shredded cheese, a loaf of bread, bananas, a carton of orange juice, milk, and a bright-yellow tin of espresso. He opened up his arms and rolled it all down onto the counter. He reached for a chocolate bar and threw it in as the clerk finished bagging.

He paid, and asked the clerk to call a cab.

We waited outside with her until a dented, lime-green taxi pulled up. Kimmel handed her the grocery bag and gave her a twenty for the fare. He held the door open. Cradling the grocery bag like a baby, she took his hand for a moment and looked at him. She hesitated, gave him a kiss on the cheek, and then she turned and disappeared into the backseat.

We walked east a few blocks, at one point dipping down through a short tunnel under train tracks, and came up to where a small park opened up in front of us. Brown palm trees rose out of the fat bushes. We walked along the black rails of the fence, cut diagonally across the street toward a window aglow with beer signs.

Kimmel stopped a few yards short of the bar.

I handed the guitar back to him.

The guitar seesawed underneath his grip. "Remember in college," he said. "My thesis. Before I had to leave."

I laughed. His thesis was on, sort of cannily, the French Air Force in World War II.

"I'm constantly thinking about it," he said. "Not going back to that in particular, but more the sit down, systematic kind of life. You know, to just go back and work out one simple problem, some minor modern European dysfunction . . . To keep it close and work it out over a long period of time. But doing this," he raised his guitar slightly, "everything is so fragmented. And now I've lost the context."

I remembered in college, reading an early draft of his thesis. It was lively and acidic and fascinating. There *was no* French Air Force in World War II. All the French planes had been destroyed on the ground by the Luftwaffe before the war had really even begun. Before the German tanks began rolling over everything in sight. So how could there be a thesis? But he'd pulled off this greatly accurate send-up of French bluster. Kimmel, I suddenly realized, was an academic at heart, and if things hadn't happened the way they did, if he hadn't been kicked out the spring of his senior year, he would have gone right into graduate work and probably would have wound up living his life in the perpetually cloistered, quiet swing of a school.

I stood there, caught between opening the bar door or saying something. "You got kicked out of college," I said. "So what. Go back." I motioned to his guitar. "Drop that, if you really want."

"But I need to make a living. Do you know what it's like to finally have a little money coming in?"

A group of men came out of the bar.

We stood there, silent under the rush of music and voices until they passed and the door closed. "But then, you know," he said, "I've been broke long enough not to care so much about the money."

"How's that?" I asked.

"I don't want to be broke again," he said, "but I know I can handle it."

"But what if you no longer have what you now have ahead of you?"

He stood there watching the empty corner where the men had disappeared. "You know, Hay," he said. "One night I was up late with Burt and a few other people. We were sitting around the Jamaica Plain studio and I had my guitar. I started singing a song, some la-di-da song. Somebody asked me what it was. I said I'd just made it up. Everybody went, 'Ooo what a great song . . . You just came up with that? . . .'"

He stared at me. "But Hay, you have to understand, I didn't like the song. In fact, I hated it. Thought it was stupid. It had an obvious sentiment and said too much. But everybody loved it and Burt got the board all set up and I recorded the song against my better instincts. Now it's out and people yell for it. Even tonight, that girl we just put in a cab, I noticed, was yelling for it. I think she, I think they are idiots for liking the song, but I nod and play the song and I hate it. I really, you know, hate it."

"Well, stop playing it."

"No. You don't understand," he said. "The point is that I don't have any control. The song started as a joke I couldn't stop. A song I could not help making up." He shook his head. "It's the song that man in the fur coat is offering me a hundred thousand dollars for more of."

He laughed with a stunted bitterness. "This whole kind of life is like starting a joke you can't stop."

"Being broke," I said, "that kind of life never seemed funny to you."

Kimmel put his hand on my shoulder. He had a firm easygoing grip. "I care about the money I make," he said, looking at me. "But money from men like that, from men in fur coats . . . I guess it's a matter of patience. Money, like everything else, matters where it comes from."

"Kimmel, if you do something stupid, but get paid for it, why should you care?"

"But then with songs I like . . . it's not enough. I don't care enough."

"It's just guitar music. Are you telling me you're too smart, but not smart enough to also be dumb enough?"

"I *cannot get lost in it*, you understand?" He stood there glaring at me.

He dropped his eyes. "Except in the fall back."

"What's the fall back?"

He shrugged, took a step, and pushed against the bar door.

I grabbed his arm. "What's the fall back, Kimmel?"

He gave me a skeptical glance, shook my hand off his arm, and pushed open the door. I followed him into the bar. Will was there with a couple of girls. Golden beers in front, they looked up at us with shiny, expectant faces.

Kimmel and I stayed up drinking the end of the absinthe. We sat behind the rails of the second-floor landing of my hotel, mute with the warm glisten of the green liquor spreading inside. The sky hung like a high black canopy over the oyster glow of the city. The dim stars seemed artificially round. Kimmel, close by in the dark, bristled with silent poise. Once, he put his hands through the rails and I thought he was tying together the legs of a bird.

Cars passed by under us. People occasionally came and went in the cool night, alone or chiming in groups across the parking lot and into their rooms. A last push of humidity was in the dry air. Summer going, going, gone; absinthe and sighs, folding chairs, a long station wagon with the back sunk down and nothing in it. The absinthe was a spell. I did not feel Kimmel there anymore, nor did I feel Will asleep in the room. There was a famous depiction of the nativity scene. The look on Joseph's face in the manger's glow. His eyes are closed but he is picturing something. He is smiling. I thought of nails. My hands were out as if to explain.

3

I woke once during the day, jumped up, and crouched naked in the teenager's room. The carpet was thick, and my feet rocked back and forth on the soft burrs. The house was silent, and my ears ached with a hollow drumming. The muscles in my calves suddenly constricted. My head pulsed and I grew dizzy. I lay back down. I lay there for a long time, looking up into the blue-filled skylight. I slept again.

When I woke it was pitch-dark through the skylight. I needed a flashlight, water. My neck throbbed. I needed to find aspirin. I fell back to sleep.

When I woke again it was blue through the skylight.

I went into the bathroom and cleaned myself up. I rinsed the tissue out of the cut and rinsed my neck. My eye was puffy, circled purple and my head felt soft with a deep soreness. I found a small jar of Advil in the cabinet. I took four, the burnt orange pills leaving a sweetness on my tongue in the instant before I washed them down. I drank glass after glass of water. Water was all I wanted and I could not get enough of it.

I dressed from clothes I'd found in the teenager's closet, pants, a black T-shirt—a purple frothing gargoyle clawing its way around the side—and a still-tagged red, white, and blue Tommy Hilfiger sweatshirt he must have gotten one disenchanted Christmas. I creaked open the bedroom door and surveyed the hallway. It was a black slate entrance hall with a roof slanting upward over white-carpeted stairs. By the door was a small Japanese rock garden.

I climbed the stairs and came up to a large, white-carpeted living room. A black wall of windows overlooked the ocean. By the windows, two black leather sofas faced each other, a glass coffee table between them. It was a big room, with an open kitchen and dining-room table to my left.

I noticed the phone on the kitchen wall. I picked it up. No dial tone. The line was dead, a good sign in terms of anyone coming around soon.

A pad of paper by the phone was headed:

THE FACE CORPORATION
MUNICH
The International Capitol Headquarters
Commanding Re-Information Agent/
Harding Stylus L&2 System

I remembered Leonard saying something about Germans.

I opened and closed a few closets. Everything in the closets—the towels, sheets, soaps, and medicines—was layered in precise piles. There was a rental sterility to the house and a clean surface order. The house was void of small unnecessities.

Past the kitchen was a narrow, walk-in pantry. I went into the pantry and took inventory. The shelves were amply stocked: gourmet canned soups, boxes of pasta, rice, and crackers, jars of olive oil and tomato sauce, a sack of potatoes—still firm, marmite, bullions, teas and coffees, Ceres juice boxes, a case of Pellegrino water, two expensive-looking bottles of Bordeaux, and a twelve-year-old, unpronounceable brand of Scottish single malt. I had an odd, sickening sensation when

I saw the booze. I felt sweaty, with a thick indigestion as if I'd had too much meat the night before.

The refrigerator was mostly empty: a red wax wheel of cheese, an unopened carton of orange juice, a stick of butter, and a jar of red jam. Nothing perishable. I took a glass out of the cabinet and poured some Pellegrino. But the glass smelled of boiled eggs. I poured it out, dried the glass, and put it back in the cabinet. I had no appetite, but I made a plate of cheese and crackers. I suddenly felt dizzy. My neck hurt, the scab shifting and breaking up painfully.

I needed to sit down.

Wooden stairs led to a loft platform. I took the Pellegrino bottle and climbed the stairs. There was a thick white carpet strewn with pillows and cushions and squared with low bookshelves. I stood in the loft for a moment. To the south I could see the yellow mustard disc hanging over Santa Monica. To the north, corralling the bay, a hill rose up like a buffalo shoulder.

There were tire tracks on the beach and the beach was empty.

I looked down into the living room. The house was empty. I could just feel it had been empty for a long time.

I lay down. A side table was piled with dried out fashion magazines, and the low line of shelves was jammed with beach-house paperbacks: Robert Ludlum, Larry McMurtry, Anne River Siddons, John le Carré.

I looked at the books, ran a finger across the dust on the spines.

I stretched out across the cushions and looked out to the sea. It was a good spot, suspended over the water. Safety in a world of water. The ocean was a dark blue, iced by a filmy layer of white sunlight. The ocean, I finally understood, is a barrier to light.

To the south, coronets and pelicans rose off the water as a man in a red wet suit kayaked through a spit of rocks. Reddish strands of seaweed fluttered in the current behind the rocks. He rowed past the house, heading north, and I instinctively shrank back.

When I looked up again, the birds had floated back down to the rocks where the kayak had passed through. They stood along the rocks, silhouetted black against the dusty western sky. They watched the kayak's progress like old men in small towns watch traffic. I lay back. On the table by my head, the magazines rested in silence in the silent house.

I slept.

When I woke, bright light like interrogation hit my eyes. The sun had tumbled down onto the ocean from above the house, and I squinted down into the big blue Pacific as waves snapped over and withdrew. My eyes followed a retreating wave into the sea, but the brightness blinded my eyes, pounded my head, and I could not hold the panorama the wave disappeared into. Even the ocean seemed uneasy with its own motions, as if it were exhausting itself.

Safety in a World of Water.

And for the first time since my accident, I remembered Will. Years ago, when we were all just out of college. He was driving. Kimmel was in the front seat. I was in the back. They were talking about some old, harsh boarding school master with a kind of cautious affection, as if he were somehow beyond real judgment. They were still impressed with the fascistic strangeness of their boarding school: hard cubicles, barking masters, slave boat rowing. A car cut in front of us and suddenly we were sliding. Will was holding back Kimmel with one arm and then trying to steer out of the slide with the other. I'll always remember Will's instinct that way. The car bumped over something, bounced hard, and I hit the ceiling and was thrown into the well of the backseat. There was one long tilt, as if we were up on two wheels, and then the car fell and jerked to a stop.

I was on my back. Above the sun broke through the clouds, trampolining in and out of the sky.

We climbed out of the car, stood on the off-ramp oval of grass, and stared at the two flat tires. We patted each other on the back, half-stunned in the cold and smoky fall air. We were all right.

The other car had pulled over. A small, elderly Chinese woman had climbed out and was walking over to us. She had on a faded old blue sweatshirt and black slippers. She came up to Will and spoke in halting English, but with a defiant certainty, "I no see you boys."

Will stared angrily down at her. "Oh man, you cut us off. You almost completely wiped us out."

For some reason, she patted him down, his pockets, his ribs.

He pulled in his elbows and drew back. "Jesus." He couldn't help laughing with dismay, as if tickled. He took a few sidesteps away from her in a kind of buffalo shuffle. "God," he stared at her. "Weird."

I saw the peeling letters across her sweatshirt:

Sea World

Safety in a World of Water

I began to laugh.

I couldn't stop laughing. Will and Kimmel were staring at me. The Chinese woman looked deeply concerned. She thought my head had been hurt and I was becoming hysterical.

I got myself together and looked down at her. "Safety in a world of water," I said.

She nodded at me. "Yes. Yes yes yes."

I gave her a hug. She held me tight at the waist. She had no idea what was written on her sweatshirt.

As a boy, I'd had the very same shirt. Finn Theiss, my great-grandfather, had built Sea World.

Finn, at the turn of the century, was one of the richest men in America. He lived in a brick mansion in Shaker Heights, owned islands in Canada and in Miami, and had a huge ranch along the coast of Venezuela. His company made the gravel. Ballast for the railroad lines spreading west, and then, with the coming of the car, for the new roads. He had bustling, dusty quarries all over the Midwest and became famous in his time for converting them, when they were spent, into clear lakes and pine forest parks. Finn's first roads were legendary for having the shine of the moon in them—a guiding, pearly light as if from St. Peter. This was because the early gravel was full of centuries of Indian skeletons, cut out from ancient mounds, the bones ground white and luminous under wheels.

Late in Finn's life, after the auto explosion of the twenties, he had begun to believe the roads were choking the country. He was embarrassed at what was happening. The roads he'd built were running over his own old hunting grounds, over his youth. Even in Canada, where they'd used to caravan for days by horse and mule to get to his cabin, it was now just a straight three-hour drive from Detroit, and the purpose of the place, its pristine solitude, was gone.

People were beginning to die in cars in large numbers, and he never forgave himself for the accident (which happened in Daytona Beach, of all places) ending Annie Oakley's career.

He believed roads, like fences, would cover the West. That Americans would become dangerously restless without a frontier to conquer, and there would inevitably be technology making the last, vast open space—the sea, an inhabitable frontier. The roads were pressed to the shores, and Finn saw, at road's end, piers extending across the placid, clear bays of Miami to an octopus-shaped city: talons of bathysphere dwellings plunging underwater, broad steel-grate promenades, and rising, glowing glass skyscrapers.

It was a simple, midwestern mythification of the sea. The New Deal was in its early, idealistic swing, and rich people had big, public ideas. Americans had to have a frontier to conquer. If it was no longer west, it had to be what had been passed over.

In 1932, Finn had been a silent partner (to stave off potential embarrassment) behind one of the first bathysphere tests. The big steel ball, with quartz portholes for eyes, had been tossed into the Atlantic Ocean off Pensacola. Inside was a scientist Finn had met in a Miami jazz club. The bathysphere had sunk right down four hundred feet. When it was hauled back up to the surface and opened up, the scientist burst out alive and wide-eyed and talking wildly about the deep ocean's "infinitesimal experience, man as miniscule as an atom on a new frontier."

The Miami papers ran a few short pieces, but the country was deep in the Depression, and nobody cared.

But Finn saw it as a huge breakthrough, and with a recalcitrant sliver of 1920s blue-skies optimism, he began looking around for a sympathetic architect.

Addison Mizner was a child of the West, of fenceless horizons drawing him to the sea. He had been a gold miner in the Yukon and had, in the twenties, rose Gatsby-like to fame as a Florida architect and bon vivant. He made his fortune designing beach houses for the new Gold Coast wealth of the Florida land boom. He weighed over three hundred pounds and his heavy Spanish architecture—all medieval grandeur and "moneyness" had become instantly passé after the crash. He had gone bust in 1931 trying to build a new city of gold, a baroque Venice on the Sea in swampy Boca Raton (which means "rat's mouth").

In 1932, Mizner's only commission had been the new Palm Beach Post Office. His blueprint—a surprising minimalist about-face—was his first attempt at modernism. A kind of international-style glass box, the blue glass entrance sloped away at a forty-five degree angle, shimmered in the sun like a hard ocean and slanted down at a thirty-degree angle, as if about to engulf (or slice the heads off) the citizens dropping off their mail. The design had been rejected and Mizner had destroyed the blueprint. But Finn, hearing about the building, had asked Mizner to dinner.

Broke, fat, and in ill health, Mizner waddled into the Everglades Club with a chow dog at his heels. He ordered two plates of eggs scrambled with caviar—one for the dog—and his own bottle of champagne. Finn at first told Mizner he intended to commission him to redesign his Miami house, and then he mentioned his idea for a city at sea.

Mizner didn't miss a beat. He immediately began to sketch buildings on the white linen. Glass structures set in a bay and shaped like radio towers. Connecting the towers, he drew skyways of glass. One of the skyways wound down into bleacher-like terraces around a glowing oval of water. In tiny letters across the water, he wrote, *Blue Arena*.

"Ocean makes sand makes glass," he told Finn by way of explanation.

Before the maître d' intervened, Mizner had drawn, with a quick precision, a small, archetypal city at sea. On the last linen napkin, he drew, with a final, contemptuous swirl, a small beach house lying on the horizon of shore.

Mizner died a few months later of a heart attack, his only surviving attempt at modernism on Finn's linen. It was a prototype of glass, and flamboyantly unbuildable.

But Finn was undeterred. Based loosely on Mizner's designs, he proceeded to spend a fortune over the next few years building his city at sea on a scruffy coastal avocado grove just north of Miami.

In 1936, three years after Mizner's death, Finn completed the nation's first seaquarium. The central structure was a glass tower on a moated spit of peninsula, where, from inland as you approached, it *appeared* to rise out of the Atlantic. It was a trick probably only gratifying to midwesterners, but a lot of them were beginning to come down to Florida.

Adjacent to the tower was the blue glass aquarium—round as Mizner.

Sea World.

Its espoused purpose was to pursue the idea of inhabiting the sea: a true marine center for studies. To this end, Finn hired engineers, scholars, divers, animal trainers, and scientists amenable to his vision and acceptable to a generous salary during a depression.

It goes without saying Finn lost millions.

Finn's Sea World closed down in the fifties and the name and slogan went to franchise. But the original structure still stands in Miami, now a water slide and mega-bar called Aqua Slam.

There is still, hovering by the bar's main entrance like a hapless chaperone, a plaque with Finn's profile.

It turned out only oil rigs ever inhabited the sea.

Just like Epcot Center, Sea World had genuine scientific beginnings. "Safety in a World of Water" had originally meant a future utopia at sea for everybody. But the Florida tourists wanted giant fish in giant bowls. "Safety in a World of Water" came to mean *you* were safe from *them*.

4

I moved into a ground-floor studio in West LA provided for me by the production. I arrived with no furniture, and did not buy any. I slept on a mattress on the floor, my clothes in a pile. After two weeks, the landlord accused me of making porn movies.

I worked long hours getting the show set up. I'd been hired as a producer, and it was a big break. The production was for public television, but we were spending all our time okaying bands with our sponsors: American Express, AT&T, and a consortium of sneaker companies. The show was about new American music, but the underlying reason for the show was to bring teenagers over to public television. There was a pock-faced girl from Nevada with a country voice like a rasping, billowed sail, and a group of kids from some Tampa Bay shit hole who made beautifully menacing instrumental music. Otherwise, the bands being booked onto the show were a joke. A humiliation.

It had been a month since I'd left Helen in the hands of her father and the nurses in Raleigh. Since I'd walked out of that ward for the last time and got in my car. It was all too recent to consider, but nights—driving home from work along Santa Monica Boulevard, or lying alone on the mattress—I could not hold off thinking of Helen. Not as I'd left her, but as she had been before she'd become sick. She'd been fading for so many years, and now that she was definitively not at my side, there was a huge absence inside me, crushing inward on itself.

Helen's beauty was in her expressionless face. In her flat gaze and still mouth. She always had a youthful, languid dissociation and she gave me a feeling of deep silence. It was a good, grounding feeling. She was tall, with smooth pale skin and shaggily cropped blonde hair. Things inside me would unfold under her brown eyes and cautious voice, smooth out until they were flat as a table between us. We'd lived together so easily, splayed asleep all over each other in our bed, and sleepwalking around our junk furniture. I don't know what we ever did, or how the time we spent passed. I knew we weren't cynical to each other and we didn't talk much except when we'd drink and then she'd become curious about all sorts of little things in my life I'd never considered of any interest. She never talked much about her life, but there was an unconscious ease of motion between us and I took that empty contentment as a good sign. A sign of unnoticed happiness.

And at the time, I'd thought her detachment was a kind of boredom. She was so unreadable. I'd watch her sideways at the movies. She would sit stone-faced through the chase scenes, trip-ups, shootings, romantic conclusions, and arty travelogues. Silent except for an occasional abrupt, husky laugh, and then she would glance at me with an embarrassed smile.

We'd walk out, and if we talked about anything, we'd talk about something else. But it was such a mystery—to not venture a word about a movie right after seeing it. Somehow, though, I could tell she liked the breezy stuff, the happy endings.

The evening it all started, Helen was running a bath. I looked in just as she was pulling off her T-shirt. This seemed to bother her, and she turned her back, folded her arms modestly across her breasts, and stepped into the bath.

I came in, sat down on the rim of the bath as she slipped in. I reached over and turned off the faucets. She lay there, her body disappearing under the peaks and ripples of white foam. She slid completely down under the water, and came up with her blonde hair wet and dark and there was a ring of foam. She stared at the water. There was a new, strange tension to her face.

I smoothed her hair behind her ears, brushing off the foam. "Are you all right?"

She nodded, closed her eyes. I kissed her forehead in the steam. She didn't open her eyes. Helen had been brought up well, had a certain Southern smoothness and also a Yankee restraint. Her self-regard had always been so nonchalant. And she'd never had any first-relationship, petty certainties about the way things ought to be done. "Okay, sure," was her same response when I'd ask if she wanted to move in together to an apartment I'd found on Fifth Street, or drag a broken sofa home off the street, or take a bus up to Vermont and go skiing. And we'd get on some nine-hour bus ride and read and stop and eat fast food in silence and be happy in it. And she didn't even ski.

Some long weekends we'd rent a car and go up to her aunt's in Maine. Helen could read in a car without getting nauseous, and to me this represented some mysterious, well-bred integrity. Helen always read when she traveled. With chatty strangers next to her on buses or trains or planes she could smile, turn her shoulder just so, put her book up. She had an instinctive kind of sweet deflection. She could use a kind greeting, like no one else I ever knew, to end the conversation. Strangers could never, in all my time with Helen, find a way in.

But maybe her distance, all along, was a supreme form of introversion. A self-conscious kind of containment. She was never morbid, until that moment in the bath. Fatalistic, but as she lay in the bath with her eyes shut tight, I realized something new had come to her face. Come dark and quick as a summer storm, and it would not leave.

Her eyes were still closed. She was breathing so slowly, as if practicing. "Hayward," she finally said, "everything suddenly is just pounding through me, but it's like there's no pulse."

"I can't explain," she said. "I'm scared. I've been having the strangest dreams. A blue, vaporous man standing by our bed. A blue, vaporous finger pointing at my temple . . ."

I sat there at the edge of the bath, listening to the water's echoes and looking at Helen's softly bulging eyelids. I felt a last few seconds of calm between us. And then I stood, reached for the towel.

She opened her eyes. She slowly got up out of the bath, resting a wet hand on my shoulder for balance as water sluiced down her body. There was a matchstick flicker of light between her thighs and an easy, upward curve to her breasts. Her skin had grayed from the bathwater, and I wrapped her in the towel.

Five years later, the illness had set into her limbs like concrete. For the last three of those years, I had been going back and forth between seeing to her in southern wards and production work in New York. When I was offered the job in LA, I finally understood there was no chance of return for her, for us, and I packed a bag and drove down to the Raleigh ward one last time to say goodbye. She was by the big windows overlooking the highway. Her hair was dyed white blonde, frizzy and wild, and she walked with an old lady's halting woodenness, eyes cemented to the ground. Her body had swelled from the medication. She sensed I'd arrived without seeing me, and sat down at the window to wait, staring at the cars passing by below. When I approached, the cars below seemed to flee out from underneath her feet. She turned halfway toward me as I sat down, and before I said a word, her lip quivered and she considered me out of the corner of her eye with astonishment.

I'd seen Will once in LA, a couple of weeks after Kimmel's Tucson show. He'd just finished up the Manson piece, and he had a party in his hotel suite the night before he headed back to New York.

I came over early. The door was propped open with a leather-bound menu. Will was on the phone, cutting up lemons and limes at a makeshift bar. He was cutting right through the fruit, into the grain of the hotel's antique desk.

I stood at the door and watched him for a few moments. He set down his phone, and scooped up the wedges and dropped them into a bowl. He turned and began wrestling with the big bag of ice he'd had sent up. He tore off the top, hoisted it up and over into the metal bucket. Ice flew out all over the place. Will went at things with a hard abandon. Rowing contained his impulsiveness, but I'd seen him play hockey a few times. He could drop his shoulder and wind and bend through a crowd immediately to the heart of the boards. But then he'd trip up or accidentally catch some guy in the jaw with his flailing stick, and a fight would erupt. There was an assuredness, and then there was a bear-paw indelicacy—an almost slapstick balance he'd always seemed to be able to maintain.

The rest of the cubes poured down and clanged into the metal, then the rush of ice muted itself. He looked up and saw me. "Oh," he said. "You have a date coming tonight."

"I'm not in the mood," I said.

"C'mon Hay, it'll be good for you."

"Just don't introduce me, all right?"

We were looking at each other. There was a speck of amusement in his eyes.

"All right?" I repeated.

He shook his head, loosening the last clinging pieces of ice out of the bag.

People began to arrive.

I stood in the kitchenette with my drink. I did not introduce myself to anybody. Will was genially drunk and a good host, greeting everybody and pointing new arrivals to the bar. Most of the guests were friends from the places he worked—twenty or so well-dressed people standing around the hotel suite chatting. A tall, familiar-looking woman with a long, pretty face arrived with a balding man. The man wore red-rimmed glasses and a white, tab-collared shirt. The woman had rich, brown hair and her clothes were the shimmering green and brown of a live lobster. She came in and seemed to know Will and everybody else there and you could hear her voice over everybody else. She never seemed to actually touch anybody, only bounce her finger just above a shoulder by way of a greeting. She did this to me, introduced herself as June Foote. She was a publicist in New York, where Helen had once worked. She'd known Helen. I introduced myself. She nodded in recognition, asked about Helen as she reached toward Will. He grabbed her finger and roughly squeezed her hand until she fell off balance. He caught her at the waist, righted her, and pulled her against him. She laughed like a little girl before she pushed him away. He held out his hand, and they shook with an exaggerated formality. She introduced Will to the balding man. Will nodded, and as they shook hands, he pulled the man slightly toward him. The man looked surprised, and they stood there in deep conversation.

I went for another drink.

When they'd finished talking, Will came over to me. "See that guy?" Will said, waving his drink.

"What guy?"

"The guy I was talking to. In the fucking architect glasses."

"The red rims?"

"Yes, the red rims. And that candy striped English shirt—Turnbell & Aston, Ashford & Simpson, Turner & Hooch . . . whatever the fuck they are called."

"You know what those shirts are called," I said.

"He's Albert France," Will said, ignoring me. "He writes for the *Times*. One of the dance guys. He's also out here to see the Manson ballet. He hasn't seen it yet, but he's gonna run it down."

"How do you know?"

"He was drunk the other night at a dinner, and he told me so."

"Why?"

"Some kind of moral preemption. Manson groupies don't fit his idea of ballerinas. All that deviant bending—I mean, doesn't he realize basically that's what a ballet is?"

"Will, how many ballets have you ever actually seen?"

"France has seen too many. That's the problem. The ballet's moving to New York in a few weeks and he's treating Manson's arrival at Lincoln Center as if it were a quality-of-life issue. He told me he cannot accept the concept. He said, unlike Broadway, there's no off-Ballet."

"And the conceptual producer knows. I told him. I had to." Will shook his head. "He was going to come tonight. Can't you just see him coming in," he said, reaching out and pressing his iced gin against my arm, "a flying wing of those ballerinas in perfect V-formation behind him. Like bowling pins all creamy white and up right, and then deviantly bending to make their drinks . . . "

He looked around the room. "I mean, why do you think I had this fucking party in the first place?"

"There's always going to be someone like that," I said, "in the way for no good reason."

"And you know, Hay," Will said, "the conceptual producer is this lifetime loser abstractionist with a ponytail and beard and these little darting eyes. Sort of an avant, skronky flake. But a good guy and I had to tell him, you know, because this Manson thing is his one and only shot . . ." Will was staring at France. "And now, here comes Albert France . . ."

He went over to the bar.

He mixed two gin and tonics, spun around, and walked directly over to where France and June stood. He nodded politely to June, and handed France a gin and tonic.

I could see the look in Will's eye as he raised his glass.

France raised his.

"Tonic for the disease," Will announced, "and gin for the niceties."

He took a long sip. France took a sip. Will poked a finger into France's chest and began to yell at him.

France stepped back, alarmed. He waited until Will had finished, and then began to speak with slow consideration. He'd apparently taken the toast as some sort of old-school invitation to verbal duel.

But Will suddenly reached around like he was grabbing Albert France's ass, and came up with his wallet. He ran over to the window, and flipped the wallet out. The hotel suite was on the sixth floor. There was total silence. All heads were turned.

Will turned back and stared at France. "Run it down," he said.

France stared at the open window.

June's constant, broad smile was gone, and she looked cold and imploringly at Will.

France turned and hurried out of the room.

"People don't drink gin anymore for a reason," June snapped.

She grabbed her bag and followed France out. She stopped at the door, turned, and walked back to where Will stood. "Even when you're being thoughtful," she said calmly, "you're being thoughtless."

Will's mouth was hanging open. He was beginning to look mortified.

I stayed late and got drunk with Will, but before leaving, didn't have it in me to duck him and his setup. Monica was a pretty blonde film publicist. She wore couture pantsuits hemming in her natural plumpness. She was older than me, a real big-haired, big-boned man hunter. We wound up going out a few times. I couldn't figure out how. She had an over-polite, midwestern way of making something seem agreed upon, even though I hadn't said a thing. On our second date, she gave me a furious blowjob, and then curled up and cried. On our third date—at a Mexican restaurant, she brought me a homemade sponge cake—the bottom of the cardboard box dripping and sticky with syrup, drank five margaritas and then told me she had a gun in her bedside drawer.

A few days later she walked into the production office without warning, greeting me with her steely coiffed hair and numbing cheeriness. She sat on my desk, swinging her keys and talking about lunch at Fred Segal.

My boss Leonard was standing nearby. He rested his bulbous eyes on her and told me, right in front of her, I could do better.

Leonard was blunt. He was a television producer, an obnoxious money hustler who treated you well so long as you were on his side. I liked him because he was good at what he did and had no qualms about side effects, about the little, sensitive fuck-overs I'd been taught all my life to care so much about. He was older looking, but I could not tell his age—fleshy face, steel-rimmed sunglasses pasted over his eyes. His darkened hair made his fake tan look like shoe polish.

We were friends. I don't know why. We spent a lot of time in his purple Jaguar, going all over LA meeting with managers and seeing bands. I'd talk to the bands, and he'd talk to the managers. Once, I'd politely told him his orange linen shirt was too gaudy for the band, the War Winks, we were on the way to shoot. The War Winks were being petulant about being filmed—even though nobody knew who they were, and hadn't yet signed the releases in his briefcase.

Leonard was nervous about wasting a day of money, and wanted to make the right impression. He stopped the Jaguar at a vintage store on Melrose, went in, and then came back out in a purple bowling team shirt.

I looked at the shirt.

"What," he said defensively, "I thought these kids were from Orange County?"

The War Winks were rich Bel Air kids; high-irony fake nerds with industry parents. The shirt couldn't have been worse. And it matched his car.

I looked at him. He looked down at himself, and we both began to laugh.

I took him back inside, and the nice Goth girl attendant in white face and witch black, her arms wrapped in chain metal, helped him find something more subdued.

One day in the office, I played Leonard Kimmel's record. Thought maybe I could help there.

But he didn't like it at all. "This is obscure," was all he said.

And I couldn't get Kimmel on the show.

One Saturday, Leonard took me on a cigarette boat to Catalina with Natalie Wood's daughter and a record company president. We drank beer on deck and the sun glittered in our eyes. We saw two baby whales, powder blue in the green sea. We talked and drank and got along great, everybody putting their arms around each other. When we returned and docked, they all wanted to go and get sushi.

I made up an excuse, and went and had dinner in a Chinese restaurant in Santa Monica. The Jade Chalet.

Helen was still in the Raleigh ward. The money I'd left for her bills was disappearing fast, and I didn't have much more. Helen's father had called a few days before to ask if it was all right to sell the Annie Oakley Warhol. I'd had to tell him it was a fake. Helen and I had had it on the wall of our place on Fifth Street, and along with most everything else in our apartment, I'd left it there for her father to pack up and hold onto for her. My father, way back in the seventies, had picked up the fake Warhol for nothing in the Georgetown Junior League Store. He'd given it to me when I'd moved to New York. Annie Oakley's face in the portrait is a chalky, ghostly blue, her hair stringed purple, and the medals on her chest ribbed with electric orange. A frontier of white lay ahead. Her eyes, fixed on the horizon, had a severity and honesty Warhol's slashes of neon panic could not leaven or penetrate.

I finished my rice and shrimp and took out a pen. I wrote a last check to Helen. I wanted to write her a note.

The world, I knew, had narrowed down to one sort of room for her. All white and gray, a rubbing alcohol smell, and a parking lot outside the barred window.

A fortune from the Jade Chalet:

You will wake up one morning and the
blankets will be Diebenkorn canvases.
You will wake up into ocean parks,
full of a deep, Diebenkorn blue
because a bed is a sea and a sky to lie between.
You will sell them and be rich.
It's better to be sick if you are rich.

But as I read what I'd written, I realized the last thing she needed to hear was abstractions. I no longer knew how to wish her well.

I tore up the note.

The waiter came and took my plate. I ordered another beer and asked for the bill. The day I'd met Helen, I'd come down into the lobby for a soda. I was working in the dark, shabby dubbing room of a big production company on Forty-sixth Street, and my eyes were still adjusting to the bright lobby when she'd crossed right in front of me—rough blonde hair, dressed in jeans and a forest green sweater. Brown eyes. No jewelry, only a worn brown leather choker around her neck. She had a slow, spaced out walk and a slight stoop. I watched her step into the revolving door, swing outside, and the sun seemed to implode her hair and then I could not see her.

I followed her. I looked up and down the block. I was about to turn back when I saw her. She was sitting on a bench in the little triangular park across the street. The park was perpetually in shadow from the midtown buildings.

I crossed the street, walked right up to her. "Hello," I said.

She looked up at me. Yellow leaves were scattered around her feet.

"Taking a break?" I said. I sounded like a coworker, all matter-of-factness and heavy-handed.

"Yes."

"Me too." I said, standing there.

She steadied her eyes on me, still trying to place me.

"You don't know me," I said. "Hayward Theiss."

She didn't say a word.

"We work in the same building."

She nodded.

"Are you going anywhere?" I asked. It was the short week before Thanksgiving.

She nodded again. "Home."

"What are you going to do when you are home?"

"Sleep," she said, eyeing me with a hesitant curiosity. "Don't you sometimes just love sleep?"

"Sure, I guess."

"It's like that feeling when it's snowing. But without the exhilaration. Just the softness, the peaceful part."

"Where's home?" I asked.

Her father, she said, was a professor in Raleigh-Durham. Her mother's family was from Maine. Her mother had been a scientist.

"What kind of science did your mother do?"

"I don't even know. There were always frozen animals in our freezer."

"What kind of animals?"

"Birds," she said. "Frogs, snakes."

She looked up at me and frowned. "You know, when I was a girl," she said, "my mother, when she'd send me off to school with my brown lunch bag, sometimes she'd try to do something special before she'd go off to work. Sometimes she'd make me a grilled cheese sandwich. Wrap it up hot. She didn't get that it would be cold at lunchtime."

"And she was a scientist . . ."

"Yes," she nodded, "that's the thing."

We were silent. She was looking at me. "Hayward?"

"Yes?"

"No, I mean, the name. It sounds Southern, but I've never heard it before. Where's it from?"

"Ohio. I'm named after my great-grandfather's springer spaniel."

"Really?" She laughed. "A dog?"

I nodded.

She was smiling. "You're named after a dog? What *is* your family like?"

I looked at her. The question, unfortunately, wasn't rhetorical. I was suddenly confused. I had no idea how to answer. There was only my father, and although my father had always been good to me, he was sort of a mystery and did not talk much about the past. He felt his past generations in his blood and that was enough. Time had passed, now it was gone, and there wasn't much to say. I didn't have any reference points; the family tree was like a Pollock—thick-coated spinouts, furiously buried symbols, flicked hints, and stop-start lifelines. Pissed on. About the only thing I knew for sure was I was named after that stupid dog. I did not want to tell Helen this. It seemed anemic. I thought of Sitting Bull, Annie Oakley's adopted father, and blurted out, with a mixture of sarcasm and stridency, "Well, technically, I'm related to Sitting Bull."

75

She shook her head and looked at me. "But I mean your father and mother? Sisters and brothers? Your *family*?"

5

I passed the days in the sunny loft, reading spy books and staring out at the changing patterns in the sky and the ocean. I had no idea how many days had passed. I knew I'd hit my head, and there was a vacancy, a short-term kind of immediacy, and a physical leadenness to my deeper desires that made me think I was operating with a serious concussion.

I'd been aware enough not to make a single mark of my presence. I did not shower, for fear of noise from the pipes outside, and never used lights. The teenager's room was apart from the rest of the house, off the entrance hall by the garage, and seemingly cut out as an afterthought. I slept in a sleeping bag on top of the teenager's quilt. The bed was hard, the room had only a skylight, and I slept soundly. Every morning I would roll the sleeping bag up tight with my clothes and put it back in the closet.

From behind the locked door of the teenager's room I could hear a car coming in the driveway, and have enough time to slip out underneath the house. My only concern was someone coming in while I was up in the loft. But the loft was the best place.

I cooked once a day, from cans in the deep pantry. Simple, nourishing, one-pot dishes: chicken broth with black beans, rice with canned carrots or artichoke hearts, pasta and sardines. I did not have much of an appetite and I'd hide the leftovers away in the vegetable bin, clean the pot, and put it exactly where I'd found it. The pans were stacked in a sequence of size, and I would make sure to replace them as such. I used the same bowl and the same spoon and fork every day. I used a green Pellegrino jar for water. I'd gone through most of the Pellegrino. The tap water had a slightly sulfurous mustiness, but it was water.

I'd have tea and microwaved oatmeal in the morning, and always be startled by the sound of the beep. Everything was one pot or microwaved, easily disposed. Like a stock boy, I kept moving things to the front of the pantry to make it seem as full as I'd found it.

I double-bagged what little trash I generated, and put the bags under the house.

I kept to the bedroom, the kitchen, and the loft. I craved fresh air. But I never risked even cracking open a window. It was safe there—I was sure I had not been seen. But it was also a glass house.

I'd been out once, when the sun was strongest, to see if I could see into the house from the beach. It was a big risk, but I had to know. I put on the purple goblin T-shirt and a pair of the teenager's gangster-rap black shorts, which came down over my knees. When the sun was high in the west, I slipped out under the house. I edged down the sand alley. The house next door had two windows overlooking the alley. But the blinds were always drawn and Leonard was long gone from there. I stepped into the last patch of foliage before the seawall. A couple came down the beach with a dog. The sun pressed into my eyes, and as the couple walked by, they bended and folded like candle flames. The dog stopped, sniffed in my direction, and looked right where I stood.

Farther down the beach, a woman sat reading under an umbrella. Beyond her it was empty.

The dog caught a new scent, turned, and trotted on with his nose skimming the sand.

I stepped out of the foliage, over the low wall, and down the steps to the beach. I walked to the water's edge. I turned around and tried to see into the house. Through the black glass I could just see the arm of the leather sofa, muted by sunlight, and nothing else farther in. The house reflected back a smoked crystal light, as if the inside had been covered with a dark foil. It looked closed up and empty. No sign of life. It was like a great big, black mask in an empty museum, no light through it.

The house to the right, I knew, was now vacant, and I'd become familiar with the routines of the people on the other side. The man was at work in the Valley or Santa Barbara or LA or wherever it is you commute to from way out here. The woman, in a velour sweat suit, was off in her black Cadillac SUV to the gym or yoga. Everybody wore sweat suits out here. And gold jewelry. And had black dogs.

I looked beyond the line of beach houses to the peaceful bowl of land above. The bowl was lushly green, strewn with white houses like pieces of trash. The distant peaks of the brown mountains rose paper thin against the blue sky.

Water rushed up and over my feet. It was frigid. I looked down. I was standing on a clean, cold slope of sand. Artfully dotted around my feet were a tiny white conch shell, a smooth maroon rock, a clump of green-bulbed seaweed, and a charred piece of wood. It was strange to be in the spot I stared at most of everyday. The water rushed back up over my feet. I reached down and grabbed the conch shell before it washed away. I held the shell in my hand. I noticed a flat blackness, like tarmac, up in the shell. It was alive.

The sun had warmed my face. I felt tired.

I waited until the beach was clear, and went up and slipped back under the house.

Coming up into the closet, I stumbled over a box of the teenager's stuff. The junk of his youth tumbled out—a basketball, old electronics, a leather jacket, black-metal CDs, and a pile of Japanese comic books and Swedish porn magazines. I pulled out one of the magazines and opened it up. A naked blonde teenager played with herself and licked the thigh of an older, dark-haired woman. I felt a twinge of involvement. Their eyes were closed and they seemed genuinely intimate, but my involvement became only curiosity, and I stared at the girls having sex the same way I stared out over the ocean.

I boxed up the stuff, went upstairs, left the conch on the counter, and made tea.

As I took the tea and headed upstairs, I glanced down at the conch shell. There was a centimeter trail of sand grains and wetness. It had tried to move.

I boiled water, dropped the conch into the pan.

I pulled it out, and carefully disgorged the mussel from the shell with a lobster fork. I rinsed the shell and set it on the counter to dry. I took the mussel, dead but still glistening, and went down into the closet and buried it in the cold sand underneath the house.

I went up to the loft, scanned the paperbacks for a new book. I'd just worked through the le Carré, and was now getting into the Ludlum. I noticed a romance novel by Sidney Sheldon. Sidney Sheldon, I remembered, had written the screenplay for *Annie Get Your Gun.*

I'd seen the film on television once. Annie Oakley's big shooting contest with Frank Butler had been decorously reenacted.

I remembered, despite the numbingly affectionate theater of the scene, the match between Frank Butler and Annie Oakley had actually occurred. My great-grandfather

Finn had set it up. He'd set it up to make a lot of money, which he did.

Annie Mozee (Oakley was a show name) and Finn had both grown up in Darke County, Ohio. They had been poor farm kids, and hunted game together in the county's lumpy meadows, cornrows, stream beds, and dense clumps of woods. Annie had a long-barreled, cap-and-ball Pennsylvania rifle, taller than she was. She was a miracle shot. One in a million. Otherwise, her childhood, like Finn's, was dark and hardscrabble. One long chore. She called the fields, *out there*.

Annie, in her early teens, made extra money by shooting game. She would wrap her kill in silvery green swamp grass and take it to the Katzenburg store in Greenville, who in turn sold it to the thriving hotels in Cincinnati. Her birds always sold for a good price because they were, without exception, shot clean and in the head. *Quails will fly straight for an opening in the trees. A grouse will seek cover. It can drop from a bare tree as swift as sight, and can skim like a bullet over the ground. Doves fly out of a grain field or a patch of ragweed, swerving and swooping in wild, unpredictable pattern. You wait then. You don't sight them. You just swing with them, and when it feels right . . .*

Katzenburg said later, after she got famous, "She had a feeling about her. She had eyes clear as light and brought with her a feeling of far away."

Annie, unbeknownst to Katzenburg, had started in 1875 to sell her birds straight to the Highland Hotel in Cincinnati. Straight to Finn. He was the buyer. Finn, still a teenager, had moved to Cincinnati the previous year, and had gotten a job at the Highland. He worked hard, low down in management, and used all his connections to the country, to the German and Quaker farms, to secure reliable, cheap stocks. Annie's birds were highly prized, and all the other hotels began buying birds from Finn.

In 1876, Annie turned fifteen. She put down her rifle and left Darke County—with its premonitions of the scope of the world in its town names—North Star, Russia, Frenchtown, Versailles—and followed Finn to Cincinnati. Cincinnati was a bustling city in 1876, overrun with people fleeing the depressed east. The West had been mostly conquered by that time, the last buffalo hunt had taken place, Custer had been slain and avenged, and it was the gateway cities now, Chicago, St. Louis, Cincinnati, with their industry and new, spastic flux, that were untamed and wild. Cincinnati's cobblestone streets were clogged with riders and carriages pressing through the air full of horse dung and smoke. It was the first gateway west and big steamboats rung out as they set out loaded with grain. The wharves and stockyards were alive with sailors, laborers, Easterners, soldiers, immigrants, and criminals, all transient and flowing west.

One afternoon, Annie came into Finn's ground-floor apartment in the Highland. A strange man stood there, his shoes broken and dirty. He held a silver platter in one hand and two candlesticks in the other. Annie, without missing a beat, walked right in and right past the thief, reached into the pantry, and pulled out Finn's shotgun. She cocked it and pointed it at the man, told him to leave. He took a step forward. She shot a hole in the wall two inches from his head, and he dropped the silver, turned, and ran.

A valet heard the shot, rushed over. A crowd gathered and the police came. The hotel managed to keep the incident hushed up, but what was Annie—not even sixteen and living with her older sister on Fairmont Hill—doing in Finn's apartment in the middle of the afternoon?

But Finn had just enough luck to endure the scandal. Bourbon had recently been invented, by mistake, in Cincinnati. A ship's hold of rye had caught fire, and the burnt barrels were thrown out to a junkyard. A wood salvager eventually cracked open one of the barrels. The oak inside had turned to charcoal, and out flowed nectar gold and brown as loving eyes.

Finn became the first in Cincinnati to ever *formally* serve bourbon. The only place it was made was across the river in Kentucky, and in well-to-do Cincinnati anything Kentuckian was frowned upon as hillbilly. Kentucky bourbon was assumed to be a bootlegger's drink for sailors. But Finn made up an English-sounding brand and a Pennsylvania bottling address, priced it at the Highland as if it were a delicacy, and it instantly became fashionable. By the time Annie had blown the hole in the hotel wall, Finn was making the hotel so much money from liquor sales, not only was the minor controversy ignored, but he'd already been made a manager.

Finn and Annie were in Cincinnati together for two years. On most Saturdays, accompanied by Annie's sister, they would walk up Fairmont Hill and sit outside at Schuetzenbuckel's Beer Garden. Finn drinking the malty beer, and Annie soda or tea. Finn would dance with Annie's sister, then Annie. Over and over until her sister would drop out. And then they would go on, swirling around to the brawny German rhythms.

Sundays they would go to the Quaker church on Broad Street, and then dine together back at the Highland's banquet room.

It was an idyll, a kind of glowing respite in both of their lives.

When I was young, my father had two ancient photographs, wrapped in onion paper and tucked into cardboard. He kept them in his change drawer amid pipe cleaners, broken gadgets, and buckeyes. When he was away, I'd take them out. One photograph was of Finn, the other of Annie. Under each photo, the gold-etched script read: *Green & Connolly Studios, Cincinnati, Ohio, May 21, 1877.*

Finn in 1877 had grown into a barrel-chested young man with a long, doubting face and gleaming eyes. His mother had died in childbirth. His father, my great-great-grandfather, had been an abolitionist Quaker farmer and a stretcher bearer for the Union. He had been killed at Shiloh. If he had been a soldier he would have been too old to fight and would have never been in any danger. At Shiloh, the Union troops were pinned against the Tennessee River and were being slaughtered. Finn's father was running back behind the lines for bandages. He was caked in mud, and the Red Cross on his chest could not be seen. He was shot on sight by Bull Nelson's troops in the driving rain, mistaken for a retreating deserter.

Finn, consequently, had grown up dirt-poor. He'd gotten by as a sort of local migrant worker on the larger, more affluent German and Dutch farms, and his eyes in the photograph are full of a hard desire.

Annie's face in the photo is serene—her eyes wide, dark, and intense. Her face is slightly down turned, as if she is embarrassed by the focus of her eyes. Her hair is long in thick, dark curls, and she has a dark color, looks shy and also a little wild. She is not smiling, but her lips have a youthful, expectant parting, as if she were in love.

But Finn and Annie's life together in Cincinnati changed abruptly in the summer of 1877. Just two months after those photos were taken, Finn set up the shooting match with Frank Butler depicted in *Annie Get Your Gun*. Finn set everyone up, really. He'd known what Annie could do when she'd arrived in Cincinnati two years before, and had forbidden her to shoot in the city's galleries and arcades. On occasional Saturdays, he would take her out to the country for picnics, and she would practice her shot in some quiet, unseen field. Finn forced her to wait years, until the most lucrative possible moment, to reveal her talent. And the moment arrived when the famous, touring sharpshooter Frank Butler came through town calling for challenges.

Annie, secretly prompted by Finn, came forward. She was an unknown shot, a woman, and a hick. The odds against her were staggering. Finn managed to have Annie delay the match two days while he went around quietly accumulating bets, the largest wager being a year's salary against half ownership of the rival hotel, the Globe. They shot real pigeons, raising the stakes even further. *We used two traps, gun below the elbow, one barrel to be used. I shot a muzzle loader, but it was a good one. Mr. Butler won the toss and took his position at the traps.*

His voice came quick and even. "Pull."

"Dead," called the referee.

I then faced the traps. My knees were shaking. I lined the gun up, then dropping it quickly below the elbow, called, "Pull."

I too grassed my bird in good time. Spectators flocked in on all sides. The scores kept even. Mr. Butler's twenty-fifth, a quick-climbing right quarterer, fell dead about two feet beyond the boundary line.

I had to score my last bird to win. I stopped for an instant before I lined my gun. I saw familiar faces. I knew I would win.

It was a stunning victory for a woman back then, and Finn was on his way with a stack of cash and a certificate for half of the Globe Hotel.

A few days after the instantly famous match, Annie, by complete chance, ran into Frank Butler outside of Wiswell's gallery. They talked politely about guns, and then Frank Butler revealed to her how much Finn had collected from everybody in town. Annie had not seen a penny.

Annie stopped receiving (or visiting) Finn. She stopped speaking to him.

Finn, soon after, sold out his share of the Globe and moved to Cleveland. His take from the match had been the seed of his fortune.

Annie's notoriety from the match had been the seed of her fame. A year later she married Frank Butler, but she did not take his name. She changed her name to Oakley, and joined Buffalo Bill Cody's Wild West Show.

But aside from my father's photographs and Annie's brief recollections, most of the story is just menu history. I'd read about the bourbon and the shooting-match bet on the back side of an ancient, preserved menu from the Globe. It hung on the lobby wall of the boxy white Hilton that had replaced the Globe in the early fifties (the Hilton is gone now too, replaced in the late eighties by a glassy, businesslike Embassy Suites). The menu, yellowed with age, had been butterflied and framed. One side liver and onions, black pudding, pike, pickled beets, the other side anecdotes about the old hotel.

But why Finn and Annie went their separate ways isn't menu history. It didn't make for friendly summation. The truth was, they were cousins. When he'd leave his apartment door in the Highland unlocked for her, it was incest.

Finn's and Annie's mothers were sisters. Annie's mother had never told her children she'd had a sister. Her sister, Finn's mother, had shamed her family, run off at fourteen with an older, Irish Quaker laborer, married, had a boy, and died in childbirth. Her husband had died at Shiloh.

She'd become only a long-buried stranger's name.

Apparently, when Annie's mother told her all this, Annie, flush with local fame from her victory over Frank Butler, and already receiving lucrative overtures from touring shows, made an immediate, calculating decision not only to leave Finn but also to never speak to him again.

A year later she hit the road as a sharpshooter. That sort of cousin stuff was all right out in the country some places, but intermarrying was also exactly the kind of rural compromise both Finn and Annie must have been so determined to get away from.

It *was* difficult, even back then, to go on and accomplish anything married to your cousin.

But there's another story.

Finn, in the summer of 1877—his pockets full of good prospects after Annie's win, had asked Annie to marry him. She said yes—knowing they were cousins, and wrote to her mother about the engagement. Her mother immediately came to Cincinnati to get her. She took her back to Darke County. Nobody saw her for a year. In all the retellings of her life, nobody can account for this year, other than to say she was hidden away.

A year later, she left for the Wild West.

Finn, a year later, appeared in Cleveland with a son, and began to build roads. And both Annie and Finn, even with all their youthful success and wealth, became these two quintessentially solitary, wandering Americans. As if cursed to wander around stuck in some myth. Stuck in the convenient sadness their great first love was really only mundane blood love, rather than something more unusual.

6

Most weeknights Leonard and I worked late. He had this red-braided pot called "herejuana" he got from Sheryl Crow's dealer. He smoked at his desk at night, on the phone while watching footage. I tried it once, and found myself alone in the dark office at 2 A.M., the only light the plain blue screen of my computer, a paper-thin ocean I was trying to put my hand through.

Most weekends we'd be out in the Valley, working on audience-less band shoots in various soundstages. One Sunday afternoon, the shoot actually came in on time, and I went out afterward to a bar with a couple of the cameramen. To my surprise, the Redskins were on. Playing Miami. The Redskins were the only sports team I could ever muster any interest in. They were a great success during my flailing adolescence, and in a weird way, I still looked up to them. They were down by seventeen in the third quarter. The cameramen were beginning to bother me because we'd made friendly wagers on the game, and now the Dolphins were driving again. One of the cameramen was an actual socialist. He wore a pin with a red fist and drove a big, square seventies sedan, as if making a point about waste. He had a hot tub and had once invited a couple of us over to use it. I'd laughed. I had thought he was kidding. I was still too embarrassed about this to apologize. But he didn't like me much anyway. I was younger, and his boss.

The Dolphins kicked a field goal.

"Nice kick," said the other cameraman. He was one of those perfectly styled outdoorsmen I only ever saw in Los Angeles. Tall and black-haired in jeans, plaid shirt and work boots. But then he had tattoos up and down his forearms. I never saw anyone so outdoorsy with so many tattoos.

"That was a nice kick," he stated again, recognizing the obvious with a sure, hearty voice, as if he were made of oak and you of tin.

It was a fifty-one-yard kick splitting the posts.

"Of course it was a nice kick." I muttered.

"C'mon Hay," the socialist said. "Just a game here."

I looked at him, at his pin. "As if it's not so obviously stupid," I snapped, "as a system, in terms of what people really want."

He held up his hands, opening his palms in a kind of "I give up, no intelligent life here" gesture. He'd done it with this kind of rabbity, Robin Williams effeteness.

The Redskins got the ball back. They ran for a yard. On the next play, the quarterback threw a ball directly into the back of his tackle's helmet.

"Goddamn." I said.

The socialist shook his head. "You can't believe in this stuff too much."

"Look, fuck you. The Redskins are losing and I don't need you telling me it doesn't matter."

"C'mon guys," the forester baritoned.

The Redskins ran on third down and lost a yard.

I got up and went outside for some air. It was pleasantly cool, and beginning to get dark out. Standing under the bright halogen lights, in the carbon-dioxide ambience of busy Little Santa Monica Boulevard, I calmed down and felt for a moment my own decent health, felt okay after a hard week of work, and not the usual Sunday fear of death. But the weight of good health was going to increase the fear of falling through. Helen slipping down the wall rack of the Bleecker Street pharmacy, falling right asleep, incredibly, as the panty-hose eggs rained down around her. Helen had been young, ready for good young things. Not old-aged roommates in paper slippers babbling complaints. Helen, like everybody else, wanted an occasional cushion of pleasantness in her life, and it was only when I took her out to Café des Artistes that we hit the ground running. It was our third date, and a huge, risky expenditure for me. I'd had a string of dead-end, low-wage production jobs, and didn't go out for good dinners. The last expensive place I'd been had been a few months before, on my twenty-fifth birthday. I'd put on my father's blue Brooks Brothers suit, too light for the cold, wet dusk, and deposited my inheritance at Manufacturers Hanover Bank on lower Broadway. I'd been presented with a pink deposit receipt for $370,000, the end of Finn's fortune. I'd immediately withdrawn two hundred dollars, and taken a cab to the Old Homestead at Fourteenth Street and Ninth Avenue. I'd sat down, my young arms loose as jelly, ordered a T-bone and a bottle of expensive red wine, and celebrated my birthday alone at that fading, musty steakhouse.

When my father was a boy he lived in Miami every summer, working at Sea World, feeding the dolphins and sharks. As a young man he spent summers in Venezuela, doing construction work and drinking five-cent glasses of clear rum in whitewashed Caracas bars. Finn opened up a lot of worlds for a lot of people. In the latter years of his life, he traveled all over the world with a large entourage of family, friends, and servants. One of his best friends was Howard Chandler Christy, the artist who created the Christy girl, a Twenties turn on the Gibson girl. Christy's studio was in the building above Café des Artistes. One night after a fire had gutted the restaurant, he got drunk, went down, and thinking it would all be hastily painted over, spent the night into the day (supposedly with the help of Salvador Dalí, who was also living in the building at the time) covering a wall with cherry-lipped, naked versions of the Christy girls, swimming and swinging in their own orange Eden. Fearing retribution or eviction, he was hired to replicate the murals on the rest of the walls and it became a great sensation, his biggest success. In every way, Christy girls should have been pandering and tacky, but as Helen and I saw, they had a strange seriousness and magic in their expressions. They lived in a rare, youthful world unto their own; it was impenetrable and it fascinated people.

Helen and I sat down at Café des Artistes surrounded by those girls. Helen was looking around with a curious but restrained smile, the restaurant light softening her hair into a lamplight gold. She wore an iridescent blue dress and the same worn leather choker around her neck. We sat in a small banquet between a leaded window and an oil-green copse of trees. Behind Helen, a naked blonde swam by, her eyes gleaming back at me.

The waiter came and I ordered, with a put-on fatalism, a three-hundred-dollar bottle from the "Celebration Wines." Helen was both embarrassed and pleased. Café des Artistes was not a place for gourmands. I told her it was really only thirty dollars. She seemed let down. The waiter came up cradling the bottle. She couldn't help a smile. It was all right by her because it was obvious that I was not a gourmand. That I'd just pointed to something I didn't understand and smiled. She liked that.

We were drinking the wine and we were looking at each other. The wine was so expensive we couldn't help feeling drunk. We finished a second cheaper bottle with the buttery food, and she began to ask me questions. Simple questions about my family, my past, and suddenly some synapse in my brain opened up and I began to speak with antic propulsion about so many things because not only was I finally having a good time with someone else but also, because I was grateful for this feeling. I suddenly felt the need to explain myself. But like Annie Oakley's whole life and myth, I didn't know what was true about my own past. I wanted Helen to know that from the outset. I wanted things to be clear with her. But as I talked I realized there were too many contradictions, and that maybe nobody wanted to hear somebody's history that is not only full of lies but also censored. My father and I weren't really from Washington, D.C., although we'd lived in the city for decades. But we also weren't from Ohio anymore, or the Eastern Shore. Growing up, until we'd moved out to the Eastern Shore, we'd never owned a house, just rented various ones—always suffused with a vague ache of womanlessness—along MacArthur Boulevard, or down below Wilson High School, in colorless middle-class neighborhoods with furniture rented and set down all at once out of large department-store trucks. (For some reason, my father kept all his inherited furniture in a storage space in Tyson's Corner.) We were Quaker, I told Helen, outwardly modest, even-handed, and generous, but also withdrawn inside and judgmental. We were also Catholic and felt the Catholic dismay of sin, but then the idea of salvation was a joke. We were broke and then we weren't. My father had a two-hundred-thousand-dollar Shaker side table in storage, a series of expensive BMWs, but the food was always frozen, the soup canned, the hotels motels, and the restaurants dumps. (Until of course, I was faced with taking you out, I half-joked to Helen to no response.) Our ancestors were conscientious objectors who died in wars. We were neither Democrats or Republicans (my father rarely voted and once we went to a John Anderson rally at a car dealership). We were decent athletes but tended to be depressive and, except for the Redskins, hated the hoopla of the games on TV. We drank a lot but did not handle it well.

She raised her wineglass and, to my relief, finally laughed.

I never knew my grandfather. Neither did, apparently, my father. My grandfather was in his fifties when my father was born, and died before I was. He was an alcoholic country lawyer with a bad temper and a generous streak (he impulsively passed out college scholarships as if he were campaigning for mayor). My grandmother was sweet and simple and died when I was twelve. I never knew anybody on my mother's side, and beyond my father's sister, a corkscrew-haired owner of a small gallery in Philadelphia who we used to spend summers with in Colorado, and who'd taught me how to tie my shoes and button my sleeves when I was young, I had nothing to do with any of my relatives, and they wanted nothing to do with me. Growing up, the more I'd learned about all my relatives in the last century, the more it seemed that the family line was made up of travelers and quick-change artists, whether they were politicians, pool players, bankers, priests, marksmen, stretcher bearers, or even inventors. My father's great-uncle, a missionary, had invented reflector sides for trains, but had gone off to Peru soon after and had never bothered to get a patent. In the fifties another relative, Roland Theiss, invented "The Happiness Machine," built to test the happiness of women. "How's your love life?" or "What kind of future would you like to live in?" He would ask young women whose fingers he had strapped down in leather rings to a table. He would read the quivering needles on the mysterious box—electric wires curling from the leather to black metal—studiously turn a dial, and then announce the results.

He was really just a traveling shill for the Studebaker automobile company. They were promoting a new model called the Lark, and the plan was to get the machine in all the local papers and then crown a woman, with great fanfare, "Miss Happy as a Lark."

The machine could not, as each woman would inevitably ask, make you any happier. But Roland, apparently ever the opportunist, still managed to pick a lot of them up, promising that upon further exploration, it might.

I'd put my wine down and stopped talking. Talking had been too easy, as if it had all been for the girl behind Helen, swimming by.

Helen was looking at me. "It doesn't sound like you've ever told anybody any of this before."

I was looking back at her and I felt a certain, weighty contentment, as if on the verge of a long sleep. But whatever weight of possibility, history, or expenditure I began to feel, it was leavened by wine and white linen fleur-de-lis and the murals of cavorting girls around us that seemed as young and blank as we felt. She felt the blankness, too. She told me so, almost apologetically as we rose, "I don't feel any of that rich food at all."

Finn had been a tough young man. But the bad luck he and Annie had with each other early on might have been what had set them on such rigid, successful courses. Sometime in the eighties, I'd asked my dad about Finn's gravel fortune. He said most of it was gone. "I blew a big pile of it with Ray on a uranium mine investment in the seventies."

I asked him why we always seemed broke back in the seventies.

"That was a funny decade," he said. "The years just seemed to burn down like a pile of leaves. Money didn't matter much then. It was the last time the world didn't feel like it was progressing."

I waited outside the restaurant after dinner. Helen had gone to make a phone call, and when she finally came through the doors, she came out on the edge of a glaring, overhead light, there and then not there, contained in her weary, incandescent carriage. She had carriage, as if half asleep on another plane of insight. I'd never fully understood or saw too many benefits from that plane, but I'd understood somehow, right then as she'd moved toward me, she had suffered more than I had. She knew more about it.

And then, a few months later, there had been a phone call.

One Saturday afternoon, I was running an errand in her neighborhood and I suddenly wanted to see her. She'd stayed over at my studio a few times, but I'd never been up to her place. I called from a pay phone.

Her phone rang and rang. I hung up, dug out the change, and tried again. It rang. I was about to hang up when, to my astonishment, a man answered. "Hello."

I froze.

"Who's there?" the voice asked. It was Southern, but clipped. Hurried sounding.

"Is this Helen Conover's apartment?"

"Who is this?"

"This is not Helen Conover's?"

"She has left."

"Where did she go?"

"Who is this?"

I said my name.

"What do you want?"

"I wanted to speak to Helen."

"Helen?"

"Yes."

There was a long silence. Then a muted burst of conversation. There was the noise of someone moving around. I could hear his voice, but nothing he was saying.

He came back on the line. "Hold on."

After a minute or so of dead silence, she came on the line. "Oh, hello?"

"Helen?"

"I'm sorry. I have to go. I'll have to call you another time. Thank you."

She hung up.

There was something off in her voice, an artificial politeness, as if a toothpick had been caught in her throat. It was not guilt or embarrassment underneath, but something more serious. More like a strained timidity, as if she'd just been hit.

I did not see her for months, and when we started back with each other, the phone call was never mentioned.

I came back into the bar. The forester saw me and pointed up at the screen. The Redskin safety had intercepted a pass and was running in the clear down the middle of the field. He was looking up at himself on the JumboTron as he ran, as if the play were only really happening if he saw it up there. As if he felt the need to relive the play before it was even over. But maybe I had it wrong. Maybe he was just looking up to God. It was midway through the fourth quarter. The Dolphin offense was held on three plays. The Redskins got the ball back and scored again on a hurry-up drive. A few minutes later—down by six points, they were on the Dolphins twenty-three with one last play. The quarterback, a big-boned, long-ball passer, got flushed out of the pocket and lumbered, as if in slow motion, down the sideline. Unbelievably, no defenders came into the screen. I still do not understand where the Dolphin secondary was on the play. He fell into a linebacker near the goal line, and fell over like a drunk into the end zone.

It was a great, freak play. The quarterback couldn't out-run a steamroller. The Redskins won.

The socialist threw thirty dollars on the bar and left. The forester gave me a sound pat on the back, handed me a twenty, and drove off in his spotless, vintage Ford pickup.

I stayed at the bar, soaking in the surprise win. I ordered a hamburger, another beer, and grabbed a pile of papers from atop a video machine.

As I ate, the bar around me began to empty, and the noise around me thinned. Sunday night.

I finished the *Times* and began to leaf through the *Weekly*.

"Kimmel," I said out loud.

There in the corner of one of the listing pages was his photo. He wore a frayed black blazer and button-down shirt. He stared out with his tricky dark eyes and deadpan face. There was a caption:

> Kimmel's slim, cranky songs are imbued with a Kinksesque, wry detriment and a beautifully tired tune-fulness. Just drums, guitar, and vocal, the melodies roll on with a ramshackle, skeletal looseness as if about to collapse to the floor at any moment. Whatever the songs mean, they all seem to start at the end of something, and hang around like dead flowers you can't toss out.
>
> Last time through, however, Kimmel's drummer was tossed out. Wildeyed and drunk, he dropped his sticks mid-song, went into the audience, and beat his fists on his own singer's shoes to the point of real physical detriment.

He was playing in some Silverlake club. I checked the date. He was playing right then. I kicked myself for not having checked the papers before. He hadn't bothered calling, but I felt a rare rush of good feeling. It was a good coincidence if I could still catch him.

I signaled to pay.

I arrived at the little club and everything, of course, was running late. Kimmel hadn't come on, but I could not get backstage. I got a beer, sat down at a little round table, and waited amid the sparse crowd.

Eventually the taped music stopped and the dark room went darker. The club manager came onstage and made a few announcements. While the man was still speaking, Kimmel shuffled in behind him. He wore the same jacket and shirt he'd had on in the newspaper photograph. He waited until the man finished, and then stepped forward and muscled the microphone into position.

"Somebody else's song," he mumbled by way of an introduction.

Oh I am an English nobleman,
a nobleman am I.
My dignity would be besmirched
if you hit me in the face with a pie.

It was a funny song. Nobody laughed. They wanted Burt for that.

The next song I'd heard before, but he sang it this time in a bewitching style. A simple but desperate love song with a magic, internal momentum, it began with a soprano, almost glammy hopefulness, and then descended to a repeated chorus . . .

Same blue shirt,
same blue tie,
dirt underneath,
overcast sky.

And then as the song ended, his voice seemed delicately strained, fated to break up like ice cracking . . .

I never meant
to be this kind of man.
I never set out
to do the things I can't stand.

The verse was his only real confessional attempt, and I wondered if it was the hundred-thousand-dollar song he hated so much.

Kimmel's talky singing the rest of the show was quiet and scornfully miserable. His voice had a brined reserve, sounded disinterested. There was no Burt, and without Burt, the songs had no drive and the humor behind them was lost. As the show progressed, his singing digressed to a hoarse whisper, and the crowd barely noticed when he'd start or end a song.

At one point he stopped mid-song, as if remembering something. He pressed the top string of his guitar and mis-hit it. There was a vibration, as if he'd scraped his own bone, and he looked vacantly out over the chatty, disinterested crowd, the memory gone.

As I stood and watched Kimmel play, a nagging feeling took hold. Kimmel, in the years since college, had somehow been winding himself down. It was as if underneath whatever he was doing with career, people, health, and even with his future, he was on some kind of strict subliminal timer. As if he knew exactly when he would run into a hard wall of failure. There had been some of the old tartness in Arizona—although much of that was an absinthe-induced pissing contest with Will, but there was something consciously reductive about him. But maybe I was wrong. Maybe Kimmel was now just spinning along under an even more inscrutable cover, knowing exactly where he was going. Either way, since college, he'd been disappearing more and more into something I had no idea about.

I remembered the spring of our last semester, when Kimmel had begun to change.

Will had invited us down to his stepfather's house in Palm Beach. He was over on the Gulf Coast for crew training, and the plan was to drive down from school and meet him at the house. Will had described the place with great animation. It had been designed, coincidently, by Addison Mizner, and Will said it was like an opium palace inside, a Moorish transience of rooms made of the weightiest silences. The house floated on marble water, full of decadent, orange air and teak dark as coffee.

Kimmel and I, excited, did the drive in one shot. On I-95 in an ice storm, a tractor-trailer skidded out ahead of us, jackknifing and coming to a rocking halt across three lanes. We were lucky and I just managed to swing us around the back. There was already a white sedan crushed up under the trailer.

Shaken, we detoured to Charlottesville and bought cocaine from a boarding-school friend of Kimmel and Will's—a fraternity president at UVA. The last thing I remember of the drive was trying to hold a knife blade full of cocaine under Kimmel's nose as he drove through a freak North Carolina snowstorm.

I woke at dawn as we pulled into rainy, languid Palm Beach. We found the keys and remote for the gate, as instructed, in a padded envelope. We passed through the gate, then drove down a narrow, white-shell drive, through deep, curling foliage, wide tongues of green leaves, and thick orange and red bushes. We came onto a broad lawn with ruler-straight royal palms and slouching coconut palms spaced out across the grass. Beyond the green was a chipped pastel wall, and then the green, surging ocean.

To the right was a graying stucco caretaker's apartment over a garage, set back and protected in the foliage.

There was no house.

Will was not there. In the apartment there was a hot plate and a mini-fridge, sparse, wicker furniture, and two cots. There was no phone and no message.

We went to town for food and supplies. On the way, Kimmel announced it was too humid for his gabardine suit, and we drove out to an outlet and he bought jeans, a few plain Oxford shirts, and a windbreaker. As soon as he came out of the store in the new clothes, there was less of a surface to confront. Just a college student in jeans and clean shirt, finishing up his thesis and ready to move on into other things. But standing in the rainy parking lot, Kimmel suddenly seemed to be at a halt inside, carefully considering directions. It was as if he believed there was a way to be in college, and then a way he had to figure out to be once he was out.

It rained all day. We unpacked—Kimmel's luggage a cardboard box full of books and papers. We explored the property, made dinner, and went to sleep early. We could feel the world outside, the teeming highways of Florida on one side, the ocean on the other, heaving against the property. But the big lot was walled off, lush, and placid and we would not be bothered. Some time in the night, Kimmel's cot gave out, the springs poking up in disarray. He put the mattress on the floor. But then there were so many mice, he had to hurry and build a wall around the mattress with all the books and stacks of papers. Occasionally throughout the night, a mouse would manage to hurdle the wall, and I'd awake to his alarmed gasps.

In the morning, he dismantled the walls and rearranged the books and papers in random but tidy piles. He folded his sheets and blanket into a perfect, square pile, and carefully leaned his guitar against the wall. He sat up cross-legged on the mattress, and placed on his head a crown he'd triangulated out of paper. He looked at me with a supercilious purse of the lips, and held out his mug. "Now, get me some tea," he said, beckoning to me with a sheikh's dismissive, back-handed flip. "You there, get me some tea."

Kimmel, for the rest of the week, worked on his mattress on the floor, surrounded by the stacks of books and papers. He somehow had it all organized in his head, knew right where to go for something. He would reach two inches up into a random stack and come out with exactly what he needed.

Afternoons, we'd take breaks and play soccer with a tennis ball in the drizzle. At night, we played backgammon, read, drank tea and a little whiskey left there, crouched and protected like dogs in a den while the wind whipped down the hollow of the rain gutters. When we talked, it was about work or music or about getting a house in Maine for the summer and swimming and reading. But we could hardly pay our expenses at college. He was on a full scholarship, and got a little money to live on from somewhere. But I never saw any of his family, ever. And he never asked about mine.

As the week passed he played his guitar more and more and spoke less and less. Sometimes he'd play at night, and under the sound of the rain, it was lovely to go to sleep to.

He'd sit up and play for hours. He really began to get lost in it, in a fragile way, when there were no words.

The day before we had to leave Palm Beach, the rain gave out (we had not heard from Will, and nobody from his family had ever come around). We drove over to the discharge channel of the Riviera Beach power plant. The concrete-encased plant, with its huge rusting metallic pipes and tower, loomed uneasily over the manatees hanging around in the warm, polluted water. We stood on the crab-grass in our jeans and bare feet, pressed our fingers into the chain-link fence and stared down at the animals. The man-atees were big and gray and scraped up, most of them had these big gashes from the blades of boat engines. Big rings of blubber suffocated their weird, doglike snouts. They basked listlessly. Dozens of them, rolling over each other like fish in boxes in Chinese markets.

"Why don't the sharks come for them?" Kimmel asked with flat-voiced amazement. "Where are the sharks? Look at those things, they're like floating turkeys."

He looked at me, genuinely frustrated. "It's a feast. Where are the sharks? Why don't they come and get them?"

"I would, if I were a shark."

"I don't understand this."

It was a hot day. The sun was finally breaking through the withdrawing clouds and the heat burned like fuel in the air above the grass. Big boats churned by in the channel, and we could see the lines of cars gliding over the causeway. Kimmel could not take his eyes off the manatees. "Do you ever think that you are born to grow," he finally said, "that even, to a certain age, you can barely keep up with your own growth? And suddenly, in a moment, it stops. And then you are grown. And it just becomes a matter of fending off?"

Through the fence, out over the ocean, I saw three storks skimming the water in a neat line. My eyes followed them down the shore until they disappeared. The lime-green ocean fluttered with light. "I think it's a matter of becoming too ambiguous," I told him.

"But that's all right for now," he said. "Besides, ambiguity can make it necessary for people to comply."

"Comply with what?"

He let go of the fence, dropped his arms, and turned to me. "With what you want."

"Why?"

"It makes them curious about you," he said.

"What do you want people to comply with?"

"I don't know yet." He gave my arm a squeeze, and we turned around. At school, Kimmel had the nicest habit of hooking his arm into yours when walking around. He did it with men, women, professors, parents, and students alike, making no distinction other than liking you. But there was also a quelled sadness when he'd touch you. It was as far as he was able to go. And if you touched him, you'd only feel him pulling away.

On the way back, we stopped at a gas station. I got out and checked messages.

Will had finally called. He said he'd made a better boat and hadn't been able to cut practice short and come over. "But," he'd said on the machine, "I hope you are enjoying the house."

I hung up. Got back in the car. "Will left a message."

"What did he say?" Kimmel asked.

"He said enjoy the house. I mean, what house?"

I went up to the stage after the show. Kimmel was on one knee, coiling up a cord. I said his name and he heard my voice and slowly looked up. His face was gaunt in the bright light and his eyes were dark hooded and flickerless. He seemed frozen into delayed reaction, and it was only after

I'd said hello a second time that he motioned for me to come around the side of the stage.

I followed him downstairs. He got me a beer and we sat and tried to talk. But he seemed distracted, getting up, and with a moody, concentrated hunch, disappearing out of the basement dressing room every time this shaggy-haired guy in a thick navy sweater came back in. He seemed to be on the end of a long tour. Various people familiar with Kimmel nervously milled about the long, narrow room but didn't talk to him. I asked Kimmel how things were going, but he was vague to me about how he was doing because, I got the feeling, if he ever subsequently failed, you'd never know he'd been trying (the show had not been well attended, and his record, as well as Burt, had disappeared). The guy in the sweater sat down across from us. He was drinking a beer, wordless and spaced out, his leather boots up on the table. There was a big mirror on the wall behind him, and I could see a kind of eye signaling going on between him and Kimmel. I turned and asked Kimmel about it, and he said the guy was traveling with him. Then he got up again and disappeared again. I caught a vague whiff of pot, and something else more acrid and burnt beneath it. Kimmel, I finally realized, had become druggie.

I sat there for a minute, finishing my beer in the unpleasantly mildewed dressing room. There was a sinister, teenage basement vibe growing, and I got up to leave. As I made my way to the door, Kimmel came up and leaned into me with his hands in his pockets. We looked at each other for a moment.

"Do you want to go and get something to eat?" he whispered.

We walked around the corner to the Café Industry. The room had a golden hue and there were all sorts of books and magazines lying around. Kimmel and I ordered beer. The waitress put down some bread but neither of us ordered food. He said he was heading to San Diego the next morning. The tour was ending, and he was going to stay down there a while. He did not ask about Helen or Los Angeles or anything else in my life. But he knew, in a way, I didn't want to talk about any of it.

"What happened with Burt?" I asked.

"Nothing, really."

"He was heckling you here last time?"

He looked at me. "You read that?"

I nodded.

"I paid Burt to do that."

"What?"

"I paid him to heckle me. The shows were getting boring," he shrugged. "Anyway, it was getting to the point where all he wanted to do was beat me up."

"You can certainly have that effect on people, Kimmel."

"Well, he certainly did a good job."

Kimmel looked up. A sharp-nosed, gangly girl in a silver dress and a black crew cut had come up to our table. She'd recognized Kimmel from his show, and she leaned over our table and tried to speak with him.

He smiled nervously up at her in silence, letting her hang there with her stumbling sentences.

As she walked away, he said to me with flat-voiced amazement, "Her top lip is bigger than her bottom lip."

We got a pint of whiskey out of his car and walked around the spiderweb streets of Silverlake. It felt good to be out with a friend in the marbleized night of the city, sliding along in the low-lit air. On the commercial blocks, the buildings were all the same height, and except for reflections of light above on the passing clouds, I felt as if we were indoors. Kimmel kept on glancing up at the sky as he walked. It seemed representational, Kimmel with all his distance and the feeling of light on clouds.

We walked by a deli, a fruit stand out front. I found an old pleasantness looking at the produce. Banana bunches opening out of tins like umbrellas, pears wrapped in paper, loose piles of bamboo and fern. I remembered as a kid being interested enough to break the needles and smell them, pick at the sap, and roll it between my fingers. Taking a pinecone home to the adults, who'd put down their crystal glasses full of liquor to inspect the hard flower.

Next door to the deli was a café painted with Rasta colors, and whispers came from the dark, "smoke" and "aceed."

Kimmel went in and bought a small, clear plastic bag of pot.

We walked up a hill, along stucco houses perched beyond square garages. We crossed a small park with a baseball diamond, and came back down a street of rundown wooden houses. We wound up sitting on the steps of some old columned bank. I'd drunk most of the whiskey and with the pot, my body felt like a black flame, permanent in the night.

Kimmel had his arm around me. I was crying, but I could barely tell.

7

One night, I could not sleep. I lay in bed, flashlight at my side, the Ludlum folded across my chest. I wasn't thinking of anything, but all of the sudden I was no longer tired.

I got up, went upstairs, and lay down on the black leather sofa. The black sky sparkled with stars. Mirroring the stars, I could make out the distant yellow dots of oil rigs, minuscule, agitated lights wavering on the fragile horizon line between the sky and the sea. I thought of Finn and his choices and his failures. Had he built it all for her?

I saw myself asleep in the glass reflection. Some time in the night I saw myself standing at the glass, as if at a chalkboard, tracing the famous figures between the stars, illuminating them across the night sky with glowing lines drawn out of the stars themselves. But there were so many stars, and they would not sit still. They lost their distinction where I'd drained their glow, and I could not find the universal shapes in the spaces between. I drew a mass of frenzied, glaring lines, violently crisscrossing what I could not connect, scratching out the last, cool tarp of darkness and then I was awake in the bright morning.

The day had climbed up the walls, and the sun was in my eyes. My cheek was sweaty against the leather. I heard an engine close by.

I sat up and squinted down at the beach. A Jet Ski buzzed by just offshore, the driver kneeling in a black wet suit, staring in at the houses.

He did a little loop and puttered to a halt just to the north of the house.

A man in a white robe, holding a mug of coffee, stood at the shoreline. He looked like the actor Ron Silver. He probably was. He pointed in one direction.

The Jet Skier pointed in the opposite.

The man motioned with his mug, shook his head.

The Jet Skier jerked up his arm and gave the man the finger. He fired the clutch and the Jet Ski roared as it rose up and planed away south along the shore.

I stared until the Jet Skier was a speck off the breakers and the man had disappeared back into his house. When I was younger—right up to when I'd arrived at this house—desire, alcohol, and confusion would blend into strange conviction running through my head like empty freight trains barreling west. A kind of conviction I could never coordinate with my body. Now, there was nothing. I'd given up on too many lives—Helen, Will, Kimmel—and I didn't trust second chances with people. When you give people second chances, you know even less about them. In a second chance is irrevocable distance—people no longer reveal themselves through mistakes. Buffalo Bill Cody killed seventy thousand buffalo in seven months as part of the campaign to starve the Sioux, and was the first to avenge Custer by murdering a Sioux child (a lodge of Crow scouts cornered the boy in the Dakota woods; it was right after Bull Run, and Cody, dressed in a full-length fur coat, stepped forward and shot the boy at ten yards). He then reinvented himself as one of the first great public champions of the Sioux, hiring Sitting Bull to tour with his Wild West, once the Sioux were decimated.

The conquest of the West, according to a Larry McMurtry paperback I'd skimmed from the loft's shelf, was first a story of heroes, then of publicity, then sprawl.

Water, too much or not enough, will someday probably take care of a lot of the sprawl. There certainly wasn't too much water dripping down from the mountains around here.

But heroes?

There were trappers, explorers, ranchers, and surveyors venturing out alone before anybody was writing about it. But from the beginning, if they didn't work for the government, they worked for companies: Kit Carson for Jacob Astor's American Fur Company, Jedediah Strong Smith and Daniel Boone for the Rocky Mountain Fur Company, "Bangall" Mike Fink for the Mississippi Keelboat Company, R.C. Keith for the Swan Land and Cattle Company Ltd., and "Pony" Bob Haslam and "Buffalo" Bill for the Wells Fargo Overland Stage Line. They weren't heroes. They were company men.

It was the Wild West Show publicist, "Arizona" John Burke, an ex–drama critic from Washington, D.C. with dandyish appetites, who reinvented the lives of these men, himself as a long-haired cowboy claiming to be a native of Pima Indian territory and a hero of the Sun Dance.

"They were all plain, laconic men," Wyatt Earp wrote in his autobiography, "but Major Burke's program made a badlands saga out of them all."

Annie, according to Major Burke's Wild West promotional sheet, grew up eating bark and lizards, raised mountain lions in the Black Hills, killed her first Sioux with a slingshot at age eight, and joined the Wild West at fourteen. Annie herself had surprisingly little to say about all her time with the Wild West. *We traveled in day coaches. We made nearly all one- and two-day stands. When an all-night run was necessary, we carried our mattresses and blankets and our seats were made into beds with boards, which we carried to spread from one seat to another. I believe that we originated the Pullman idea to become common years later.*

One evening the boy who did this work had lost two boards that went under the cushions. The coaches stopped near a board fence and the boy got off to pry at a board. But it held. It was dark and the boy climbed over the fence, for he thought he saw a board sticking upright in the ground. With a yank he pulled it free and tossed it over the fence and returned to the car with it.

I slept undisturbed, but in the morning I spied letters on my bed board and I read "Here rests in peace the remains of Joshua Pepper."

Everybody knows the stories of the West. By the end of the 1890s, the stories were already so worn out, even the Wild West Show was having trouble interesting anybody.

Finn, in the 1890s, was living in Cleveland. His mines, deep in the momentum of a gilded age, churned out more and more ballast for the railroad lines. For tracks connecting the cattle and mining towns—set out on the prairie distinct as stars, to the cities of the Midwest and the Northwest. He had married, but his wife had died giving birth to their only child. There were employees to raise the son and the infant girl, and Finn kept moving, traveling ceaselessly through the West, Canada, Florida, and South America, peering alone into his mines, walking alone through his pristine parks. In photographs from around then, the bad luck he'd had with women was in his eyes, his gleaming gravel eyes.

He would go sometimes, when the cash-strapped Wild West would cross his path, buy a ticket, and sit anonymously in the half-empty bleachers and watch Annie shoot.

Annie, to keep up her career, found she had to go further and further into the world, and the further she went, the more she went alone. More and more she went back to the private European shows, to the European arenas of the Wild West, and to the men there in the thinning circles of turn-of-the-century aristocracy. Dressed in a white, crushed-lambskin cape in front of a corner of red brick grandeur, laughing and raising and pointing her finger at Lord Yates. Dressed in knickerbockers and an Eton-style jacket, raising and pointing her gun at a lascivious French count bursting into her Saint Germain des Prés hotel room like a thief with a present of an automobile scarf and a lewd proposition. Raising and pointing her gun, there are dozens of photos of her with the sad circus eyes of an elephant: eyes worn down by thousands of dead-on, absurdly staged shots, eyes worn down by her endless, dreamlike prome-nading. *Dain Salifour, king of Senegal, after witnessing one of my exhibitions in Paris on July 12, offered Col. Cody 100,000 franks for me.*

"What do you want her for?" Cody asked.

"I want to take her back with me," said the black King. "My people are not safe in the small villages; the man-eating tigers carry them away and with her such wonderful skill, the danger would soon be past. Release her."

Witnessed the celebration of Pope Leo XIII on the anniversary of his coronation. He was carried around on a throne by eight men who passed between rows of soldiers. He seemed scarcely able to raise his heavily jeweled hand and distribute his blessings, and his heavy crown was on a royal purple pillow borne before him.

A beautiful girl with a psyche-knot lay on her left side with her head pillowed on her arm. The terror had overtaken her so quickly that there was not a sign of struggle. Her dainty nightrobe stood out plainly under the lava.

While at Marseille I was escorted to the Château d'If on the island of Monte Cristo. This small island stands in the Mediterranean, just off the mainland, and was made famous by Dumas. The attendant sold to three different people in our party the "original key" to Monte Cristo's cell.

A letter with a photograph from a pointed chin Welshman got down to business. He had seen me shoot. Would I marry him? He had a little money and guessed that I had saved up some. "Yours until death us do part, your darling ducky." I sent a .22 bullet through the place where brains should have been. I then wrote across the narrow chest of the rest of the picture, "Respectfully declined," and off it went.

He came without display except that his coachman and footman wore the usual royal livery and his carriage bore the royal insignia. His voice was low and kind and after a half-hour's chat we went into the arena, for he said he would like a coin that I had marked in the air with a bullet. He had just placed the coin in his pocket when a bucking horse charged toward us. The rider had mounted some distance off. I just had time to say, "We are in danger here," but the prince's reply was, "I don't think that he will hurt us." I knew better and leaped to his side just in time to shove him over, holding on to his left arm as he went down to his knees. The infuriated beast struck his right shoulder. The prince only smiled as he was dusted off. The next day he sent to me a diamond bracelet with the crown and monogram of the prince.

We went today to the butcher shop for a Christmas turkey. The dealer had been arrested the day we'd arrived and set camp for making counterfeit pesos, but was released when he proved that his money contained more silver than the Spanish government money. The dealer asked them if they would have a wing, a leg, liver, or a gizzard. He could not believe that anybody would buy a whole turkey. Two hundred beggars followed them and the turkey, and the butcher sent an armed guard along with them.

The Emperor was confined to his rooms, being barely able to appear once a day for ten minutes at the large window facing the square. There the people flocked and waited that they might wave to him. "War mad," I started to say to my manager and the same words came from him at the same time.

She'd tried to settle down with Frank Butler in Manhattan, New Jersey, North Carolina, Ohio, and on the Eastern Shore of Maryland. But Frank Butler could not give her children, and, like Finn, she could not keep still with someone else. Her striving to maintain success, and the restlessness accompanying success, would lead to her death. She wanted to be loyal, but her eyes were on the horizon. There were targets there. The pull to the distance was the most certain feeling.

With the American fortunes of the Wild West seriously fading, Annie turned to the stage. Westerns on Broadway. But even theater audiences had tired of the West's heroic exaggerations, and the plays were flopping. Her acting career went nowhere. If you look in the Columbia Encyclopedia under Annie Oakley, it reads, after a brief bio, "complimentary tickets came to be known as 'Annie Oakleys,' for reasons still disputed."

A second chance came. One spring day, she went for a horseback ride in Central Park. She had just returned to New York from a tour of Germany, where she'd shot a cigarette out of Kaiser Wilhelm's mouth. *We left Kaiser's game preserve in the morning, and visited Magdeburg, Braunschweig, and Leipzig. There was a spotless town near Leipzig with a wonderful bologna factory. But, behold, my manager accidentally*

*entered a factory inner gate that was supposed to be kept locked
and found one pen full of horses and the other of dogs.*

Riding in Central Park, she came across a group of men
surrounding a man peering into a large black box on legs. It
was Thomas Edison. He was experimenting with live
motion in film. Edison and Annie knew each other well. It
had been the Edison Electric Illumination Company of
Brooklyn lighting the Wild West whenever it had played in
New York in the 1890s. It had taken two and a half tons of
coal every day, and the whole system, the most light man
had ever produced, was engineered daily by Edison himself.
Brooklyn was one of the last places the Wild West drew a
good crowd, and it was because of the bright lights on the
show rather than the show itself.

Edison asked her about the cigarette shot. It was already
famous in America (in 1914 it became "her most famous
miss"). He asked her to come to his Black Maria studio and
take a shot for the kitograph camera. He explained to her he
wanted to attempt to catch the flight of a bullet on film.

The following week, when Annie arrived at the Black
Maria studio—a black glass roofed room revolving on a
track to face the sun, Edison had her dress up in her famous
white fringe and rhinestones. As she loaded, lifted her gun,
and pointed it across the studio, a stout man appeared wearing a spiked Teutonic helmet, a fake mustache, and medals
on his chest. He turned his profile to Annie, and popped a
cigarette in his mouth.

The Kaiser, in New Jersey.

But Annie enjoyed the reenactment, and Edison invited
her back.

She returned the following week with her friend
Elizabeth Custer. (Elizabeth Custer, a demure, well-bred
woman, had years before gone to see the Wild West Show
in Brooklyn. She'd wanted to see the reenactment of the

Battle of Little Big Horn. She'd wanted to see a reenactment of her husband's death. She'd been impressed by Annie's performance, and at tea after the show, discovered they were neighbors in Greenwich Village.)

Edison could not believe his luck.

Shot in West Orange, New Jersey, Annie Oakley starred in, and Thomas Edison directed, the first-ever motion picture Western. Incredibly, the first Western consisted of Annie Oakley (Sitting Bull's adopted daughter) saving Elizabeth Custer (the wife of the general killed by Sitting Bull) from ax-wielding Sioux and Lakota Indians hired from the last of Cody's (Custer's first avenger and Sitting Bull's first apologist) Wild West Troupe.

The Wild Women of the Wild West was a stunning success in the five-cent peep shows and nickelodeons—there were lines around the block in Boston, New York, New Haven, Cincinnati, Chicago, and San Francisco.

The footage of Annie and Elizabeth no longer exists, the negatives long destroyed in a Black Maria fire. There is a catalog script of the shots somewhere in storage in the Edison library, in Fort Myers, Florida. There are still a few promotional placards, with Elizabeth Custer all dolled up and Annie Oakley all holstered up, which pop up occasionally at Western memorabilia auctions and are inevitably bought by wealthy lesbians from Aspen or Taos.

8

A production break came. Two weeks off. Leonard went to France to try and sell the show to European television. I needed a rest, but didn't have anything to do.

I drove around Los Angeles during the days, in greater and greater loops until I'd reached the artichoke and strawberry fields. I drove the highways in a kind of slow, ambient anxiety, lost in my thoughts but eyes on the lookout. The freeways were hard charging, cars would swoop around, a face in the window contorted and outraged at my car's puttering tempo. But the driving itself was the point. I was completely destinationless.

One afternoon, deep in the inland empire, my engine began smoking.

I pulled over into the emergency lane and stopped. I got out through the passenger door as a metallic river of cars roared by. I opened the hood. There was a small oil fire. I reached back into the car and got my Styrofoam cup of coffee. I threw it on the fire. The engine burst into flames. I stepped back and looked at the cup.

The nondairy creamer.

I stood there with my car burning up. Nobody stopped. Twice, cop cars flew by. The emergency lane was studded with broken glass. Maybe it was the harsh afternoon light or the relentless pulsing of metal under the hot sun, but it began to look as if the glass around my feet was from church windows. As if it were from a broken sheet of stained glass fallen off a truck—blues and reds and oranges peculiar to the big windows of biblical scenes. Some fragments looked as if they still had lead rims and a fractured image: half of a pale yellow forefinger, the dead eye of a blue fish, a red field.

I left my car on fire, climbed over the railing and down an embankment. I walked along an access road, found a gas station, and called a taxi.

I never heard a word about the car.

I stocked up on food and booze and lay out the rest of the week in bed. A green can of Heineken on my chest most of the time, daydreaming through conjecture. Burnt circles, pasted hearts, and North Carolina tobacco fields. Wild turkeys at my father's house in the Chesapeake, a bluegrass festival in the mud in Carmel, a friend reading on a sailboat off Laguna. Sun on them all. But I was drunk most of the time and deviant in terms of meaning, terrified that actual memories would only bring a thousand coffee cups of pain.

I began to have bad days from the drinking. One morning I woke up so hungover, I put on my shoes and went right downstairs in my pajamas, went outside, and began to run.

I spent the second week off back east at my father's house. I flew into Washington. He picked me up at Dulles, and we went to Au Pied du Cochon in Georgetown for a late dinner. As we walked in, I noticed the mural of the Arc de Triomphe and the Eiffel Tower was still behind the bar. Growing up, I'd had many long, silent meals there with my father. He'd read the *Post* and *Wall Street Journal*, recognize somebody at the bar and go off and catch up. I'd drink Coke and do my homework, occasionally gazing up at the pastel Eiffel Tower. The first time Annie Oakley had met Thomas

Edison was at the Paris Expo of 1889; the year the Eiffel Tower had finally been finished and the year Edison had unveiled the phonograph. He'd set dozens of phonographs up, provided earphones for all of Paris. They'd listened to marches and waltzes and stared up with worried wonder at the Eiffel Tower poking around in the stars. Annie, in 1889, was at the peak of her fame, and unimpressed with the phonograph. She asked Edison if he could invent an electric gun.

Edison said he could, and then never did.

When we sat down, my father took one look at me and told me not to expect.

The waiter had come over to pour water. I ordered a rum punch and waited until he turned away. "Not expect what?" I asked. "Money? Inheritance? That sort of thing?"

"No. I mean it in a broader sense." He put down his water and folded his hands. "When things go wrong, people tend to expect."

"And?"

"And that's all I'm saying. Don't."

"Okay," I nodded, looking around for the waiter with my drink.

After dinner, we headed out to the Eastern Shore. He asked about Helen.

I told him the last time I'd seen her—in Raleigh. It wasn't any good.

He shook his head. "You really got it there," he said. "That should not happen to someone in their twenties."

I was at the end of my twenties, and didn't know if he meant Helen, or me.

We were silent for a while. There was nothing to say about when I'd last seen Helen. But it was a relief to see my father, and right then I understood I was in trouble. Although I didn't know what it was, exactly.

And I could only guess at his trouble. He'd never, it seemed, settled into anything except his solitary house in the Chesapeake. He'd always had temporary jobs in Washington—mostly financial inquisitions with his friend Ray or the doctor. And he'd put too much faith—like Will and Kimmel with boarding school—into his time at college and his eating club, and had consequently never had many friends around later in life.

He'd never remarried, and if he ever had girlfriends, I had no idea.

As he drove he talked randomly about people he'd known, mostly names unknown to me. He mentioned Grace Slick and Gordon Liddy. He'd been acquainted with a lot of different sorts of people in Washington over the years, and he knew secret things about some of them.

"How do you know about them?"

"Well, Washington used to be a small Southern town."

"So, gossip?"

"I don't gossip, Hay."

"So how do you know about them?"

He glanced at me, kept on driving in silence. We were all the other had. Consequently we kept our distance. Rarely crossed. We were parallel. All my life I'd thought this meant dependable. When I was a kid and we'd drive, he used to turn and really stare at me. This hard look I couldn't escape. But otherwise he left me alone. He was always lackadaisically cavalier about fathering. He had a westerner's view of isolation, of space and wanting to be left alone.

But he was a midwesterner. And he lived in the East.

When I was a little boy, he used to tell me two things:

"Be adventuresome. Be accountable."

It was hard to square the two. One inevitably compromised the other. But there was a uniquely American, stalwart kind of ying and yang to his advice.

He exited the highway at Annapolis and pulled into a gas station. Fog hung on the surrounding inlets and the station's lights were liquid and oblong. He dug around for a cigar, and gently shook it out of its tube. He bit off the end. "You sober enough to switch?"

"Enough," I said.

He reached into the pocket of his blazer, and pulled out matches. He shook the box, struck a match. It flared up at the cigar's tip. "Do you know what sesquipedalian means?"

"No. Why should I?"

"Because there's a lesson in it."

"Well," I said, "what does it mean?"

"A long word." He said, moodily exhaling smoke.

"What's the point?"

"Believe what you hear."

"I'll do that."

"And more importantly," he added, examining his cigar, "believe what you see."

He smoked, staring straight ahead at the brightly lit gas station.

I looked at him. "I'm tired of fighting the lines."

"What?"

"You're full of lines."

His eyes seemed to harden.

"You're even puffing that cigar like some Vegas stand-up."

He grabbed the car door handle. "I don't know," he shook his head. "I don't know what you mean."

He got out of the car, came around, and stood at the passenger door. I couldn't see his head, just the smoke trailing down from his cigar.

We switched. A light rain began to spatter the windshield as I started the car. I could sense an old anger growing in him, but his anger was not there for me, it was just there. I drove us back up along the highway, but the entrance ramp had been blocked by construction. I got us lost, lost in rainy detour traffic in a faded, industrial area of Annapolis. We were at a stoplight. There was a shop window, curved, thick glass beaded with rain, defunct machines lit up inside. Above it was a glowing neon sign for an old, abandoned luncheonette. The brick wall of a broken-down factory filled out the block. My father seemed distant and sad.

There was stoplight after stoplight, we were still lost and he began to grow uncomfortable. "You're lost," he said. "Pull over."

I kept on, stopping and starting through the lights.

He unbuckled his seat belt and looked at me. "Stop driving," he snapped.

"I'm driving fine," I said.

"No, you're not," he said. "You're driving like you're jerking off."

I slept late in my old room, got up, got coffee, and took a long drive. New houses and new suburbs were growing like vines around his property, the rims of the corn and soybean fields all being sold off. I wandered around a shopping mall, ate junk food, played a few games of pinball, and then drove on.

I did this for four straight days.

Nights, exhausted but unable to sleep after the day's endless unraveling of time in the car, I'd lie in bed and listen to the truckers' weather station on the radio; reports of sheets of rain across I-94 in Montana, floods on the Everglades Parkway, and dry black, sparkling skies over Maine.

I'd drink three or four bourbons before my eyes would close. I'd have driven around so much, I'd dream of driving. Driving, in my removed, hungover state, was itself a dream of driving.

I'd been using my father's old black BMW. He'd had it in the garage forever. When I was fourteen, just after we'd moved from D.C. out to the Eastern Shore, my father had come home from some trip, put his bags down, and announced we were broke. The next day he'd gone out and bought the BMW. A brand new black coupe. Leather dashboard, red leather seats. It had a car phone, which he could not figure out how to use.

I had understood we were broke, and I'd asked him.

"It's a different kind of broke," he'd responded tersely.

It seemed a huge extravagance for us, and out of character for him. But he had an odd faith—odd for him—in the redemptive power of a new car.

The day after he'd bought the car, we'd driven up to his college reunion. We picked up Ray at the hotel, drove across campus, and pulled up to an unremarkably square, colonial brick house. We signed a ledger and were given name tags. We walked through the house and into the back garden. My father's clubmates were trim men in neat tweed with precise manners. They reminded me of perfect wooden sailboats. They only seemed unhurried when they talked about their families. Otherwise they were all business, in banks and firms, all making money. I could sniff a buttoned-down, reflexive disdain for my father, as if he had roared up the green lawn on a speedboat. He stood in the club's back lawn, slightly disheveled in his running shoes and plaid Pendleton hunting coat, round face, and mirrored sunglasses; his hair a loose fold over a bald patch. He held a customized orange and black aluminum tennis can of beer. He was quickly getting drunk, and had begun to talk a little too loudly to Ray—who wore Ray-Ban glasses—and two other clubmates about some high-flying sure thing, something to do with solar panels.

My father suddenly halted the conversation and rolled up his sleeve. "See this watch?" he said.

Ray and the two men looked blankly at my father.

"Yes," Ray finally said.

"A consortium of men in Washington gave it to me. They had it specially made."

"It's a Rolex," Ray said.

"It's a special Rolex."

"How's that?" Ray asked.

"It's a golden-eye Rolex."

"What's that?"

"Well, there are only five in existence in the world," my father said.

"How did you get one?"

"I told you. A consortium of men gave it to me."

"What are you trying to tell me?" Ray asked.

"I'm not trying to tell you anything," my father said.

There was a short silence. The two men turned and walked away. My father looked at Ray and laughed. Ray, with his round red face, turkey neck, and old Baltimore accent, just guffawed and took a sip of his hard liquor.

I slipped off into the back garden. I walked along an old slate path, yellow weeds hanging on in the cracks, until I came to a grassy hill. The hill sloped downward to an alley of neatly spaced, vase-like oak trees. Beyond the trees, a field stretched wide and green in front of me. I stood there for a long time. There was an announcement.

I turned and made my way back to the garden's edge. I watched as the club members crowded around a big cardboard box and began to shed their tweed. Out of the commotion, Ray and my father emerged wearing gray, polyester safari jackets, their class year stenciled in block letters across the back. They stood examining each other and laughing. They took up cardboard placards, efficiently formed two columns with the rest of the members, and strolled off like merry game-show hosts into the rich pocket of landscape and weighty, frowning architecture.

Suddenly, nobody was around. I took off my name tag. Tentatively, I walked across the lawn to where the men had been getting beer. I took one of the orange tennis cans and pulled the lever. It swarmed white into the cup. I drank fast and warily. It tasted dry and cool and better than air. I drank another. The boredom of the day suddenly dissipated and the evening's grassy freshness rose in my head like helium into a balloon. I walked down the street. I came to a tent bannered:

CLASS OF 1973

There were a few people milling around scatterbrained with big kinky hair and in leather sandals. They all looked like my geology teacher, who talked about quartz and mica and god and his powder-blue Karmann-Ghia with the same repetitive awe. I got another beer there. Nobody seemed to care. I had a few more back at the empty lawn of the club. Hours broke up and disappeared. A hum started in my ears. I beat my fist against a tree to make it stop. The dusky sky beat back down at me. I felt the heat and salt in my palms and in the summer evening. The air around me and inside me seemed to melt through my skin, to join me and pick me up and I felt as if I were floating. A lightness bloomed in my chest and I had a glimmer of adulthood with all its low voices and cigarette smoke and glass-clinking mystery. I grew confused and dizzy. I walked into the garden and began to spit. I knelt down on the slate path and began to vomit.

The next day we idled in the hotel's parking garage. I was lying down across the BMW's backseat, pale and miserable.

The sun glinted through the heavy, latticed concrete walls. My father sat there with the driver-side door open, rummaging through his brown briefcase with its combination lock and handle worn down to a shine, searching through sheets full of numbers, coffee-ringed *Financial Review*s, and glossy quarterly earnings pamphlets. He was shaking his head. He'd lost some papers he had wanted to show Ray. Ray was now running some big acronym in Washington. They'd had brunch, but my father hadn't been able to find the papers. Ray had already driven off, and he was still looking.

He pulled the car door shut. He glanced into the rearview mirror. "Well," he said, dismissively closing his briefcase, "it was always a drinking college. Take a nap. You'll do all right after." And he turned and handed me a ginger ale.

I slept and woke up and it was dark. We pulled off the highway and into a gas station. Pumping gas, my father looked worn out and preoccupied under the neon. He'd been up all night with his friends, and I wondered why they'd made him look this way.

An hour or so later we were dipping and bending on a country road, coming close to home. It was dark out, and raining steadily. Headlights suddenly came up behind us, coating the windows, and then a sedan roared past.

"That man is drunk," my father said.

I didn't say anything.

He was smoking, and the glowing tip of his cigar, like an unhinged beacon, traced helter-skelter patterns on the window as the sedan disappeared into a red speck up the road. "Speed's a crime," he muttered to himself. "A fucking sin."

Our headlights slicked the wires and lit up the geometric considerations on the yellow signs. Through the steady rain, I watched the fields waver with a sheeny mutability, then suddenly come aglow with the beams of oncoming headlights. We came around a bend and there was the sedan up against a tree and also slightly off it, as if the tree had uppercut the car hood and broke it like a jaw. One of the headlights shot up the trunk and illuminated the dark, thick branches.

We pulled over. Our headlights settled on the wreck. The driver-side door was open and the man had disappeared. Beer cans were tumbled across the seat, and there was a smear of blood across the cracked front windshield. I was staring at the wreck and the feeling was a little like seeing a bright red fox cross MacArthur Boulevard in midday traffic in Washington, D.C. Watching it trot unnoticed across the intersection and into the reservoir and feeling a new, strange kind of stillness and fear. Feeling that the borders that ruled you growing up are made of air.

I looked at my father. His eyes were locked on the car. His strict look seemed out of another, more serious, self-sufficient era. But there was also dismay in his eyes, as if the scene were the incomprehensible toll of his years, as if the tree had finally given in and evolved, growing the metal out of its trunk in some late-twentieth-century mutation of a limb.

"Bad luck he hit that tree," he said coolly, as if we'd always be untouchable in the expensive black coupe. "It's the only one around."

The day before my flight back to Los Angeles, Will came down from New York. He was waiting out front when I pulled into the Baltimore train station. He smiled, tipped a pink newspaper toward me. He held a brown briefcase in his other hand, wore red Converse low tops, jeans, and a suede blazer melted to tar at the seams.

I lowered the window.

He gave me a long look, and came around the car and got in. His eyes looked tired, and he pulled out an airplane bottle of Jack Daniels he'd bought on the train and took a tiny sip.

I turned onto the ramp, looped out of downtown, and merged into the highway traffic. We were driving out of town, past the massive Johns Hopkins hospital complex. Helen had once been in a Johns Hopkins ward. It was the same as all the other wards: gray hallways, florescent lights, a plastic smell, a waiting room with a window overlooking a gravel roof. Slow, grouchy nurses in blue scrubs. Old magazines and little paper cups and conversations negated in the blur of noise and alarm. Mysterious contests going on that everybody seemed to be noisily rooting for, but which were never there. Always some just out of reach, growing sense of hilarity without fail leading to panic.

One afternoon, the Johns Hopkins ward held a visitor-patient line-dancing lesson. I arrived in a rhinestone, but-toned cowboy shirt and with an oversize pink-foam cowboy hat for Helen. "Achy Breaky Heart" played as we stood side by side and tried to follow the dance instructor's commands. The nurses were all enthusiastically in line and swinging their feet, and one of the patients got overexcited, snuck into the nurse station, and somehow shut off the power. The country music stopped playing, the vents stopped blowing air, and the ward went dark. Helen and I stopped in midkick. Her nails, full of the relentless muscle of her disease, sud-denly dug into my palm like claws.

The lights came back on. She dropped my hand, flipped off her pink hat, wandered away, and turned on the televi-sion. She stood there in the bright room's commotion, her finger pressing her lower lip, watching a tennis match.

I looked down at my palm. She'd drawn blood, an arc of red dollops just under each finger. I wiped my hand on my jeans. The cuts in my hand throbbed and I felt an abject failure. And the fear in the failure—the way failure works on the nerves and with vertigo and confusion replicates itself—began to take over. My hands began to shake.

"That was a let," Helen said, turning with angry eyes that came at me like propellers. "A let!"

"Achy Breaky Heart" started back up. A nurse walked over and switched off the television as a chaotic struggle ensued to re-form even dance lines. Helen stood there, crazy eye of the storm, staring at the television as if the match were still on. Her brown eyes were focused so hard they looked as if they were about to shatter.

"About leaving Helen," Will said to me.

I glanced at him. I was surprised he'd remembered Helen had been in Johns Hopkins. "What do you mean?"

"You had no say."

"Why's that?"

"From what I saw, she became a ghost. She had nothing left to say for herself."

I shifted down and merged onto the Annapolis highway. "I don't want to talk about it because as soon as I start to relive it, it becomes clear that it will never end."

"For her maybe. But you need to watch out for yourself. Ghosts suck you as dry as vampires. You go gray just the same."

"It seems deeply disloyal to have left."

"You loved her?"

"Yes, Will, of course."

"So what were you being loyal to if she wasn't really there? And Hay, if it's never going to end, where are you going to be by that time?"

"I don't know," I said. "In the past, I've never been able to think too far ahead.

He glanced at me.

"I really don't know," I said, shaking my head. "But I do know there had to be something more I could have done."

When the Bay Bridge sprawl had faded, and we were on a two-lane road between cornfields, Will dug into his bag and came out with a galley copy of his book. He held it up with a dopey, proud smile. It was coming out in a month.

He opened the book up and began to read in a warm and fluid voice.

The book was based on the series of articles he'd done on a malcontent sugar heir. The heir had commandeered, converted, and lived on a giant glass-encased glowing floor at the top of his family's Greenpoint sugar factory. The floor sat high over the East River, and when the heir had lived there, it had emitted a strange, powder green light over the neighborhood.

The heir was an unstable Cuban American—a tall and black haired, good-looking homosexual. He wore a white Fila sweat suit everywhere and had a frantic disposition, as if he himself were constantly ingesting too much sugar. He was a cursed man—everything he ever did went wrong. The book, Will mentioned in an aside, was about how some people, whether it be luck or expectations, are simply cursed. When the heir would go out to dinner, the food would never be right. When he would pick up his dry cleaning, it would not have worked. Every day, it went like this, and as Will talked on, it struck me that Will liked it, strived harder even, when things went wrong. He searched out trouble in his work, in his own life. If he couldn't find it, he'd quickly grow bored, and let it grow out of him.

The heir suffered from manic episodes. One day, out of the blue, he began to give away fake jewels from a purple velour sack. A ruby to a Polish housekeeper coming back from Manhattan, diamonds to two guys in delivery trucks in front of Met Market, a piece of gold to a hungover musician in a jean jacket, a sapphire to a Dominican manicurist. A few people took the gem with a simple warm smile like it was a kiss on the cheek. Most would take it and hurry away, fearful of him or thinking it was real and fearful he would change his mind. A sweatshirt-hooded Puerto Rican kid, immediately recognizing a fake, threw a zirconium diamond back in his face.

A cop witnessed this and came over and asked the Cuban what he was doing.

"Nothing."

"What do you do for a living, sir?" the cop asked.

"I own the sugar factory."

The cop stared at the troubled Cuban in the white sweat suit, and assumed he was being taunted with some new street lingo for dealing.

He arrested him.

Undeterred by the arrest and the increasing pressures from his family and friends, his fake-jewel episodes continued. And then he began to notice something strange. Reactions were never out of the ordinary. People, he began to realize with increasingly grave disappointment, were never surprised. They mostly thought the gems were real, but acted as if they'd experienced a stranger handing them a glowing gem before, as if there were a popular television show he wasn't aware of, doing the same thing. There was no mystery to his action, and no surprise in the response.

And then he feared maybe *he'd* somehow seen it done before. He suspected he had. He watched a lot of television and never remembered any of it.

Disappointed, he turned to men he knew, and began to give fake jewels away to the men in the sugar factory as they filed out after work. The family—tough sugar moguls—had enough. They immediately came down on him. Put him in a hospital. It turned out he'd already been on medication, and the pills he'd been prescribed had probably caused his psychotic munificence.

Newly medicated and released on a bare stipend, he'd engineered his own kidnapping for ransom. It was meant to be a joke. He'd hired performance artists, and was going to use the final ransom note as some sort of punch line. But he had fallen hopelessly in love with one of the men supposedly holding him, and didn't want the kidnapping to end. The whole frail scheme had, of course, been found out, and it was all taken way too seriously by his family.

They disavowed him. The irony was that, yet again, the medication—this time the family doctor's choice of prescriptions—had caused the strange plan. The pills had given him a martyr complex, had caused him to engineer the kidnapping.

He had no money left to give, and the performance artist spurned him. He disappeared without a trace.

Will found him!

Will paused, dug into his pocket for another airplane bottle. I glanced over at him as he unscrewed the cap, took a sip, and stared out the window. There was no pleasure, it seemed, in his drinking anymore. I'd always believed it wasn't who you were, but who you believed you were going to be. With Will, it was always who he was right then. In his hard-charging day-to-dayness, he was a constant personality. But the problem was no matter what he did, he'd try to derail his own consistencies. It wasn't so much being self-destructive, it was more about the frustrations of seeing other lives destroyed. And he just couldn't help being drawn to destroyed lives, drawn to his own faculty for seeing people in their worst, mundane light. And in this light he saw only burrowing and conniving and failed dreams. And all these dreams stuck with him, more weight to drag around. And the more he cared, the more vivid the dreams. Only the booze narrowed the dreams, and more and more the hangovers were becoming all that was ahead.

He'd call late sometimes. Wherever I was, he always seemed to be able to find my number. His voice would be bathed in drunkenness, and I remember once I could hear the wood floor cracking under his feet as he paced, as if the floor itself were airing out the disbelief of his own pain, his voice clawing at the black Irish grad student cut and run back to Boston. The things she had said to him, the reasons for leaving, he'd repeated with such misery because he'd known exactly what they were going to be.

Or, was it none of that?

Was he only calling feeling my own dismal dreams as Helen lay in ward after ward? Or was he just fighting staying drunk and doing nothing more? Maybe the sourceless pain is the bewildering worst, because that was the kind in his voice in those late-night phone calls.

We pulled up to my father's house. The house, dog-eared and white shingled, lay low on a bluff overlooking the bay. In the adjacent cornfield, someone had skirted the preservation laws and a huge new house had shot up. Red brick and neoclassical with Corinthian columns, it sat on an unlandscaped square of raw grass, and rose up way out of scale over my father's house.

Inside, Will dropped his stuff and shook hands with my father. He pointed his finger in the direction of the new house. "Lobbyist or lawyer?" he asked.

"Either. Both. There's a lot of money around these days," my father said. "Fat cats and poison lawns."

Will ran his hand through his hair, his elbow bent up in the air like he was taking a picture. He was gazing at the bay through the porch windows. "Do you think we could swim that?"

I looked at Will and laughed. The opposite shore was a distant line blurred by humidity. Will had an enthusiasm you couldn't help getting caught up in. But you had to doubt it, too.

"Oh come on, Hay," Will said, catching my look and scanning the flat, empty expanse. "It's just a mile or so."

"Depends when," my father said with a barely perceptible grin. "Low tide you can walk a good deal of it. But then high tide you get jellyfish, currents. And in the middle there's the channel. You know, boats."

"What about now?"

"You could try," my father said with a broadening smile. "Water's warm enough. But wear tennis shoes. Broken shells."

Will looked at me. "All right, Hay," he clapped his hands. "You look like you need the exercise."

My father pointed to a barely perceptible needle of a cell tower on the opposite shore. He said he would drive over and pick us up. He turned, and hurried out the door.

We changed, walked a mile or so down the brown thumbnail of a beach. It was a humid, sunny afternoon. We walked into the water, against the water. Will's big legs plowed through the water just ahead of me, his shirt ballooning up around him. We made our way out of the calm empty cove, and into the larger bay. Blue plastic Clorox bottles, attached to crab traps, bobbed around us. The bottom was whipped soft, and I felt cold wisps of current and a slippery, alluvium film around my ankles. As I walked, the flat shore across the channel seemed much farther away in the water than it had from the beach. The water suddenly became cooler and greener. I took a step forward and then there was nothing.

I could feel a fresh current moving across me as we began to swim. The bay was brimming with the new tide, and after a while the current gripped us broadside and began to push us out toward deeper water, toward the edge of the bay where it chopped into white. There was a big yacht way out where the bay broadened, and a few crab boats drifted along the shore, looking for an old abundance.

Will lumbered on ahead of me, swimming with a primordial patience among the potshot whitecaps and determined current. We tried to stay inside the line of the point of the shore ahead, where the cell-phone tower receded as it rose and felt increasingly unattainable. It was slow going. The surface had begun to pyramid and foam white from winds around the point, and there was a different level of cold underneath, a serious, unlit cold.

I stopped.

I thought for an instant I'd seen a speck of a man on the far shore, watching our slow progress. As I treaded water I felt a dreamy chill to match my quickly chilling body. I held my arm up, but I could not, for some reason, wave. I had the strangest feeling. The sky above me was an endlessly broad blue, and in it was the size of the world, the mineral permanence. I felt unknown colossus ready to burst under the bay's floor, sad figurines long buried without ever having been in the warmth of the grip of a believing man.

Suddenly, I could not connect the world I was in with the world Helen was in. They were not the same anymore.

Will sensed I'd stopped. He stopped swimming and turned.

We faced each other, treading water and holding up our right arms in a strange sort of frozen greeting. Will was an ex-crew jock with a great wind. He'd go out running, disappear for hours up the West Side Highway.

"You all right?" He yelled in the wind-hollowed quiet. "We have to keep on. We shouldn't drift."

I stared at him.

"We should take off our shoes," he said.

Drops from his arm flew across me. The bay knuckled at my chin.

"It's all right," he said, digging in the water behind him for his shoes. "We have time. We have all day."

I did not move.

He bobbed there, his head just above the water, smiling at me. "Don't think like that, Hay."

He flung the shoe, wiped snot off his nose with his forearm, and then looked back at me. He wasn't afraid. "Look, if there's trouble, you know, we should stay away from each other."

I looked at him. He wasn't kidding. We were silent there in the water. A wave crowned and caught me in the chin. I took in water and coughed. I felt a vomitous clench in my stomach. My whole body shook. I let myself cough it out. And then I began to laugh.

I laughed until my head grew faint, and then suddenly something certain and reductive occurred to me, and I knew I needed to move, but also limit my motion.

"I'm serious," Will yelled, closer now.

I coughed out a last bit of water. "I wasn't laughing because I thought you weren't serious." I yelled. "I was laughing at how far that shore still is. I mean, we aren't getting anywhere."

He turned around and looked. "Yeah," he said. "Pretty far. Pretty far back, too."

I reached back in the water and got my shoes off.

We swam on, making little progress. The bay was full of river water and not too buoyant. I was swimming but not gaining a hold on the water, and my limbs were beginning to turn to sponge.

I heard a deep bellow. It resonated underwater. I pulled up.

Will had stopped just ahead of me. He was bobbing just above the water line, as if decapitated. "That was a tanker," he yelled. "I mean, haven't you ever seen them go by?"

The bellow came again, blowing down the bay. But it was otherwise weirdly quiet way out there, and I no longer had to raise my voice. "Well, now that I think about it, this channel opens way up in Baltimore harbor. But ships are rare here, and today is Saturday . . ."

"Fuck, Hay. You know? Fuck." He slapped the water. "It's not like a nine-to-five thing. Those fuckers will cut you in half and go on to Mombasa or wherever and never notice."

I looked around. Ahead, a seagull hurled itself against the water. Other seagulls circled just above. "Nothing's in sight."

He stared at me with disbelief. "Did you hear that horn?"

I looked at him. "I heard it. Look, it's not a tanker I'm worried about. I'm basically swimming sideways."

Will, treading water, had half-turned and was craning his neck, squinting ahead. "I think we're all right."

"We're out in this channel. We're in a tide, Will. You got it in you to swim out of it?"

His shoulders seemed to ease back and he lifted a finger out of the water and pointed ahead. "We can walk it."

"Right, Will. You and me and Jesus."

"No, no," he pointed again. "See that brown line there, that's shallow water, where this channel ends. We can walk in from there."

I stared across the water's surface. I could see a darker shade not too far ahead—a hundred yards or so.

We started swimming, but after a minute he pulled up.

I stopped.

He was bobbing in the water, looking back at something behind me. His expression had darkened. "Oh fuck," he yelled. He glanced toward the shallow water, then back behind me.

I hadn't heard a horn.

"We would have made it." He smacked the water. "There's no need. No need."

I turned around. Will was still yelling.

I rubbed the brackish water out of my eyes. A sailboat on motor was coming down on us. The boat was my father's neighbors, a doctor with a forty-footer who, my father had said, got seasick under sail.

We waited, treading water.

Eventually, the boat pulled up to us and my father dropped the ladder. "You guys are idiots," he said.

As we motored back, a tanker came in sight. A giant metal hull stacked with rusted maroon canisters. An Indonesian flag fluttered, rose full, and drooped with a stop-start petulance. The ship slid by us as if the bay itself were land and the ship were water. Giant wakes bloomed up through the channel, and the doctor revved the engine, aligned the sailboat, and sliced across the faces. Will bobbed and smiled and held the deck line like a field-trip retard. His skin was tight, beaded with water and he looked exhilarated.

After dinner, my father walked into the kitchen carrying a bottle. "Here, look at this, Will," he said. "I got this for Hayward." He held up a wax-sealed bottle of Blanton's single-barrel bourbon.

"You didn't tell me that," I said.

"That's because I didn't want you to drink it."

"Why'd you get it for me then?"

Will stood and grabbed the bottle. "Just open it," he said. "That's all."

Only the touristy liquor store way over in St. Michaels carried Blanton's. I could see my father getting into his new, silver BMW and making a special trip. And then, when he got back, not being able to offer it to me.

He'd been that way all his life. I was just like that, probably.

The doctor came by. He had gray hair, a narrow face, and a quiet, western accent. We got into a long discussion about soft money.

We kept on drinking. It got dark.

My father and the doctor went into the den, switched to drinking Scotch out of rhinoceros-etched crystal. They listened to Churchill speeches on the old turntable, standing like drunken officers and acting sentimental about a time when they supposed one man could save the world.

But they *believed*. With Will and me, you'd never believe we believed.

But as I watched them from the doorway, I began to sense this eating club half smirk to the whole thing. As if they were putting each other on for their own entertainment because they knew they were putting each other on to put us on.

Will suddenly came up behind me and poked me in the ribs.

I jumped. "Jesus, Will."

He pulled me aside.

I was sipping tentatively at a Scotch, and he took it and took a huge swig. "Hayward," he said, "I wonder if your father is CIA."

I looked at Will with a skeptical frown, and pointed at the wobbling men.

My father and the doctor were listening to Souza now, walking in place in tandem, clenching their fists and jutting out their chins in a drunken, halfhearted attempt at a march. But the song had begun to skip, and they had not yet noticed, and were still tripping to adjust their strides to the repetition.

Will turned to me and shook his head and laughed. We both started to laugh and the doctor and my father, hearing us, glanced up as if we'd finally gotten the joke.

9

One morning I made tea, went up to the loft, and looked over the bookshelf. I realized I was down to the last spy book. I pulled the paperback out, and stared at the cover with dismay. A post–Berlin Wall Ludlum. After lying around in the loft reading so many of those books, I'd begun to feel like a spy leftover from the Cold War: illegal in a strange country, but having no country to return to. No one searching for me, but still having to hide.

I thought of the accident—the man sitting behind the open car door, the blood dripping onto the pavement at his feet. Somebody—some authority, all abruptness and steel— actually might be searching for me.

I lay down on the loft's white carpet, warm in the sun-rays, and began to work my way through the book. The English agent was ruddy and cheerfully fearless, but sort of sad and listless emotionally, and talked this defenseless mumbo jumbo when some old lover poked around for an inner life. He was meeting a "Joe" at an abandoned trolley station. The Joe is late and an unlikely car has pulled up across the street.

But the English spy is not phased. He knows so-and-so will have so-and-so as an escort. He knows there will be a gun in a briefcase and the man to be shot will be carrying the briefcase.

Or, wait?

I leafed back through the pages. I could never keep it straight. I was always backtracking. There was something else in the briefcase, and if the man revealed what it was to the English spy, he was not to be shot.

My eyes caught a movement out in the ocean. I looked up. There was a big patch of white water. Nothing else.

I went back to the book. The English agent is in front of the trolley station. He hears the faint crunch of a footstep in the snow behind him . . .

Again, my eyes caught a movement. I looked up. At first I thought it was one of the huge yachts mauling the water. There was white, but no boat. A frothy movement brought up a spiraling, luminescent wash of water.

A body rose.

"That's a goddamn whale," I said out loud. I was surprised at the sound of my own voice. It was the first time I'd said anything out loud in weeks.

The whale seemed to twist slightly in the air, turned over, and submerged itself, its big gray tail rising up and giving the water a last smack. "Great," I said. "Fuckin' great."

I'd seen dolphins, seals, and jittery packs of surf runners moving in elastic, choreographed swarms, but this big, singular thing was something else. I watched it continue along, going under and resurfacing farther and farther out, and I had a sudden intimation of memory from another side of my own life. But I had no idea what it might be, no desire to connect the whale to anything of any even fragmentary importance. Whales were whales and if you ever saw one, you knew they could not be representational. They were one thing. If there was another thing in your life, well "Fuck you," said the whale. "Don't pin it on me."

I finished the last spy book at dusk. I read the last line, closed the book, and slid it back into the shelf.

I looked up.

The sky had turned to white, and then shot out pink. I watched as everything fell and went gray and for the first time, some of the old twilight-hour feelings, like dark black puffs of smoke, passed through me. I remembered Helen and our apartment and the slow claustrophobia creeping in. The Annie Oakley on the wall—all cosmic-cowgirled up by Warhol. How Annie's eyes were full of the same strange distance, the same severity Helen's had come to take on.

Warhol had done Annie's portrait from a photo taken of her in 1903. In 1903, when the Wild West show was in its death throes. Cody, in a desperate maneuver for attendance, began steering the show to the hometowns of its stars. He booked the Wild West into Greenville for July 25.

Finn, hearing about the show, came in from Cleveland and on July 24, paved Broadway, Greenville's main street. It was the first paved street in all of Darke County, and of itself a great attraction.

But the Greenville Wild West show turned out to be a famous mess. Finn Theiss and Annie Oakley, along with 1970s rocker Rick Derringer—"Rock and Roll, Hoochie Coo"—are Greenville's most famous products. But the suspicious tumult of the Wild West show—as if validating rumors of their past in Cincinnati—has always hung over Greenville's view of both Annie and Finn. Derringer's various drug busts have kept him in a dim light.

The day of the show had been hot beyond belief, hot beyond the town's memory, countenance, or prediction. Finn had been late in finishing Broadway. His men had just got the last yards of asphalt down late the night before. But overnight, the weather had stayed too hot for it to properly set. *The parade went on. The horses were shined up, spurs and saddle trimmings glistened in the morning sun.*

As the Wild West turned down Broadway and paraded the last fifty yards to the town square, the new road had gone soft, soft under the hooves, the boots, and the wheels of the whole troupe. The horses, lined up under riders at the front, were unnerved by the strange, sucking turf and contagiously spooked into a freeze. One brown mare turned around, and confused, as if she'd suddenly stepped into a pit, flipped.

The mare lay on her side, struggling to stand, tearing up huge swaths of asphalt as she slipped down again and again. Men skirted around her. Dogs barked, broke, and ran. The whole parade waffled and broke down into accordian-like shambles around the horse. She was wild again, and her desperate unease seemed to float up Broadway to the still half-empty square, where the parade had yet to arrive but where, on a platform adorned with red, white, and blue ribbons, the mayor panicked, suddenly rushing across the stage and launching into a speech.

He announced Annie, who was not ready. Not even onstage.

Much of the crowd turned from watching the horse, broke off from the sides of the stalled parade, and hurried into the square.

The brass band broke into "for she's a jolly good fellow . . ." and drowned out the distant, whinnying commotion. The mayor stood onstage with a silver loving cup, looking around.

He announced her again.

Half the crowd faced the stage. Half the crowd faced the commotion of the horse and the collapsing parade.

The band played the same song four times.

Finally, Annie came rushing up onto the platform and the band crashed to a halt. She wore a dark red dress, red as dried blood. She smiled, held up the cup, and began to speak. But then she froze. *I noticed a man standing at a corner below the grandstand* . . .

She was looking at someone in the crowd. Her face grew dark and she ran offstage.

Trembling and pacing under the platform, she shook off the mayor and others and rushed out from behind the stage area. A large crowd had gathered at the entrance. They cheered her appearance, crowded around her, and she could not pass through or get back away.

Her husband, Frank Butler, saw all this and recorded it in his diary. His diary is in a glass cabinet in the Garst Museum in Greenville, Ohio.

But Frank Butler did not see whom she was looking at. He saw the look in her eye and he knew it was not the horse. He began to ask himself questions, but he never found out whom it was she was looking at.

10

Will sat in the front row of five empty rows of folding chairs, holding a copy of his sugar-heir book and sipping from a can of beer. He was dressed in his old, browned seersucker jacket and jeans. I went up and sat down next to him. He leaned over and gave me a one-armed hug. He settled back and looked toward the bookstore entrance. "Have you seen Kimmel?"

I shook my head.

"He called. I think he knows about this somehow. Isn't he around here somewhere?"

"He rented a place down near San Diego. Encinitas, I think. But that was a while ago."

"I didn't call him back," Will said. "But I thought he might be here."

"Do you know what he's doing down there?"

"No," Will shook his head. "And I don't want to call him back."

"I never really hear from him," I said. "He did call me once. He sounded so drab. He just didn't have *anything* to say . . ."

Will looked at his watch. "Fuck, five minutes." He looked around the empty room. "Late setup," he said.

He took a long sip of beer, took another look around. He dug around in his pocket for a pen, and opened his copy of the book. He drew a scaffold on the blank back page, eight dashes underneath, and we played a game of hangman.

I got it without a miss, infuriating him with a series of lucky guesses without losing a single part of myself to the rope.

B U T T F U C K

He glared at me. "See, Hay," he pointed to the empty scaffolding, "that's just the kind of hanging you think you're going to get."

He smacked the chair next to him so hard it flipped forward. He was noisily attempting to right the chair when a small, round man with a big name tag stepped up to the microphone and announced him.

Will looked back across the empty rows of chairs, ran a hand through his thick, brown hair and grimaced. The only other person at the reading was Leonard. He sat in the back row reading a magazine. Will stood, went over to a life-size cardboard promotional placard of himself. He picked the placard up, took it up to the tiny stage, and propped it up behind the microphone.

Leonard cut two lines on the dashboard of his Jaguar. He cut a third on a Randy Newman CD cover and handed it back to Will. Leonard wore a big gold watch, a silk shirt, fresh pressed black jeans, and beaded moccasins. He was playing the Randy Newman CD. He thought Randy Newman was the funniest man alive, and kept on repeating lyrics to us. Will and I glanced at each other as Leonard bowed to do a line. We both hated Randy Newman.

Leonard fixed up the dashboard, and the three of us got out and walked up the lushly banked street to the party. It was a white, modern house receding down the slope of a hill in rectangles. Will had been invited by a film producer interested in optioning the sugar-heir book. Leonard—still a television producer who wanted to be a film producer—had offered to drive us up from the bookstore.

Will looked around for the producer but didn't know what he looked like. He drifted off to the bar without bothering to ask anybody. Leonard and I ran into a fat English rock manager we knew from the show. He had long golden hair and wore spectacles. He stood with a pretty, auburn-haired girl. I recognized her. She played a young horse trainer on a moderately successful television drama series, and had made one art-house film. It was a serious, Scandinavian-style comedown I'd gone to see one summer night in Raleigh. After waiting thirty desperate minutes for dialogue cover, I'd finally cracked open my beer in the theater's silence, and had immediately been kicked out.

Leonard poked me in the shoulder. "Tell them the joke."

I shook my head.

"C'mon, Hayward, tell it to them."

"A Pole, a fag, and a Spic walk into a bar. Bartender says, 'Get the fuck out of here.'"

Leonard laughed until the manager and the actress began to laugh. He had an infectious laugh. And he loved the joke. I must have told it to him a hundred times. It was, anyway, the only one I ever remembered.

The rock manager asked the actress if she wanted a drink, and disappeared purposefully off. Leonard was talking with her, and then broke off talking to her and hastily motioned to a man across the room. The man was talking to the English rock manager. Leonard bluntly excused himself and went over and huddled with the two men.

The actress and I stood in the sunken, white-carpeted living room, the big windows full of green palm fronds under the bright glow of security lights. She watched Leonard and the men, shook her head, and asked me who my friends were.

I said I knew Leonard. We worked together. I said I didn't have many friends.

"Leonard and I used to be friends," she said. "I think we still are."

A gaunt, nervous man came up and stood by us. We were standing by a table. On the table was a large, neatly dissected pink cake. He pried his arm between us, putting his dirty cake plate on the high stack of warmed, clean ones. He looked up at her like a fish just hooked. "Hello, Cathy," he said, and introduced himself.

Cathy said hello to him, and somehow at the same time looked at the dirty plate on top of the clean ones and also smiled at me. Her eyes were laughing too hard at this man. Her face was too tan and her teeth too white. But she looked as if she were still warm from the sun. Her shoulders were round and shiny, and a white halter top was slouched across her breasts as an afterthought. She was so easily pretty with her dark red hair, and slight hook nose.

"Is getting blown off an aphrodisiac?" She asked me, her eyes coolly following the man as he left.

"It's got its own peculiar sweetness, getting blown off."

"I'm told I don't like men who like me. That I'm a better accessory than a girlfriend." She looked at me.

"You want me to answer that?"

She hunched her shoulder ambivalently.

"Well, for men who know who you are," I said, "there are no complicated expectations. It's too easy to idealize a relationship with you."

Her eyes wrinkled with suspicion. "Idealize into what?"

"Into, I don't know . . . idealize a relationship into just the simple program of accompanying you. Like an accessory."

She seemed unsatisfied. "So you know I'm an actress?"

"Yes," I said, and mentioned the art-house film. I told her my great-grandmother had starred in the first motion picture—a Western, directed by Thomas Edison.

"Not a lot of dialogue in that one, either," I added.

She looked at me with a well-worn suspicion. She was losing interest. She had no reference point for me other than Leonard, and therefore no attention span. It struck me as kind of a peculiarly actressy kind of distraction.

"But that's your friend, right?" She pointed across the room to Will. "The guy in the wrinkled jacket? I saw you come in together, with Leonard."

Will stood in a small den. It looked as if he were talking to two men who had their backs to him. Their arms were crossed and they were watching a television with the importance of having something riding on the show. Will stepped up between the two men. They parted as if synchronized, and stared at him. Tidily dressed in black, with softly parted blond hair, they looked like Armani-clad, door-to-door Mormons.

"He's not from out here, is he?" she said.

"No."

"He'd better watch out for those two."

Leonard came rushing up to us. He handed us wineglasses the size of urns, full of sangria and orange slices stained red. "Drink a big sip of that and then take it to your friend Will over there. You need to get him. Right now."

"Something about those two men is making your friend very upset," Cathy said dryly.

Will was now arguing with the men. His hands were clawed over his eyes and I could hear his voice carrying.

I took the glasses, took a long sip. "I better go over there, I guess."

I drew Will out of the den and down a hallway. The two blond men had turned away with a military insolence. They were talking without pleasure and occasionally looking back at Will.

"Please don't tell me you're being snobby about this place," I said.

He gave me a sour look. "No," he said, genuinely unnerved. "Goddamn it Hay, of course not."

He was shaking with antagonism. I handed him the goblet of sangria. He took a long sip, running a hand through his hair and staring down at the hard, tan fiber of carpet. His chest seemed to sink a little and he took a long breath.

"Look, I can't translate it," he said. He stood there, frozen in thought for a moment. "You know. God, I should go and apologize."

He shook his head, took another long sip of sangria. He had a fuck-you spirit, but he also had a deep, overbearing tenderness that made him ricochet from confrontational anger to wobbly mortification. He was looking at me now, standing close by, and his free hand was clenched. "I spilled a few drops of wine," he said, "and one of those guys gave me this petulant look. And then the other guy turned and gave me *the exact same look.*"

He put his hand on my shoulder. "And there was a coldness emanating from them. I mean, this clean, German, industrial severity. And then I had this really bad feeling, watching them stand there watching the television, that I'd never shake the day-to-day shabbiness. Your life, my life. But that they'd done it."

"They're just movie people."

"Well fuck, Hay, they bother me." He dropped his hand from my shoulder and stepped back. "Don't you think I should try to figure out why?"

"Not necessarily. Mailmen bother me. I don't know why. Who cares?"

He was not listening. He was staring again at the two men. "It's almost as if they *want* to let distinctions be washed out."

"People here used to try and do that through suntans."

He hunched his shoulders and took a step in one direction and then the other, as if cringing to deflect some sudden harsh light of authority. He stopped, looked into his sangria, took a sip, and looked back over at the men. "When I interview people," he said, "whether it's about something important or trivial, more and more I'm finding they are confusing their own memories, even their own déjà vu, with what they've seen on television. It's like there's this new fear of old actuality."

"That's nothing new," I said.

"It's new because it's creating *feelings*, feelings they never had," he insisted, "from images that were never really there . . . catching something familiar in the corner of your eye— a pretty Asian girl in line for a film, a strangely familiar house. It's very subtle, and more and more now it becomes a remembered feeling—a sadness in a kitchen, the fascinating way your father shuffled cards."

I nodded. "Once I remembered my mother, sitting cross-legged on a sand dune, in a thick, white Irish sweater smiling a homebound, early-sixties kind of smile. But I don't really have any memory of her. It's fake. From some beach-party movie. It happens all the time."

"But that's just a memory you know is fake. What about the feeling it gives you? What if you don't realize the memory is fake? What then, about the feeling?"

"Those men, it's not their fault."

"Yes, it is," he said. "It's their ideology."

"Look," he said, antagonism rising back into his voice as he motioned at me with his drink. "My father is long dead. If I remember him shuffling cards, there are consequences, good and bad. But if what I remember is fake, there are no real expectations. No real consequences. I won't eventually remember a full game of cards with my father because I never saw him shuffling in the first place. But I will wind up with this huge smarmy feeling of satisfaction at the complicated way I imagine he shuffled cards. Even if he never did."

"Maybe you just don't have enough real memories of your father."

"I have very few," he said, staring at me. "And I don't want to ruin them."

He dropped his eyes and lowered his voice. "But, Hay," he said, "it can be worse in other ways. I won't ever fuck the pretty Asian girl because I never saw her in line for the movie in the first place. But I'll still have the desire. And it will be impossible to fulfill. That's sadder, in a way."

He took a long sip of his sangria. "But the worst thing is that the fake past begins to feel better than the real one. Because somewhere deep down you understand . . . *if it is fake, there are no real consequences.* It's easier, and therefore addictive."

He held his gaze on me. "Doesn't that make you anxious?"

"I know what's fake."

"You think you do, but you don't."

"Look, Will, I have plenty of memories I'm certain are real, that I don't want anymore. I'm happy for them to be replaced."

"If you replace them you're just a mole. You just dig in, and sit there. It's like if you wake up praying, you never really wake up. And that's nothing to do with religion." He stared intently at me. "Do you see, at all, what I'm talking about? I mean, over and over I have to ask people, 'But what *happened*? What really *happened*?'"

He tipped his goblet at me. "You know what I'm trying to get to in people?"

"No."

"Anti-showmanship."

He looked past me and down the hall. The two men were gone from the den. His eyes searched the party for them. He relaxed on his heels, took a long sip of sangria. "I don't know," he said, "I'm not explaining this right. I shouldn't have yelled at those men. I don't even know what I was saying."

"What were you actually saying to them?"

"I was trying to ask them, only this was after the spill— and of course then it didn't come out right—it came out angry—if they believed there was a correlation between precision and longevity?"

"What would that be?"

"Precision being self-awareness, being careful."

"Did you get an answer?"

"Did it look like I got an answer?"

Cathy appeared at the end of the hall. "Leonard's waiting outside," she said to me. "He wants to go."

Will stared at her. "Outside?" He laughed. "All right. We don't want to jeopardize Leonard. Let's go. Dinner. I'll buy."

He looked from me to Cathy. "All right?"

Cathy made a face.

He took it as a yes.

I never would have guessed.

Leonard was waiting down the hill, standing by his Jaguar.

Cathy stopped as we passed a little makeshift booth. "I did valet," she said. "I'll see you boys down there."

"By the way," she said, fixing her eyes on Will, "those guys you were talking to . . . those guys are serious heavyweights at Fox."

Will stared at her and groaned.

I looked at him. "Wasn't the producer you were supposed to meet up here from Fox?"

In the restaurant, the four of us pressed into a red vinyl booth, Cathy and I facing Will and Leonard. We ordered drinks, Cathy and Leonard immediately sinking into conversation about who else was up for the job she was up for. Will, despite everything, seemed in good spirits. He drank both wine and vodka and chatted brightly to me about a half-Filipino girl he was dating named Reina. About a piece he'd done recently on a musician named Tommy Clement, a studio bassist for the British skiffle and MOR acts coming across in the pre-Beatles sixties: Lonnie Donegan, Johnny Duncan, Cliff Richard. Tommy was a woman named Vanna, and lived in the Bronx.

In 1958, not a lot of women played stand-up bass. Vanna played with her father on the Catskill circuit. But he'd died suddenly of a heart attack, and she'd been broke and desperate for work. Women weren't allowed to audition for session work, so one day she went dressed up in her father's clothes, got the job, and became Tommy Clement. She'd been a big Polish girl with a round face and a hearty voice, and the transformation had really been no problem. She liked being Tommy Clement. Things were easier: the attire, except for the tightness of the sling pressing her breasts down, the anonymity, except for the occasional, stunningly crude thing a man would say about a woman when he thought no women were around. The only real trouble was with the musicians who turned out to be secret homosexuals. One famous session guitarist, Phil Shin, had come onto Tommy Clement, virtually tried to rape him, and found out. But Phil Shin couldn't tell anybody, for obvious reasons.

Vanna was moving into a rest home, and was selling all her old records. She held an auction in the living room of her little brick house by JFK airport. She served vodka and ham sandwiches, and Will hung around the auction while she talked about her life and showed him old photos of her and the boys. Will watched the whole auction. A few of the records turned out to be immensely rare, and Vanna made nearly five thousand dollars. When a record she loved was sold, she'd put it on her old brown turntable one last time and make the winner—man or woman—dance with her.

The magazine had killed the piece. Billy Tipton's jazzy cross-dressing story had recently come out as a film. It'd made Vanna's whole life seem redundant.

Will didn't seem to mind. "Nobody remembers Larry Doby," he said.

"Wait," Leonard said, breaking out of conversation with Cathy. "Who was Larry Doby?"

"Baseball. The second black pro player," Will said. "Poor guy, even if he'd beat Jackie Robinson to it, I mean, with that name, he'd still be completely unknown."

Will raised his eyes to the door. The restaurant was a celebrity sort of hangout—Leonard's choice—and Donald Trump had just walked in with an entourage and was standing at the bar.

Will called the waiter over, and sent Trump a shot of Goldschlager.

Trump, who probably thought it was from Cathy, tipped the awful, gold-specked liquor toward our table as if it'd been a compliment, and drank it down.

Will seemed disappointed. "Jesus, LA is a finger fuck," he said.

"Dip them in gold and you can stick them anywhere," Leonard said with a pleased lewdness.

Cathy's shoulder brushed my shoulder. We looked sidelong at each other, her eyes offended. Without shifting her eyes she somehow indicated Leonard.

We ate. We all had lobster and spaghetti with oil and garlic. Another bottle of wine came. I went to the bathroom to piss. Will boomed my name on the other side of the door. I unlocked it.

He came in, Leonard in tow. Will was holding his hands up and making a pinching motion.

"What?" I asked. "Crabs?"

"Make sure," he said with slow-voiced assurance, "before things get heavy, you get a feel of her calves."

I looked at him.

"Soft calves, soft tits." He smiled haltingly, a little bit of schoolboy shame in it. He locked the door, turned, and held up a tiny packet of white powder.

Leonard stood shoulder to shoulder with Will, the same guilty, druggie smile on his face.

"Could you try," I said to Will, "to enjoy yourself for once without the animosity rush?"

"Fuck, Hay," he laughed, his hands fumbling around with the packet of speed. "You don't have anything on her yet."

Will did a line, handed the packet to Leonard, and walked back out.

As he drew his head back, Leonard's eyes were blurry and his black hair tousled. He straightened up, offered me the rolled-up dollar, and looked in the mirror. He shook his face as if to wake himself, and told me he knew Will's last name. He'd grown up in the same city as Will's grandparents. He said he was still ashamed he'd grown up in a suburb, while Will's family's house was on the river, and had a name and a gate.

I drove with Cathy to a club on Wilshire. She had a vintage white Mercedes coupe. The red leather seats matched her hair. Will and Leonard followed us in the Jaguar, but disappeared along the way.

Cathy had some medium-range VIP clout, and we left their names at the door. We made our way inside and sat at a low glass table in one of the private back rooms. With the line of speed I felt a smoothness, like a perfect stone in clear water. The room glistened with refracted light against black velvet. A thin, jet-black woman in a white, see-through blouse appeared and took our drink order. As I ordered, Cathy stood and went off into the crowd and danced alone.

Leonard and Will eventually arrived. Will sank heavily into a chair, immediately signaled the woman, and ordered drinks. Leonard was looking around the room to see if he knew anybody, then he sat down. I asked him what was going on with the show. We hadn't been shooting on weekends, and the calls from managers and publicists were noticeably thinning out.

He gave me an impatient glance, got right back up, and disappeared off, cell phone at his ear.

Will looked disheveled. LA was not a good city to be in without a purpose, and suddenly he no longer had one here. There were strands of gray in his hair and coffee stains on his collar and it seemed as if he couldn't clear his throat. And there was something new in his eyes since the restaurant. They'd been a long time getting here, and now there was a strange distance. He was still jumpy from the speed, had a bad, rollercoaster energy, but there was something else now underneath.

"What did you take?" I asked.

He stared blankly at me. He looked up as his double vodka was set down. He took a long sip, as if through his teeth. Bass thumped the walls. He wiped a big hand across his eyes and sucked in air through his teeth. "Ask Leonard."

"What did you take?" The music was loud now, and I had to yell.

"Submarine stuff. Dark high," he said. He didn't have to yell, somehow, and I could hear him fine. "Or no. Dark stuff. Submarine high."

"You are too old to be taking something like that."

His eyes lifted and caught mine—a direct, condescending look. His face vibrated slightly.

"It doesn't seem like speed anymore," I said.

He dropped his eyes, took a long sip of his drink. He looked at me again and his eyes softened with recognition. He shrugged, drank down his drink, and pointed to the door, making a motion to go out for a smoke.

We came out of the club. Will felt his pockets for his cigarettes. There was a narrow-faced black guy in an orange tracksuit, swishing back and forth in front of us and talking loudly on his cell phone. Before I could say anything, Will told the guy to quiet down.

The guy ignored us, kept on talking.

Will insulted his outfit.

"What!" He stopped, dropping the phone from his ear and stepping right up against Will. "You can't say that to me. Do you know what I can do to you?" He seemed to spit white teeth. He had men with him at the curb in a big SUV.

"I'm sorry," Will said, suddenly self-effacing. "We don't have any money and everybody here seems so rich. You seem so rich."

He gave Will a long hard look, and then he didn't even see us after that. He got back on his cell phone.

Will elbowed me and smiled.

"Let's just go back in," I said.

He absently patted his pockets. "Oh," he said, "I forgot . . . "

He walked up to the idling SUV. The passenger-side door was open. A black guy in an orange-striped Astros jersey sat there smoking a cigarette. He had some kind of kerchief tied around his Astros ball cap.

Will asked him for a smoke.

The guy's eyes narrowed. He looked up at his friend on the cell phone. He was talking intently into his phone, and didn't notice. The guy in the car shook his head disbelievingly, reached back into the car, and held out a cigarette.

Will took it, held it up and said thanks.

The guy offered me one. I took it.

We walked down the avenue. Will slowed with each step as if he were getting heavier. He kept doing these little half turns, as if hearing something behind him. He saw me holding the cigarette. "You don't smoke," he said.

"It didn't seem polite to say no back there."

He stopped and searched his pockets for matches. He lit his cigarette and stood smoking. He slowly closed his eyes. He dropped his hands and ash fell to the ground. He slowly opened his eyes. "You don't have Kimmel's number on you?"

"What? No, I don't have Kimmel's number."

He was looking past me, his eyes drifting upward. I turned. There was a big apartment building across the avenue, inverted concrete patios rising up the face. They were uniform and bare.

"Decks," he said with disgust.

He stared up at the building and shifted his weight. He took a step sideways and for a moment stumbled. He put a hand on my shoulder to right himself.

His eyes caught mine, flashed with guilt and worry. "Reina," he said, his voice a little slurred, "would leave me if she saw me like this."

"Well, aren't you getting serious? Isn't that good?"

He swallowed. "This is the last indulgence and I have to get out of it unscraped. This chick doesn't fuck around."

"Reina?"

"Yes."

"Leave you?"

His eyes were drooping, but he held his gaze on me. His green eyes caught all sorts of weird light, and his intense, ill-starred look froze me. Then something in his face suddenly changed, eased into a kind of apologetic determination. "I really have got to get it together. When I get back, I want to go into it with her fuckin' shipshape. No dirty little crumpled secrets in my pockets."

"Oh," I said. It hit me. I finally understood. "Heroin."

He was feeling around again in his pockets for cigarettes.

"How long, Will?"

"Just tonight, Hay. Just some stomped shit with your boss."

"No, how long. Since when?"

He shrugged.

"Since way back? Why did you want Kimmel's number just now?"

He pressed his palms against his pockets.

"You are out of cigarettes, Will."

"Let's go back inside," he muttered.

I spent the night at Cathy's place, her arm over me like a lover. But that wasn't the case. In the morning, when she turned away with disinterest, I got impatient and pulled the pillow out from under her. Her cheek knocked against the headboard as she turned back to face me. Her eyes were sharp. I slapped her. Lightly. Her eyes gleamed hard and I hit her again. This time harder and her mouth had this oval wondrousness.

After a while, I got the feeling the violence in her desire was a put-on. She'd had her troubles, I guessed. She was so pretty, with boyishly narrow hips and round shoulders, you could just tell someone had gotten to her early on. But she gave sex a little too much emphasis, saw it as the one great unknown, the one great saving grace. Maybe she was right, but I didn't believe it. Maybe Will would come to see heroin the same way, and would never learn otherwise. But then I didn't really believe that, and forgot about it. And then I thought about Kimmel.

We fell back asleep.

I woke up with Cathy standing over the bed. She was wrapped in an orange towel and distractedly holding a blow-dryer shaped like a pistol to her head. It was silver etched, had a fake mother-of-pearl handle. She finished her hair, and slid the hair gun into a white holster by the bathroom door. She drifted around her apartment in the towel, singing pop tunes, and smiling weirdly toward where I lay. She made a few phone calls. Her voice was different on these calls, demanding and abrupt. She looked good standing there doing business, tanned and glistening in her burnt-orange towel. Her face, I could see now, wasn't so perfect. There had been layers on the night before to cover the flake of sun and pills. And she'd let me do things to her, I understood, because she knew I wasn't long in this town. I had none of the right enthusiasms, and anyway, nobody any-where in the country was watching the show. It was going down the drain. It was a relief.

"Um," she said, with a hollowed-out smile as I got out of bed. "I've got to go pretty soon. I called you a cab. It should be here any minute."

But I barely heard her. I was already dressing. I had not felt her at all, no matter how hard she'd made me try. This indifference, it was why she'd let me in.

I walked out of her apartment and down Venice Boulevard toward the ocean. The apartment buildings were blank white in the sun, and blue light from above sifted through a gray film. I walked quickly, feeling starved and weak and strange. Convulsions ambushed my stomach. I sat down at a bus stop until they passed.

I walked a few more blocks to a small park. When I sat down, pain crisscrossed my insides again, up into my chest. A long coiled tightness of regret sprung up through me, and all I could think of was betrayal. The yellowness of betrayal. A distillation of everything wrong with having left. The yel-lowness of looking away, of doing what you had to do to sur-vive. It was inside me and everywhere around in the cheap architecture, storm-drain concrete, mustard smog air, in the smell of piss all around the park bench. My mouth was dry and I was sweating. My fists were clenched and pressing against my thighs. Years of hanging on, waiting for a turn. But leaving Helen had never felt like a weighing of possibil-ities and then a decision, but like an ejection, in the last sec-onds before the plane hits ground.

It had all happened so fast. We were living together on Fifth Street and everything was still okay. She'd seen a doc-tor a few days after the scene in the bath, and had been pre-scribed some pills. Then one morning she woke up and began pacing. She announced she had to leave the city. She couldn't bear the sounds of machines.

I called in sick and we drove up to Maine—her Aunt's place. We opened up the house, and then went for a walk down the little road. There was a barn. Helen opened the gate and walked right into the pen full of lambs. They pressed around her and she stroked their thick, curly fur. "Aren't they just the best?" she said to me, a smile on her face.

She crouched down, her jeans tucked into her green boots, and let them run all over her. She didn't care about the smell and the goopy mud and manure. Her cheeks were red with the cold aliveness of the air. She had a flushed, dewy expression. "You are an emperor," she repeated with a strange enthusiasm, touching the bobbing sheep on their skulls. "And you are an emperor. And you and you, too."

It was the end of the day. Beyond her, the fields rolled down a hill to a stream, and the sun had just dropped behind the mountain rising up on the other side. The first thin darkness smudged the gray trees and turned the air purple. Helen stood up. The sheep had lost interest in her and were clumped purposelessly a few feet away. I reached across the wooden fence and touched her shoulder. She did not turn.

I said her name.

"Oh," she finally said without turning around. Her voice was flat and expressionless.

We continued down the road. The air was cool, gray, and wetness hung in the air from the rain. We walked along the slick, narrow lane, along the wooden fence. A horse stared at us, dark wet patches across its brown flank. We passed under the old diseased oaks, leaves shriveled black and hanging like bats. We ran into her Great-Aunt Eleanor, an old round woman in a floral dress and blue down jacket. She was poking a young snapping turtle with her big black shoe. It was struggling in the ditch between the pasture fence and the road. Eleanor wanted me to carry it home for her for the gardener to kill and make soup out of. I put my hands up and shrugged. They both looked at me with something like distrust. But I wasn't going to pick up a snapping turtle.

We kept on along the road. The field alongside the road gave way to the forest. The trees were young, frequently harvested, and their trunks swayed like ropes in the wind. Helen stopped, took a step off the road. She was staring into the rocky underbrush that rose under the trees. "Do you see those salamanders?"

"No," I said. "I don't see anything."

She took another step up the slope, looking at the ground. "They are orange."

"I don't see anything."

"They are everywhere."

There was nothing there. I did not say anything. I treated the moment like a dream, like a mutual hallucination. I tried to enjoy the dissonance, to let the moment stretch out in some way where it would relieve itself of pressure.

After dinner, we sat by the fire in the den. The heavy-lidded oil paintings muted the light from the brass lamp, and the little white television, the sound off, glowed expectantly for Monday-night football. The Redskins were on. The game was twenty minutes away, and I was turning the white knobs, trying desperately to get the little screen to level out. Helen had showered and changed, and lay on the floor in her green corduroys and white cashmere sweater. Her back was against the armchair, and her hands grasped a book. She looked spaced out and tired. She had taken one of her pills, but her face was darkened like a rain cloud.

I thought of diversions. Usually she'd read. There was a cabinet of games: Scrabble and Boggle. But neither of us were ever in the mood for the petty assertions those games demanded. The fire was dying. I gave up on the screen for a moment, leaned back, and stared as the flames eased down into an ember glow.

I looked at Helen. Her eyes fluttered with sleep.

Closed.

The room filled up with silence. A wind hit the house, and the embers cracked and flowered into small flames. Life with Helen was coming back around to silence. Not silence exactly, but something weightier—silence and increasing friction. Growing up, my life had been full of silence in cars. Driving for hours with my father without a word between us. But there had also been an ever-present, youthful feeling of coasting. Daydreams of frictionless movement until one morning, the morning after his eating club reunion, I had a hangover. Lagging behind my father in the parking garage of the New Jersey hotel, the surrounding concrete filled me with an overbearing feeling of permanence. I stopped. I heard a new sound. The air sounded like boiling water. Later, I learned people heard this as a kind of universal golden hum, a constant thread of vibration suggesting an interconnectedness. But to me, the sound only meant that there was really no such thing as silence. That you could never be apart from noise.

I'd been so quiet at that age my father had taken me to a speech therapist and eventually to Georgetown University Hospital for a CAT scan. I remember being slid into that torpedo chamber. I remember *that* silence.

I woke Helen up and got her to bed.

I lay awake, looking out the window. It was a black night, cool and silent and void of the ubiquitous suburban glow. Beyond the broad field across the road, hills rose, hiding foxes and eagles. Some time in the night, I heard coyotes calling out from over there, and then a long piercing warble of a mountain lion drifting south from Canada.

I woke up late in the night. Helen was at the edge of the bed. She sat in the dark and stared out into the trees. Her whole body seemed to list under her white nightgown.

I sat up.

"It's not that I can't go to sleep," she said in a half-awake trance. "It's that I'm afraid of my dreams. And now my dreams come while I'm awake. And now I understand my dreams are memories. Bad ones. Ones I can't wake up from."

She lay back and stared up at the ceiling. I leaned over her, pushed her hair off her face, but she did not look at me.

In the morning, I sat up suddenly. The curtain was knotted into a tight hourglass, the sun clotting out the rest of the window with a thick yellow glare. I lay back and folded a pillow over my head. Gleams stuck in my eyes like tiny floating diamonds, like cuts into a heretofore resilient, dark peace. Helen was not next to me.

The bathroom door was shut. Locked. When I came through, she was sitting cross-legged on the floor, her head drooping. Her mouth was open and her eyes looked cold as a fish's and seemed to be sliding off onto her cheeks. A blue and yellow pill was stuck to her chin, and a dozen more wobbled on the linoleum around her. I picked her up. I dragged her downstairs, got her in the car and drove like a madman the forty-five minutes to the Portland hospital. The life was draining from her eyes, and I kept shoving her with my free arm to keep her awake. The more she faded, the more terrified her eyes got. She kept staring at the green river along the road as if she couldn't bear its strength and flow. Its simple greenness.

After a week in Portland, Helen was moved down to the ward at Yale in New Haven. A nurse was assigned to her, shadowed her. But she was so heavily sedated she barely moved. She would sit on her bed in her thin white pajamas, her eyes frozen. She would not look directly at me, as if there were a residue of shame under all she was swarmed with. But something had changed in her eyes, the warm brownness was gone and there was a new, elastic darkness, a fear in them as if she could not get out from behind her own eyes.

For weeks, she barely spoke. I read, paced the halls, played cards with the black orderlies. Hearts, black jack, go fish. Nothing heavy. The girl in the bed next to Helen's was a black-haired, Latin teenager with her arms tied down. She shrieked constantly in Spanish and broken English—through unbelievable amounts of sedatives, about the holy Trinity and a man named Victor all gang-fucking her like the devil does. Her cries were lewd—both frantic and con-sensual, and it was hypnotizing how real it all seemed to the girl.

Clean-cut and hollow-eyed, diagnosed and re-medicated, Helen finally came out. We drove down to New York, stepped back into our apartment together like the first night of an arranged marriage.

Her medications, like her doctors, kept changing, and every day I counted out various combinations of beautifully designed pills: tiny black triangles of Atarax, Klonopin shaped like rose-tinged pears, baby blue bars of Elavil, Restoril—*For Sleep* stamped seductively across the capsule—peach round cushions of Mellaril, snow-white lithium, pink Xanax ovals, and Atavans—each pill sculpted into an art deco A.

I sat in offices and listened to opinions from doctors, psy-chopharmacologists, psychiatrists, physical therapists, and even one graying hippie in Yorkville with no degrees on the wall and sheep dogs all over the floor, who called himself a psychological attaché. I spent hours on the phone with health-insurance companies. They wanted nothing to do with her.

I had to quit my job.

I took her to appointments. Watched her.

We began to walk. We paced the East Village grid, Gramercy Park, Murray Hill, the chaotic patterns of the West Village, the brisk apartness of Chinatown, and gloomy, exhaust-choked TriBeCa. Midtown. Uptown. We said little and walked fast. She was walking toward something—what, I never knew. Sometimes our outings would become tedious marches, and I would be unable to convince her to stop (nor would she continue alone). Sometimes she would just stop, a curious look of recollection on her face, and we would stand there, wherever we were, stalled, her hand determinedly clenched around something: a plastic ruby she'd got out of a gumball machine, a shop-lifted radish, a penny. And then we'd move on, and I'd feel a logistical duty to keep up.

Sometimes something would happen.

One day, walking by the UN, we saw Alexander Dubcek, the hero of the Prague Spring, step out of a black limo. A few months later, while Helen was deep in a ward in Charlottesville, Dubcek died. He'd managed to outlive the Soviet Union. That evening when I visited, Helen, to my surprise and in a rare, lucid moment of connection, had torn his obituary out of the newspaper, and we sat in the ward and read it together.

Mostly nothing happened. Once we wound up way uptown in the campus center of Barnard, watching coeds bowl. "Don't you think that's a ballet?" Helen enthused.

"No."

"Just after they let the ball go, and are frozen like that," she said, transfixed by the bowlers. "Don't you think that's a kind of elemental ballet?"

"These walks certainly are."

"You don't understand what I'm saying."

"You're just dreaming," I said. "You don't know it, but you are always just dreaming."

Usually when I got annoyed, she would turn off and not talk for hours. But this time she looked at me with a faint, private smile. In her smile was a kind of born-again condescension, and for the first time, I thought of bolting. Just taking off and running. Sending in Will in a month or so for my stuff. But the sicker she got, the more I became weirdly immobilized by loyalty.

Late one Sunday night, Helen slipped out of the apartment.

I paced and paced, called everyone we knew.

An hour later the phone rang. It was Helen. "Will you come and meet me?"

"Where are you?"

"I'll tell you, if you come." Her voice was secretive, rushed, and afraid. She meant will I come and not paramedics.

Twenty minutes later, I walked into the restaurant. She was sitting alone against the wall along an empty row of tables. Her face was frozen, an angular darkness to it, and she looked confused as if by the pain she was creating for herself. Black lines, like thin branches, criss-crossed around her mouth.

I sat down. "You aren't taking your pills."

She wore her down coat, and a bright orange ski cap. There were framed photos of Italian boxers above her head. Their bare fists were taped and clenched. She admitted she'd been hiding her doses in a crushed box of tissues

170

between the mattresses. She said she had a knife in there, and gave me a quietly thrilled explanation of the process, describing the razor's ease on her wrists, the deep, soft finesse of the cut, like a sushi knife into tuna.

"You need to take a sedative."

"No."

"Please. We need to do something."

"If I fall asleep, I'll be taken in."

A waitress came, a blow-dried blonde with tiny white teeth. She looked at us, paused, and left.

Helen leaned forward. "You're good, right?"

She tried to look at me but seemed perplexed. She lay her head on her forearm. Her cheek inadvertently pulled up her sleeve and I could see two, thin dark gashes along the underside of her wrist. "When will it come?" she said, her eyes closed.

"Soon," I said.

"When?"

"It'll come."

"I'm so tired."

The waitress approached again.

Helen sat bolt upright and took my hand.

"Can I get you something to drink?" the waitress asked with a cautious brightness.

"Oh god," I muttered. "I don't know . . . two champagnes."

Helen stiffly clasped my hand as the waitress disappeared off. The champagne order had been a halfhearted attempt at levity, but its impending arrival only made everything seem worse, and we waited in silence for the waitress to come back.

When she returned and served the champagne, Helen held her glass up, staring intensely at the rising golden bubbles.

"We can fetch fresh glasses if you like," the waitress said with halting friendliness.

Helen turned her face up to the girl. "You don't believe in the friendliness."

"Um, so, fresh glasses?"

"I can hear you. Your voice. You don't believe."

The waitress set my glass down. "Okay. Well, please let me know if you two need anything else," she said, and turned and hurried off with the tray under her arm.

Helen put down her glass. I took it and quickly drank it down. I was going for mine when she took both my hands in hers and began speaking with a rushed fascination as if she only had a few moments to make me understand before the waitress came back again. "There's me and you and then this caught in my throat. Why all these fears you need to know and not charm yourself around? You have charm, Hayward, because you are completely unaware. And my eyes feel so heavy. I have to speak with so much to get out from under them. But it is not a cure or a confession. It is how you handle yourself between, I think. Are you so unaware? I'm not sure. I do need to sleep."

"Your eyes are heavy," I said. But I knew she would not sleep unless she was drugged.

"But you can't stick your arm down my throat." She dropped my hand and slumped back against the booth.

She was crying now. She'd heard her own words and knew I could not understand them. Yet she also knew she could not talk so as to make me understand. But she was trying.

"It is all different from what you know," she cried, taking up my hands again. "I won't ever be the same for what you know about me now." Her eyes grew wide again. "I always want to be with you. Not what I am now. I know somehow . . . please don't look at me like that."

"Helen, let's go. Let's go home and get your medication." I'd worked one of my hands free of hers, and drank down my champagne in one long gulp.

She watched me. She shook her head, losing her breath through tears. "I'm so sorry. I know it's not right. I'm so sorry. But it will come to you again someday. I am so scared this is true but I am scared because it is."

She dropped my hand, pressed her hands over her face. Her voice was full of urgency and shame. "It will come, I know. Not like this . . . It will come for you and it will come easy."

Back in our apartment, we had a terrible struggle when she heard the ambulance siren. She went for pills hidden in the bathroom. She got most of them down before my elbow caught her full on in the eye, and I had to pin her down on the bathroom floor and try to pry them out. She clenched her teeth and bit her lip so hard it bled all over the sleeves of my shirt. When she saw the blood she grew strangely silent. The tension went out of her, and her eyes went blurry.

I let go of her.

She reached out and touched the blood, a drop quivering on her fingertip.

I stood and helped her up. We walked to the front room and sat and waited for the paramedics to come up the steps.

At Mt. Sinai, there was some difficulty. Her eye was black and there was a suspicion I'd beaten and drugged her. We had no insurance. Helen lay tied down, sedated in limbo on a stretcher in the hallway. A homeless man lay on the stretcher next to her, his crushed foot loosely wrapped in a clear plastic bag. I could smell the antiseptic mingling with the rot, and saw white maggots tumbling out of his heel. I had no idea what to do. I called Will, and told him as best I could what was happening.

A friend of Will's family, a surgeon named Alan, arrived at the emergency room forty-five minutes later. He took one look at her, went behind the desk and into the offices.

He got her right in.

Will arrived from work a few minutes later. He helped me with the forms—I could not even see them—and paid for everything. He stayed with me, pacing and making calls.

I remember a nurse tapping my shoulder, leading me down a long hallway with giant brown arrows painted on the floor, and into an office cool and musty as a basement. I spoke to the doctor for a long time. I did not understand anything he told me. I went back upstairs and sat catatonically in the brightly lit waiting room, staring up at the television blare of a cop show, the theme song ringing around the room . . .

Will was kneeling in front of me. I must have dozed off. He told me she was finally safe and asleep. He insisted I stay nearby. His stepfather had an empty, midtown pied-à-terre. He insisted I stay there with him and not go home alone. I could come back over first thing in the morning. He'd get me up—he had to work early.

We walked over to a sour, bare old bar I knew. A sign on the wall said it was closing after eighty-seven years. I shook my head and told Will I used to hang out there. It was near an old production job and I could always count on it to be empty.

He looked at me with his long, incredulous face. "You only liked it when it was empty," Will said with a soft laugh, "and now you're complaining it's closing?"

I sat there with my whiskey, ignoring Will. But after a few sips I realized I was deep in a sudden, violent change I could not drink away.

At the apartment, Will brought me another whiskey. I drank it down to try to get tired, and made a few phone calls I do not remember anything about.

Will came back in and set down a tray with a pork chop and a cold glass of milk. After I ate, I lay down half drunk and wide awake in the tiny maid's room with a shaft-way view, waiting for dawn.

11

I walked the house at night. Inch by inch down the pitch-black hallway, pausing after each step to let my eyes adjust, the interior contours slowly coming into focus just enough to take a step. The only light was the little red eye on the alarm box by the front door. The alarm was on, always on—every door and window ready to shriek. But the house did not feel like a prison. It was as concrete a place as I'd ever found. The comfort in its isolation was magnetic, but it was also beginning to fade. It was just a structure, and I did not feel a twinge of attachment knowing I would have to leave soon.

One night, I edged all the way up to the loft. It was a black night with no moon. I lay down and began to consider where to go. I looked over the ocean for a break in the darkness. Far off on the northwest horizon, I could just still make out the flickering lights of the oil rigs, jewelling the band of horizon.

When I woke up, the dawn sky was low, full of speeding gray clouds and cracked with blue. The ocean was chopped in blacks and grays, angrily chipped white. A white light serrated the edges of the clouds, and the morning sun broke through in instances. The soft waves rose, and lime-green light poured through their backs before the waves melted back into the expanse of gray. In the huge sameness, in the rise and fall of currents undulating like the grassy plains, I began to glimpse faces. Familiar faces, strange faces, famous faces. They heaved and blended with one another and then they were gone and all that was left was the unenforceable surface and the empty desire the horizon's light shot back.

In 1926, after almost fifty years, Finn and Annie finally spoke. It was the year she died.

Finn, out of the blue, had written asking her to shoot open one of the last of the main roads he was to build. Cincinnati to Chicago.

She'd agreed.

Maybe it was a simple desire to see, one more time, someone you loved a long time ago. Maybe when you reach a certain age, that is a newfound feeling. Maybe she knew she was dying and was able to finally acknowledge her son. But I don't believe my grandfather was at the ceremony. Either way, she was finally back living in Greenville, and it wasn't much of a trip to Cincinnati. It was the last time she ever appeared in public.

Annie arrived at the ceremony in a long white dress, her long white hair tumbling out of a wide-brim hunting hat Teddy Roosevelt had given her.

Finn stood in his dark tweed coat, waiting for Annie on the big stand trestled with red, white, and blue ribbon. He took her hand as she stepped up onto the platform. They looked at each other, both old now. They looked out over the small crowd.

Chicago was not a popular town in 1926 Cincinnati. People who had not lost their sons in the war were losing their sons (and daughters) to Chicago. It was the beginning, for Cincinnati, of a long and painful demise. Only the biggest cities seemed to have life or challenge for young men. But also, Chicago was a glamorous and prosperous city and Cincinnati's new direct connection to it must have given the crowd a turgid sense of self-sufficiency, or they wouldn't have paid Finn a dollar a head to see Annie Oakley shoot air.

She turned and asked Finn where the target was.

He pointed down to the freshly poured concrete, toward Chicago, toward the West.

She lifted her rifle.

After the crack, and after the puff of smoke had drifted off, the crowd stared down the wide, dull swath of asphalt.

Finn held up her hand and shouted, "Ladies and gentlemen, Annie Oakley. Winner of air!"

She looked at him, and they both suddenly bent over laughing, as if ducking a ricochet of her own shot.

They came back up and this is the moment caught in the only photograph of Finn and Annie together. It is on display in the dining room of the Cincinnati Historical Society. My father took me there for lunch in 1979. I remember him pointing out the photo with a broad grin.

In the background of the photo, the audience—men in mustaches and hats, women in ruffled dresses shaped like bells—is scattered across the new asphalt, looking confused about the purpose of the shot. A few seem to be clapping hesitantly.

In the foreground, Finn and Annie are clasping hands and laughing as if with the delight of a sudden, good memory. A private joke. As if it were all a joke. As if the ricochet had melted, like a glass ball, the pressure of fifty years apart.

On the white border, someone had written long ago: *Winner of Air! 1926.*

Finn outlived Annie by fifteen years. He wound up in a North Carolina rest home shooting squirrels from a wheelchair, the recoil often knocking him out of the chair and sending him tumbling down a slope. He died in 1941, the year *Citizen Kane* was released. Sea World had lost millions, his San Simeon.

Annie Oakley died a few months after the shot down the road, from complications from a car accident on one of the roads Finn had built. She died in relative obscurity, and soon after her death her house in Greenville was razed. She did not become famous again until the success, twenty years later, of *Annie Get Your Gun*.

She then became more a legend than a life, a caricature almost.

She was a genius, if you go by the dictionary definition. Or she was just a good old girl with a rare talent. She is now in the dictionary. Usually the only other woman on the page is Joyce Carol Oates.

Oakley (ō-klē), Annie. 1860–1926. Amer. sharpshooter.

Often there is a photograph.

12

I had not heard from Will in a few days, and assumed he had gone back to New York. The production was off for a week—I'd had a few messages from Leonard, but he wasn't picking up my calls.

One evening the phone rang. It was Reina. She hadn't heard from Will, and had found my number, with its Los Angeles area code, scrawled on an envelope. She was looking for him.

I'd had a couple drinks, and my answers were elusive.

She grew frustrated. "Are you really even good friends with Will?"

"I've known him on and off for a long time. Well, and then never too well. Better recently, I guess."

"Have you seen that friend of yours, Kimmel?"

"No. Why?"

"Kimmel came around here a few times," she said with a strange severity. "He'd just appear, and Will, you know, would get very drunk and good-natured and take us out to a fancy dinner. He'd give Kimmel all this unwanted advice about his songs but we'd still be having fun . . . and then they'd disappear off, you know. And Will wouldn't return my phone calls and it was just a weird vibe."

There was a long silence on the line. "I didn't like that," she finally said.

Again, I didn't respond.

"Could you look for him?" she asked.

"If he's in this city, I can probably find him for you."

"For you, too. You're his friend, right?"

"Yes. I'm his friend. He's just the kind of person, you know, it's on his terms. But that's fine. I've never believed that you choose your friends. It's more who you wind up with in certain circumstances."

She was silent on the line for a minute. "You sound as if you're too careful about people."

"Maybe."

"Well, I don't understand why Will hasn't called. When you saw him, did he say anything about me?"

"Yes," I said. "Good things. Don't be worried."

"But I am."

"Please don't. I'll find him, all right?"

"All right. Call me if you do. He'll tell you he'll call me. But he might not." There was a pause. "He's got work here, you know. His editor is calling. What do I tell him? How was the reading? Was there even a reading?"

"Reina, I'll call you."

"I'm sorry. Right. Of course, Hayward. Thanks."

"Did I see you get off a bus?" Kimmel asked.

I nodded.

We were sitting having coffee in the grill across from his dumpy motel. I'd left messages for him all over the place. When he'd finally returned my call, the number had been his booking agent's office, and I'd tracked him down in LA through them.

Kimmel raised his eyebrows. "I thought you had a job."

"I do. But I don't have a car. Did you know nondairy creamer is a plastic explosive?"

"You should get another car. The bus is no way to make it around here."

I looked at him. "What are you doing in LA?"

He looked out the window. His face looked softer—slightly bleary. His thick black hair was beginning to recede, and his eyes were dark and latticed with creases. He was gaining weight, his face and neck beginning to round out. He smelled like an old suitcase. "You know," he said, "it's difficult everywhere without a car. When I started to tour—up and down the East Coast, up and down the West Coast, down the Midwest to Texas—I'd take the train once in a while. Go alone by train. You know, to avoid Burt. But the train stations were so empty, the trains, too."

His eyes followed the wires down the boulevard. "I like that feeling," he said. "But those trains were too empty. And the station was never a station. It was a post office, a real estate office, a bistro. And too many times there was no place to wait indoors. Only the platform."

"It's not that way in Europe," he added, picking up his coffee. "Only here."

"Have you seen Will?" I asked.

Kimmel sipped his coffee, holding it up close in front of his face. There was a long pause. He was suddenly impatient. It was like this sometimes with Kimmel and Will. As if I'd *had* to ask.

"I just did, in fact."

"Where?"

He set down his coffee, leaned back, and looked back out the window.

"Look, Kimmel," I said impatiently. "I'm trying to find Will. He's been missing. Reina, his girlfriend, she's worried."

"He's with this guy. The guy knows you."

"He's here?"

"Yes." He nodded.

"Wait? The guy . . . Leonard?"

"Right."

"Will's still out here hanging around with Leonard?" I looked around the grill. I took a sip of coffee, leaned back. "Fuck. Wait, what are *you* doing up here?"

"I came up to see Will," he said flatly. "But that Leonard fellow . . . I turned around and left."

"You came up to see Will? That's nice, Kimmel. What were you guys planning to do? Go for a nice healthy lunch at Erewhon? Go swimming, jogging? Do a spa treatment?"

"Hay, please. We met for dinner. Will insisted on brains and eggs at some medieval diner. I had to come up anyway to meet with my booking agent, you know, because I've been canceling an awful lot of shows recently . . . But Will showed up with *your* friend, and they were all fucked up. Embarrassingly so," he said, glancing up with a flash of anger. "And so I left, brains still on the plate."

He shook his head. "Will can have *those*, for all I care. Disgusting stuff."

"Suddenly you just can't deal with Will when he's like that?"

"Like what, exactly?"

"You tell me. You were with him."

There was a long pause. "That friend of yours," he said, "I see his type a lot—his type has tried to manage me. He's no good."

"Why did you just leave? Why didn't you do anything?"

"Do what? It's Will's life, it's private."

"Interfere, for fuck's sake."

"What?"

"Interfere."

Kimmel glared at me. "How was I to know he was missing? Who are *you* to determine he's missing?"

He signaled for the check. "All right," he said, sliding out from the table, "enough of this. Goodbye, Hay."

"Wait, where is he?"

Kimmel stood up.

"Where is Will?"

"The Beverly Wilshire," Kimmel said, and turned and walked out.

The check came.

I took a cab over to the hotel. Will had not checked out. I took the elevator up. The door was unlocked.

Cathy lay on the bed, in her underwear and a T-shirt in the room's bleak light. Will sat next to her, cross-legged in a white robe, his hand gripping her thigh. He stood up when I came in and shouldered away from me. He was out of it, pale and shaky, stepping over old room-service trays looking for matches. The room smelled like rotting bananas. There was a guitar pick and a tiny Ziploc bag on the top of the television set. A bottle of Virgina Gentleman and a bucket of ice rested on the bedside table. Leonard stood by the glazed window, murmuring into his cell phone. He glanced up at me, went back to his conversation. The phone jack had been pulled out of the wall.

I walked over to Will, grabbed his shirt with a fist, and gave him a look.

"All right," he said, sitting down on the bed with his head sunk in his hands, "I know."

Behind him, Cathy had pulled the covers over her head. She lay completely motionless underneath, her knees up in a pyramid.

I took Will's rental-car keys and threw his things into a bag. I held up the half-full bottle of Virginia Gentleman.

"Not both. Not that shit," I said to Leonard, pointing the bottle at the Ziploc bag, "with this."

Leonard shrugged, the phone still pinned between his shoulder and ear.

I got Will in the car and we headed to the airport. He sat slumped against the passenger door, his eyes sunken and mouth open, nearly passed out but still smoking a cigarette. The drugs and booze had run coarsely through him, and his hair was streaked with gray strands. I remembered him years before in New York, cutting through the subway crowd ahead of me, jumping the exit turnstile for no good reason, and bounding up the Astor Place steps into the mouth of sunlight.

We curved off Sunset. "Why are you doing this?" I said as we slipped into line for the 10.

"It gives me time," he said, as if I should have known.

"Oh, bullshit. Time for what? It's a fucking clearing-house. It clears everything out."

"No. It gives me *time*." He moved his arm woodenly, and the ash dropped off his cigarette.

I accelerated onto the 10. "That's arrogant. You're arrogant. You do that stuff with a sneer."

He leaned forward. I thought he was going to throw up. He wore wide-whale, chocolate cords, and a black Adidas windbreaker two sizes too small, buttoned up to his neck. His shirt collar poked out like a broken kickstand. He turned away from me and put his hand on the car door handle. He was staring down at the highway, transfixed by the way the speed made the concrete so vivid. How the concrete froze just ahead, seemed to pause, and then rushed by.

He came out of it, sat up suddenly as if poked in the back. "And now I'm okay? Everything's all right, with you, going to the airport?"

He turned to me. "Fuck you, Hay. I mean, what the fuck have you done?"

"No, Will. No punk theatrics, please. I'm taking you to the airport. *You* are fucking up. The bottle is in your bag and that is all that is going to get you back when I leave you and turn around and go home. Consider it a gift."

He looked at me. "Reina can't know," he said slowly. There was an anxious emphasis in his nasal voice, "You can't tell her. I can't take her heat right now. I've got to get to New York and check into a hotel for a few days. Pretend I'm not around and clean up for her. She's not gonna take it if she finds out."

"She has to know, Will. What if you're on the floor going blue and she doesn't know what the fuck is going on?"

"I need her around, get it? If I'm going blue, I'll need her there. She'll know enough to call an ambulance."

I got him to the gate.

We were taking sips from the Virginia Gentleman, a stereophonic din of CNN above us as far as the eye could see. He was sitting up, leaning forward, his hand cupped over his eyes like a visor. He'd searched through his bag and there were clothes scattered around him on the airport carpet. He'd told me he didn't have anything hidden.

His flight was announced.

I stood up and got his clothes together and stuffed them in his bag.

I stood over him. "That's you."

He kept his hand over his eyes, but I could see that they were wet and angry. He looked like he did not want to go and did not want to stay. Everything seemed like it was ending, and I did not know what to say.

"What is it?" he pleaded. His cracked voice held empty spaces of disbelief.

"I don't know."

"What it is?" He kicked under his seat.

"I don't know. I'm sorry."

I sat back down, picked up the bottle, and took a sip. When Helen would get bad, the only way I could stay up all night with her was to sip bourbon. I got used to it.

Will was now slumped sideways in his chair. His eyes were closed, but there was still this subtle belligerence toward me.

First-class passengers and passengers needing special assistance were announced.

"I could probably get you on now," I said, tapping him on the shoulder.

"Poor Helen," he mumbled. "Blue-blood poor with red-rimmed eyes." He made a sound that was almost a laugh, but the laugh was a false start and something else broke up his expression into confusion. He was too washed out for antagonism.

"Forget it, Hay," he said, trying, with a frustrated sigh, to sit up. "I'm not going back. Let's go down to Nevada instead. Or New Mexico. Desert air, you know, dry-out air."

"I have to work. You do too."

He shrugged.

High rows were announced.

"You are a fool, Hay," he said after a long moment.

"Why's that, Will?"

"Why do you think Leonard's lying around my hotel room?"

"Because your grandparents' house had a gate."

Will turned and looked at me. "Because there's no show."

"What?"

"There's no sponsor. You don't get it. Show's off. The sponsor balked. Show's down."

"You're serious? You better be serious."

187

He shrugged. His eyes fluttered and he seemed about to nod off again.

Middle rows were announced. The line at the gate stretched out into the concourse.

I took his ticket out of his bag. Took his phone, walked off, and called Leonard.

Thinking it was Will, Leonard answered. He was taking a production job in France. The show was off.

Low rows were announced. The line still extended out past the check-in desk.

I called Reina.

I went to the desk. I bought a first-class ticket, and upgraded Will's. Reina's advice. She knew more about Will than he wanted to believe. It had been this way before, and this time came with a promise of rehab. And if getting on the plane meant, for Will, going into rehab, it was necessary I come. And, if he was going to make a scene on the plane, it was probably better to do it in first class. You could get away with more.

I stood over Will with the new tickets. It was the last boarding call. "All right. We're going. I'm coming with you."

Will's face was exhausted and cloudy, and he made a vague noise of consent.

I kicked his feet.

He opened his eyes slightly with what I thought was relief.

"Get up," I said, holding out the tickets. "First class. Because that's the way you look."

13

I sat up in bed. I'd heard a noise. The front door alarm
. . . but it could have been a truck backing up outside.

I lay back down. The room was cool, the early morning
sun bright through the skylight. The more I'd been thinking about having to leave the house, the more I slept.

But I had a strange feeling.

I got up, cracked open the bedroom door, and listened.
Nothing. The red alarm light was on.

I went upstairs, looked around. I went into the bathroom, looked down and froze.

On the toilet seat was a single yellow drop of piss.

I stood there, stunned. I hadn't used that bathroom in
days.

Someone had come in while I'd slept. I had to leave the
house.

I turned around, walked over to the window. The driveway was empty. I hurried back downstairs.

I dressed in the teenager's high-tops and baggy jeans, the
gargoyle shirt, and the Hilfiger sweatshirt. I took an old
brown Gucci bag out of the closet and stuffed in the clothing I'd been wearing the night of the accident. I needed
money now, and dug into the pants pockets. In the front
pocket was my identification and a few crumpled twenties.

In the back pocket was a folded-up bank envelope. Flattened and water stained, I assumed it was from some forgotten withdrawal I'd made while ricocheting around Santa Monica on my intricate drunk. But it was suddenly familiar to me. I looked at the bank insignia. No bank I knew. I opened the envelope. There was a check inside from Will's estate. Six thousand dollars. It was wrapped up in a typed invoice stating compensation for two first-class plane tickets Los Angeles to New York LaGuardia. As I slid the check back into the envelope, I noticed handwriting across the top of the folded invoice. A phone number. Reina had written her name and her phone number. I stared at her handwriting. I couldn't believe it.

I carefully folded the paper around the check and put them back into the envelope. I zipped the envelope into a side pocket. I stood in the room and listened for a moment. Not a sound, inside or out.

I went into the closet, down through the hatch, and climbed out from under the house. I made my way down the sandy alley and stood in the foliage. The ocean glistened like a new version of itself. On the beach, tiny waves swished and turned over with a quiet exactness in the calm, steely morning. A young girl stood at the water's edge holding a boogie board, a black wet suit falling down limp from her hips. She was rail thin and blonde. She wore a bright red bikini top and kept tugging at the strap under her breasts. I thought of Reina's hard, pubescent-like body and for the first time in a while felt an automatic pull inside. I remembered facing Reina on the street in New York. It was the last time I'd seen her. She had looked so pretty, her black hair and calm face and pushed-out lower lip. I remembered looking at her and thinking eyes are hours and hours are jewels of light.

For the first time in such a long time, I looked out at the ocean without seeing it through glass, and in its noise and tang I felt a slight exhilaration. I walked down onto the beach. The sun was breaking over the mountains in rising, crystalline rays and the beach glowed like snow. Ahead, the morning surfers bobbed in the calm waters of the palm-fringed lagoon.

I slipped under the colony fence and came up off the beach. It was a cool morning, the air still wet with the dew on the saw grass. I crossed a wooden bridge, toward the mountains and the high, pale light. There was a sandy path and two more bridges over muddy, chemical smelling lagoons full of trash and decaying plants. Pools of ghost shrimp caused ripples in the shallows.

I came to a green lawn with a wood beamed greeting center. A big sign read:

MALIBU LAGOON STATE BEACH

Behind the lawn was a large parking lot. A young blond surfer stood barefooted by an open jeep, tugging at the wet suit zipper behind his neck. He turned as I approached.

He raised his hand and motioned to the zipper. "A little help?" he said.

He was slightly bowlegged, tan, and muscular, and his board had all sorts of world championship event stickers: Perth, San Onofre, Biarritz. He was sponsored, a pro.

"It's flat," I said.

"It's okay," he said.

I helped him with the zipper.

He shuddered for a moment as I drew it up close to his neck. "Just please go slow there," he asked nervously. "I get scared I'm gonna pinch the skin, I always get someone to do that."

I tugged it gently at the end, lifting the zipper up off his skin.

He turned to face me, and shook my hand. "Thanks," he said.

He smelled like wax and vitamins. He turned and loped off with the penknife board tucked under his arm. The weird intimacy of drawing up the zipper—I suddenly felt like crying. But I could hear the rush of the highway, and the feeling quickly became scattered.

I walked toward the highway.

Across the highway I could see a Texaco station. There was a mall behind it. By the mall was a government building of some sort, a red and white radio tower, and a broad field. To my left stood a brick wall paralleled by a chain-link fence. I walked along the fence, feeling conspicuous next to the roaring highway. The highway seemed, unbelievably, to be ten lanes. The hum was deafening. Occasionally, in a car blowing by, I could make out a lazy hand on the wheel, a serene, empty gaze, and I stopped worrying about being conspicuous.

Directly ahead of me was another mall. Just before the mall turnoff, there was a private road blocked by a booth and a gate. The entrance to the colony. A fat man in a black uniform sat in the glass booth. I walked past him and into the mall parking lot. I spotted a coffee shop.

I had chorizo and eggs and two orders of fried potatoes. An old man with a sunburnt face sat at the counter next to me. He wore plaid pants and a yellow golf shirt. He kept looking at my old brown Gucci bag.

I finished, paid, and left. The man came out right behind me. I stopped, looked into a newspaper box, and let him walk by.

As he passed, I saw him staring down at the bag. An old, Lufthansa airline tag was attached to the handle, the name and address long worn away.

I walked around the mall. But the exploratory jitteriness quickly wore off, and I felt a rising unease. What had that old man been looking at?

I had no idea where to go. I began to think about going back to the house. A terrible idea. Someone had been there. Someone had come in. But my unease was rapidly building into panic.

I walked into the over-air-conditioned drugstore. A television was on in the bakery section. A reel of college football highlights, a nightmarish repetition of indistinguishable touchdowns and hyper, goony nonsense around each one. I looked at the painted faces along the rail, fists shaking in a synchronicity of triumph. Triumph was a cold feeling, made you cold as soon as it set in.

I bought aspirin, a toothbrush, and a bag of pistachio nuts. Muzak played overhead, a syrupy melody and I remembered the words:

. . . so unreal, life was just a Ferris wheel . . .

I paid, slipped the items into the bag.

I stood outside, next to the candy machines and the pay phones. I did not see the red-faced man.

My head felt full of a thick gooey distance. I'd forgotten to buy tea. I was low. But wasn't I *not* going back to the house?

The Ferris wheel out on the pier. The police radios and the lights on the trunks of the palm trees. And then I'd been standing on the beach, dumbfounded after the accident, and the Ferris wheel had come alight and begun turning, somehow indicating a direction. I had gone in that direction, and now I was out here.

But I could not stay out here.

I couldn't remember where to go. The highway was just across the parking lot. Where were all those cars going? I worried that like those cars, as soon as I began moving, I'd begin forgetting.

All the time I'd spent lying around the loft, I realized, I hadn't been forgetting, I had been not remembering. There had been an awareness underneath my sore, empty head, a careful sidestep around everything that had led up to me coming into the house. And in the house, the only lives I'd allowed myself to remember were from a hundred years ago. But the more I knew I had to make a move, the more I began remembering Reina. Wondering where she was.

Of all the people turned and gone from me, there was Reina, standing on the New York sidewalk. Looking at me and wordlessly offering me a second chance. But I hadn't. There were bad, backhanded vibrations there. She was somehow still Will's. It was too much like incest, too much like a kind of betrayal impossible to ever feel right about. I mean, who, other than Will, could ever say it was all right? In a way, I understood he wouldn't care. But that was just one way, and not enough of one.

On the street in New York, I'd walked away from Reina. And New York that day felt like a hundred years ago.

I hurried back the way I'd come. Back through the lagoon and under the fence. The colony beach was mostly empty. I walked straight up to the house in broad daylight. A reckless thing to do, but I didn't care. There was a man a few houses down on a beach chair, and he turned his head as I climbed the steps.

I slipped under the house, came back up into the cool, shadowy room, and lay on the teenager's bed, my heart beating wildly.

14

Reina came out of Will's bedroom. She went into the kitchen, ground beans, and set the kettle to boil. She was a boyish twig of a girl with long brown fingers, jet-black bangs and flat, shiny cheeks. Her feet were dark and bare, and she wore a black dress. I lay on the sofa, pretending to sleep as she fixed the coffee in the French press.

She headed back to the bedroom with a mug in each hand, and pushed the door open with her foot. Before she went in, she glanced back at me, saw my eyes were open. Her face was like brown glass. It woke me up behind the eyes, like Leonard's speed. I lay there for a minute, motionless, shaking off a feeling.

I got up, showered, and dressed in some of Will's clothes Reina had laid out. I made more coffee. I looked around Will's loft. The big kitchen opened to a couple of sofas and a rowing machine, and farther along a few heirloom antiques were set at random against the wall. But the long room was otherwise bare and you could feel the pressure of wealth underneath. I could hear them talking in the bedroom, and then it went quiet. She was driving him up to the center tomorrow morning.

Will came out without acknowledging me. He sat down at the kitchen table, scowled, got up, and paced. He turned the television on. A bright, nauseating morning chat show. He turned it off. He got himself coffee. He sat back down.

Reina came into the kitchen. She had shoes on now, and the big canvas bag hanging off her shoulder drew her dress tightly across her small, lemon-shaped breasts. "I have to go," she said, looking at Will with a severity. But there was also a kindness in the disapproval.

He stood.

She looked at me, curiously this time. She couldn't tell if I was a part of it all.

"Hay's a good guard," Will said, noticing her look and coming over and patting me on the back. "We'll put him on an hourly stipend until I'm in."

"Just give me the money that you owe me for the tickets," I said.

"Just keep him moving," Reina said to me, motioning toward the big duffle bag of hockey equipment she'd dug out of the closet.

"Like a forced march," Will said, picking up his coffee mug.

There was a long silence. Reina stared at him.

Will glanced at me and raised his mug, "Sober isn't funny."

Reina went to work. Will took a nap.

Will woke up and wanted to get some air. It was raining. I borrowed a Patagonia. Will put on his grandfather's old, pale yellow Macintosh. We stepped out onto the rain-spattered street. Will's face was going gray as the concrete, and his lips had a blackish hue. He hadn't had a drink yet (he was trying) and he felt dizzy. We went into a Dominican place just off Canal, great piles of steaming food in steel troughs behind glass. A few items on the menu had been added for all the new people in lofts. I ordered the "arm omelet" (the *F* had been erased by grease) and two coffees. Will's arms were crossed as if keeping himself warm, his head nodding like a tulip. I was hoping it was from the Valiums Reina had given him. That he didn't have something hidden.

The food was set down almost immediately. I stirred, thick café con leche moving slowly around my spoon. The restaurant had a good meaty smell mixing with the smells of wet wool, humidity, and Windex. The silvery steel at the counter flashed and glinted with the bustle of people inside, and yet the little crowded restaurant felt full of an overcast loneliness. I looked out the window, steamed and studded with drops of rain. You could see the lines of rain slicing across the building across the street, across the people and the cars, and then you couldn't.

I looked at Will. I pushed my rice and beans in front of him.

He opened his eyes. He stared down at the plate, slowly took hold of a fork, poked around, and came up with a mouthful. He closed his eyes.

We walked through Chinatown and up the Bowery. A misty drizzle lay over the buildings. He ducked into a deli and came out with a sandwich and a little packet of Dexedrine. Which was fine. Just so he didn't go east toward the old, hard stuff.

The rain eased. We sat on wet benches in the little park off Mulberry Street and read the papers. He was coming awake now. He unwrapped the sandwich. As he ate, it seemed to fall apart in his hands. He stopped, held it up with a groan. Mayonnaise had squeezed out the back and had left a greasy, curdled hole on his grandfather's raincoat. He stared down at himself.

We continued back up the Bowery. He stayed close to my side, twinging in his shoulders as if catching every noise like a pellet against his skin. He stopped. He shook his head, his eyes closed. "Hay," he said, slowly blowing out air. "It's like a gray flank against me. This dreadful fucking pressure."

I looked at him. "It's all right."

"There's a deli just up ahead," he said, his hands shaking.

"Sure."

"I'm going to have to have a beer."

"Sure, Will," I said. "It's all right."

Will walked into the deli to get a beer. I drifted ahead along the block, gazed into the window of a new boutique. A pretty girl with brown, rice paper cheeks sat on a stool.

Reina.

I shrunk back. Was that Reina? She'd been bathed in blue neon, and around her were single shoes on velvet stands lit like jewels. The façade was new, all glass, and she, like the store, had seemed impossibly delicate under the four stories of brick tenement above; vain and transient and beautifully undaunted by the sweaty linoleum history—the cast-iron stoves, sweat-pot food, crackpot accents, no-wave casualties, and rotting, graffitied bricks. I leaned forward, glanced back in through the glass.

She was closer to the window now, floating a dress across the room with her hook.

It wasn't Reina.

We walked back to Will's apartment, got the hockey bag, and caught the subway uptown. I watched Will play pickup hockey. He'd had a few beers, and played loose and aggressively. He had a nice goal. A two-on-one rush where he came to a quick stop for a slap shot. He hit the puck and it took off in a hard, steady, rising line.

Will looked better after the game. There was color in his cheeks and his eyes were clear. As we sat and waited for the train, he told me as a kid he'd used to play in the same rink. Heading home on the crosstown Ninety-eighth Street bus, he'd get hassled once in a while by the young Puerto Rican gangs. He'd push his way through and get out the back door. He was fast on the pavement, and would get away. One day, he'd had enough, and had stood and fought, a skate in each hand as weapons. They'd stolen the skates, and from then on, he'd get singled out every time: thumped around religiously and mugged for his bus pass, dollars, quarters, dimes, Redskins or Rangers scarf, whatever equipment he'd risk bringing home. Everything would get stolen. The next week his mother or nanny or whoever would push him out of the Dakota, and it'd happen all over again. But the muggings hadn't bothered him too much, he said, because back then, the city streets had been so full of dog shit, he'd come home from school every day insane with nausea.

The train still hadn't come. Will stood up, paced back and forth in front of me like a pent-up teenager ready to skip town. He was dressed in black jeans, a paper-thin, Italian oxford shirt, and red Converse sneakers. The strap of his hockey bag was tight across his chest. Beads of sweat clung to his forehead. He stopped pacing. He seemed to remember something. He lit a cigarette. It hung onto his lip and as the train approached, he closed his eyes and the breeze hit him. His eyes fluttered with a strange sensuality. The cigarette fell, and with his open mouth and shut eyes he looked like a sleeping child struggling with his dreams. You could feel the pressure of the coming train on the rails and imagine the hard rhythms and adventurous cacophony inside his head.

Back at his apartment, we played backgammon. He played at a furious pace, sipping from a can of Beck's, bantering all the while. His mouth was open, a cigarette hanging on while he clanked his pieces all over mine. Doubling the big-wage cube at every opportunity.

He only looked up when the phone rang.

Will picked it right up. He nodded. "Tonight? Well, even tonight, Reina and I would love to come. It's good timing for me, kind of a last gasp, as I'm going into rehab tomorrow."

He nodded and then laughed. He stood and began pacing with the phone. He seemed a little high-wired, to be running a little too smoothly, facing all this too easily. I had my doubts.

"Thing is, June," he was saying, "we've got a friend here who would have to come, too." He looked at me. "Hayward Theiss. You remember Hay."

"No," he said after listening a moment, "that would not be possible."

The door of the loft creaked open. Reina came in.

Will looked up. "Hold on," he said, and cupped his hand over the receiver. "It's June," he said to Reina. "A dinner tonight for some thoroughbred socialite. So she's being prickly about Hay."

"Must have been a late cancellation to call us," Reina said without a beat, hanging up her coat on a peg by the door. She paused, casting a glance on the smear across the Macintosh.

"Apparently, her parties are pretty precise," Will nodded, his hand still over the phone. "I told her we were three. A no-go, apparently."

"You told her it was Hayward."

"Yes," he said. "June's tough. She wants . . ." He glanced down at the receiver. "Wait," he said, holding up a finger.

He lifted his hand off the phone. "June," he said, "hold on just another second."

He walked over to the sofa and stuffed the phone into the cushions. "God," he said.

"We don't need to go over there tonight," Reina said.

"That's not the point," he said.

He looked at me. "You remember June, the publicist?"

I nodded.

"She's been waiting her whole life to jump in a sailboat with one of the Kennedys."

"Will," Reina said, shaking her head, "let's just . . . it's pouring rain outside."

"Let's just go get dinner," I said to Will. I glanced at Reina. Her cheek, I noticed, was glitched by a scar. It was small, under her eye.

"Where did you get that?" I asked, pointing at her cheek.

"From glass," she said.

"Recently?"

"No," she said. "A flaw from childhood."

Will stood impatiently by the sofa, his arms folded. "June's still on the line. What should I tell her?"

"Wait," Reina said to me, "Isn't June a friend of yours?"

"Not really, I'd say."

"How do you know her?"

"June was a work friend of Helen's."

"Are they still friends?" she asked.

"Well, they were work friends. And Helen doesn't work there anymore."

Will, exasperated, dug into the sofa for the phone. "Hello, June, still there?" he said, and walked away across the room.

Reina stood there in her black dress, her eyes still on me.

"But, you know," I said. "Once when Helen was ill and running from me, she for some reason called June, and June had recognized something in Helen's voice. She got Helen to meet her, and dealt with it. Got her into the emergency room, got her meds all straightened out. She did everything right, or as right as you can, and I owe her for that."

"I know about Helen," she said plainly.

I shrugged. I didn't want to talk about it with her.

"But why isn't June letting you come to dinner? Isn't it your birthday?"

I looked at her.

"I just heard Will on the phone telling her . . ."

I laughed.

"Maybe the problem is that Helen will be there," she said, looking at me.

"I wouldn't count on it," I said.

"Good," Will said, coming back and handing the phone to Reina to hang up.

She handed it back to him.

He held it without seeming to notice. "Eight o'clock," he announced. "A drink just before dinner."

He held up a forefinger. "One, she said."

He looked at Reina, his mouth brimming with a smile. "Just one, and then we are taking Hay out to dinner. It's his birthday."

"You'll do anything to keep tonight going," Reina said.

June greeted us at the door with a half curtsy and a high, arched voice like a child playing duchess. "Happy birthday," she said to me.

Her brown hair was sculpted and shining in perfect waves off her forehead. Behind her, I could see well-dressed people in rich dark wools and cashmeres. There was a smell of a roast, and red candles gleamed over cheeses. June, as we passed by, gave a mock exhausted laugh at the sight of Will. Will wore a rain spattered suede jacket, and the left leg of his pants was coming uncuffed.

Reina stayed by the door, chatting with June. Will and I made our way to the little bar near the kitchen. He poured me a glass of red wine, and told me not to worry about the invite dispute. June, he said, was shaped like a kingpin now and her youth was over. She'd done all the right things—a good job, the Colony Club—spent plenty on clothes, yet had got nothing she'd wanted—namely, a husband and child and the necessity to quit working. As a result, she seemed to lean too hard on her parties, watched them too closely, and had become instinctively protective about their success. It was, as Will said, nothing personal.

I turned and looked around the room. The party had a serene, controlled hum, but I had a funny feeling. A presence I couldn't see. I heard a bottle clank, and I turned around and saw Will putting a gin bottle back on the bar. A dribble ran out of the corner of his mouth.

He held a glass. I reached for it. He stepped back, smiling, and then frowning as he backed into a pretty, black-haired woman.

He turned to right her.

She stepped back out of his reach. She studied him for a moment.

He apologized.

She held out a thin, pale hand, introduced herself as Marina Rust.

He nodded, waving his glass toward her. "This is your dinner."

"Yes," she said.

He fixed his eyes on her. "You wrote a book a few years ago."

She nodded.

"I read your book."

"What did you think?"

"Rusty," he said.

I reached over, took his glass, and went into the kitchen. I smelled the glass. Straight gin. I poured out the drink. I looked up. Reina was watching me from the foyer. I froze. She wore a purple shirt cut like a kimono, white painter's pants and white sandals. Her hair was an ink black swoop, close cropped and purple where the light caught it. I looked back at Will. He had retreated to a quiet corner of the apartment and stood gazing into a bookshelf.

I went to the bar and drank down another glass of wine. I was nervous, but something, some blasé crust, had suddenly shaken off me. I put my wine down and put my hands in my pockets. I looked over at Will. He held a book and was staring at me. When I caught his eye, he looked back down.

I walked out of the kitchen, up and alongside where Reina was standing. She gave me an unreadable, sidelong glance. Her eyes seemed to be made of bits of glass and it was hard to settle on them through their broken-up light. She continued talking with a curly-haired girl. They were in a long conversation. I waited, turned to leave. I felt her hand on my sleeve. "Oh, Hayward, will you get me a glass of red wine?"

I turned back to her. She gave me a hard look, but there was also something lighthearted, almost teasing in it.

"All right," I nodded.

I came back with the wine. The curly-haired girl was gone. Reina and I leaned against June's wall, holding our glasses. "Do you think he'll go," I asked, "in the morning?"

"He'll go. This time at least."

"You think it will happen again?"

She looked at me. "It doesn't just *happen*." She sipped her wine. "Anyway, it's happened before. I mean, before me. Right?"

"Probably."

"Since when?"

"I don't know."

"You don't?" She looked at me. "You really don't know? Or won't say?"

I shook my head. I suddenly felt exhausted from all the long days with Will.

Her gaze softened. "You don't look so good."

"Long week. And apparently it's my birthday. Not one of my better days."

She smiled. "Happy birthday."

"It's not really my birthday," I said.

She took my hand. "Of course it is. Come with me."

She led me through the kitchen and to the bathroom. She closed the door and turned to face me. She smelled dry and clean, like mountain air. The noise and music had muted. I had the feeling we were going to kiss. But she just stood there, looking at me.

"I know what to do," she said.

"For what?"

"For your birthday," she smiled. "Now, turn around."

I faced the mirror and laughed at the sight of myself. She stood beside me, looking at me in the mirror. "I'm going to make your eyes nice."

"My eyes aren't nice."

"They are nice. But you look tired." She was digging around in the cabinet drawer, pulling out eyeliner pens and various compact tubes. She turned me around and sat me down. "I'm going to make them cool and dark. They are already dark, but I'll make them a prettier dark."

There was a knock on the door. "Please wait," she said.

She did my eyes. She worked close up to me, and I was transfixed by the movements of her shoulders and breasts and arms and of the nearness of her purple shirt. It felt good to feel her fingers across my face. It had a tremendous, calming effect.

She announced, after a few last dashes, she was done.

I stood.

She pressed her hand in the small of my back and turned me around to face the mirror.

I smiled. Black semicircles, a black focus under my eyes. I thought of the white, rude-boy singer of the Specials. I thought of Will and Wendell Blow and the strange, smoky air of Georgetown way back in 1980.

"Dinnertime," June announced through the door.

I turned to Reina. She was looking at me. She looked pleased.

We opened the door. A man brushed by us and into the bathroom. Will stood with his back to us, saying goodbye to June. June was watching us from over his shoulder.

Will saw her look, turned around, saw my eyes, and began to laugh.

We sat in Raoul's, under brassy light in one of the booths up front. Will gave me a long, curious look. He began to point, then just sat back. "You look like a raccoon," he finally said.

"I think you look good," Reina said.

He shook his head and smiled weirdly, looking away toward the door. "She did your eyes . . . "

The waiter came. Will asked about red wine for the table, and tried to slip in an order for a gin and tonic. Reina stared hard at Will while speaking to the waiter and politely correcting the order.

Will looked up at the waiter and ordered Beaujolais. He pronounced it, glancing back at Reina, "boozy lay."

When the waiter left, he leaned forward, dug behind his back, and came up with a present wrapped in aluminum foil. He dropped it unceremoniously on the table. "Happy birthday," he said.

I unwrapped the present. It was a long, uncracked, hardcover Galsworthy.

"Thanks," I said. "From you and from June's shelf?"

I opened the book and read the inscription out loud.

Hay,
Hate to say it but thanks.
Love,
Will
P.S. Please refrain from fucking my girlfriend
while I'm in rehab.

Reina frowned and hit him on the shoulder. "Ugh, Will. Gross. And June will notice."

He hunched his shoulders with a bright, defensive laugh. "Well, we can't give it back now."

The waiter came with the wine. We ordered. I held up the Galsworthy. The book gave off a vague mildew smell. The cloth itched my fingers to the touch. I put it down and looked at Will.

Reina took the book and began to flip through it. "June will of course immediately notice it's gone," she said. "It's a first edition. Probably worth a lot of money. Although," she broke into a stuttered laugh while rereading the inscription, "not anymore."

I shook my head. "Well, thanks. I still sign cards 'best' or 'sincerely.' I can never bring myself to put 'love.' It seems patronizing."

"Way to put yourself out there, Hay," Will smiled mockingly. Then he caught himself. "Well, that's not fair, you've always been sort of private. At least you're consistent."

"I'm private," Reina said.

Will looked at her. "If you were so private, you wouldn't have said that."

"You seem private," I said to her.

"I," Will said, "I am private."

"No, you're not," Reina and I both said.

"Sure I am. But neither of you know it yet."

Reina turned and asked him how, exactly, he was private. They started going back and forth in a kind of teasing disagreement. I finished my glass. The red wine felt like a velvet stage curtain dropping inside, coming to rest in lazy, warm folds. I felt an abstract, sun-stoned faithfulness. They were sitting close together across from me, arm in arm and smiling and talking. Will could never properly shut his mouth, and I could see his teeth. I looked at Reina's hand clasped around Will's. Their eyes mixed on the table's liquid surfaces as the steaks were set down, glistening with butter.

Will took a handful of french fries and leaned back and glanced with a ruddy pride at her. "Oh, man," he said through a mouthful.

He picked up his knife and fork and leaned forward and went at his steak.

We were eating and after a minute I noticed Will staring at a piece of food on his fork. He was chewing, and he made a sour face. "This food tastes awful."

We both looked at him.

He took a big sip of wine. "No, really. It's awful."

He spat out a gristly clump of meat. It fell on the table. He pushed it under the rim of his plate. He tried Reina's steak. Made a face. "It's like vinegar and ash," he said glumly. He swallowed painfully, pushed his plate away, and filled up his glass.

The next day, I went down to my father's house to rest.

We had a quiet dinner. He went up to his room and I went up to mine.

I undressed, took a shower. When I came back into the room I noticed a small bag of white powder, the contents a slightly sandier color than Leonard's speed. It rested on the sleeve of the shirt I'd borrowed from Will. It had fallen out of the pocket. I poked a finger into the bag and tasted the powder. Heroin.

I picked up the phone, called Will's apartment, and left a message for Reina.

I sat on the bed. I was so tired, but I could not sleep. I'd been drinking so much, I did not want to drink anymore. I took the bag, and dug out a small pile on a key.

I lay back on the bed, turned on the television, and flipped through the channels. I felt a nausea, then a melting. I thought that this was not building. Building is warm faith and dutiful breath. Not cathedrals of dry coolness and gray, sullen arches. I thought this with the heroin in my blood. But I also thought it about Reina.

I woke some time later. I sipped water and coasted through the channels again. I fell asleep, woke up again. *Annie Get Your Gun* was on A&E. I watched with horrified, stoned fascination as this overeager wolf girl with a hearty hick accent did a two-step, a string of dead quail bobbing around her neck. She sang and danced a hokey shuffle.

It was a caricature just snuffing out any grip I'd had on who Annie Oakley actually had been. I was about to click it off when there was this striking moment. Annie had just joined the Wild West and for the first time she sees a life-size poster of herself. She is dressed in white, just as she is in the poster. She reaches out and touches the larger-than-life mirror image of herself. A strange, sad look crosses her face. She looks bewildered.

Frank Butler steps into the frame, and with a big grin under a white hat, he dips into a baritone croon and the moment is shattered.

My father and I walked down the beach the next evening. The beach was short arcs of sand interrupted every few yards by rock jetties wrapped in chain mesh. It was dusk and the light between the water and sky was yellow and compressed, like the light in a refrigerator. There was a soft rain and the air was cold. I could hear the wind snapping my father's red plastic coat and see where it was wet and stuck to his ribs. His hair was wet and pressed thinly across his balding head, and he occasionally pushed streams of water off his face to see. He walked slowly, bent over and picking at the shells and rocks. He was good at finding things in the spit-up minutiae and litter of sea glass: a piece of driftwood smoothed into a wing, the red quill of a partridge, a peso slipped from the pocket of a Spanish tourist. Once when I was a kid, he'd seen a movement in a tide pool far ahead and had rushed forward. He'd reached down into the pool, dug around, and come up with a huge, wagging sea bass. He'd thrown it up on the sand and knocked it out with a big rock. He'd taken it back to the beach house on stilts we were renting, showed me how to gut and scale, and roasted it for lunch.

We came to a walkway over a reedy marsh. The marsh separated the bay from a small, freshwater lake. Beyond the lake the trees were fading from orange and red to gray. The doctor stood with poles on the lake's shore. He wore a yellow slicker, his gray-white hair under a black rain hat.

We tied and baited our lures, and stood in the rain casting for bass.

The doctor's house was nearby, and at some point he put down his pole and went to go get some beer.

Just after he left, my father got a hit. He reeled hard. The fish wavered, swiveled back and forth against the taut line. I dropped my pole and picked up the net. I could see the fish zigzagging in the shallow water, then suddenly— behind the hooked fish, a gigantic bass came up with his mouth wide open. The huge bass, in a flash, broke the surface and swallowed the hooked fish. We both jumped back and my father jerked the rod. The huge bass spat out the hooked bass and disappeared. The hooked bass heaved in the wet saw grass. My father lurched for the fish, but stood up abruptly, dropping the fish and staring at his hand.

The hook was in his finger, the feathered lure dangling effeminately.

He looked at me, and back at the lure. He shook his head.

I laughed.

"I should probably laugh now," he said. "But this hook is clear through my finger."

The doctor came back with a little cooler of beer. He stopped, stood, and stared tentatively at my father's hand.

"Could I have one of those?" my father said.

"Oh, oh right."

"It's ridged," my father said as he took the can of beer. "The hook. It won't come back out. It's going to have to be pushed through."

"Well, let's go look through my garage," the doctor said. "We'll find something."

"Garage?" I asked. "What kind of doctor are you?"

"Well, I've never had to remove a pronged hook stuck through a forefinger," he said defensively. "I tell you that much."

When we got to the doctor's house, he handed us towels, made us all drinks, and took us on a tour of the house, the hook still sticking out of both sides of my father's finger. He showed us his toy soldier collection in the basement, rows of tiny, painted men behind glass, frozen in action. He showed us his antique wicker wheelchair, supposedly one of Roosevelt's, and the bay views from the upstairs rooms.

We finally sat down in the doctor's den, my father in the wicker wheelchair. The doctor had grimaced as it'd crackled, but my father had given him a look, and he hadn't said anything.

He made my father a big glass of Scotch, handed it to him, and went to look around for tools.

The den was dark—forest-green walls with Currier and Ives prints. I sat down on a brown leather sofa and gave my father a look.

He nodded patiently, and said the doctor was recently widowed. "He's lonely. He's afraid we'll leave when the hook is out."

In pain now, he drank half the drink in one gulp and then dunked his finger into the rest.

The doctor came back with a knife sharpener.

"No," my father said, "we have to cut it first, before we push it out."

The doctor left, came back with a metal cutter. He had a drink in his other hand. "Give me that drink," my father said, "and give me those scissors. I'll cut it."

He drank the drink, cut the hook's eye, and pushed it out with the knife sharpener.

The doctor gasped.

My father silently leaned forward, his eyes squeezed shut as blood spattered the newspaper the doctor had laid down around the wheelchair. He looked old, pale, and shaky. I rested my arm across his back.

We stayed a while, and then we walked home. The doctor offered us a ride in his golf cart, but my father, drunk and blanched, insisted on getting air. The rain had eased and the lights from the opposite shore twinkled. We walked in silence. I had a mistrustful feeling, as if not enough had changed. As if we hadn't kept up. We'd lived in the same houses for decades. We'd driven the same Eastern Shore farm roads. My father had always had a quiet knowledge of shortcuts and paths. In Ohio, in Maryland. But they were no longer there. They were now main routes and roads. Highways. All the paths were roads. Everything was speeding up around us, and between us, nothing had closed in, nothing veered off and nothing had changed. It was still the same parallels, the same jokes. He had this one joke; it'd come up every once in a while when he'd had a few beers. The short version was . . . he had a Halloween party, he came as himself, nobody recognized him.

My flight back to Los Angeles was delayed. I sat at the gate, staring out over the tarmac at the big planes.

I had not heard back from Reina. I wondered if she checked the messages at Will's place. I did not know her number, did not know where she worked or lived, or even her last name. The only message I had was from my landlord. The production was not resuming my lease, and he was putting what little I had in storage and billing me.

I tried Will's number from the airport pay phone. It just rang and rang.

I called again. The same.

I walked around, bought a bottle of water and a newspaper.

I sat back down at the gate. Across the way, the people were headed to Nashville. The people at the next gate over were headed to Detroit. Nothing distinguished one group from the other. Bodies sat on the verge of obesity, round faces staring blankly as if at a tape loop of airport passersby.

I read some of the paper, went and tried Will's place again.

"Oh," Reina answered spacily, "Hay."

"Are you all right?"

"Where are you?" she asked.

"In an airport."

"Oh."

"Reina?"

"See, Hay, I've been wanting to reach you. I just . . . I feel so terrible."

"What is it?"

"Wait," she said. "What airport? Are you nearby?"

"What's going on?"

"Will died last night."

When I finally spoke, Reina was still there. "Are you okay?" I said.

"No."

"How?"

There was a long pause. She'd already had to say it so many times. "It was a car. He just went off the road, you know. Some guy came to get him. Somehow snuck him out. They went to a bar. There were drugs, I imagine. But then Will took the car. I think he was coming here. I mean . . . I hope so. Or I don't. I don't hope so. I don't know."

Leonard, I thought, and everything began to rush in.

15

There were voices. Drilling. A chink then a blow.

I jumped out of bed, rushed upstairs and looked out the kitchen window. The noise came from the side of the house, toward the road. But I could not see over the trees and the foliage to the front of either neighboring house.

A chink, then a blow. A chink, then a blow.

The noise came over and over again. I paced, looked out other windows. "Christ, it sounds like they're hammering now. They're going to put up five stories in ten years with a hammer and nails."

I was yelling.

I went up to the loft, to the small porthole window overlooking the mountains. From there I could see two white-dusted construction workers. They sat on the curb, talking quietly. The morning sun cleared a palm-tree shadow and the hood of their truck gleamed hard down into their eyes. The on-and-on sun.

A gleam in the neighbor's foliage caught my eye. There was a hole, and I saw robotic, steel scaffolding that had appeared overnight, a few tall beams—the skeletal scale of a next-door addition eventually dwarfing this house. I stood there. The beach house I was in suddenly felt low and old, lost in the sleepy shadow of construction melancholy. My life in the house had taken on the quality of a dream, one not worth repeating—no one to repeat it to in fact—and I simply couldn't find my way back into how it'd been before. And I couldn't move forward out of there. And now the noise was hammering away at the present.

I sat down on the loft's carpet. I would not let myself connect the drop of piss on the toilet seat to the construction noise outside. Until I'd seen the drop of stranger's piss, I'd begun to believe there wasn't a trace of my presence, and had therefore stopped worrying about anybody seeing me. I didn't even feel myself there. The windows were black, the lights were always off, and my bare feet made no sound on the white carpet.

I sat in the loft for a long time, under the construction's echoes. I stared at the wood floor at the carpet's edge. The pattern on each block of wood was like the sun in a different state of day: a melted crescent, a perfect circle, an age ring strewn off in an elastic algorithm. The rays on some blocks compressed into black lines, and on others opened up into graceful ovals of space—a bowed sun flare, a reddish, tubular bloom. In the loft, all I saw was sun: sun on glass, on water, on wood. I could see my reflection in the wood's silicon gloss. My own face, well worn with isolation. The pattern of shadows moved. I looked up. Outside, the sun had just come over the mountains. The light hit the sea, and I could see the coronet's luminescent, dark blue necks and the pelican's yellow-banded heads. The water around the spit of rocks went translucent, and underwater, green waves of seaweed clung to the submerged rocks. I watched two of the birds take off over the water, rise, and veer away to where I could not see them anymore. Again, the view was motionless. A glassed frontier, glassed in.

I heard a beeping. The alarm's warning.

I stood.

The front door creaked open.

I backed up into the loft.

I heard a step, buttons pressing in a code. The alarm was now off.

Someone was downstairs.

16

Reina and I sat in a coffee place off Cooper Square. It was a few weeks after the wake. She looked pretty in dusty blue jeans, her dark, thin arms under a laced white-cotton shirt. We talked a little. She said she was leaving the city for a while, going up to her mother's house in Massachusetts. She didn't say much else, and I could feel a barely perceptible resentment coming from her.

She pulled out an envelope. "For the plane tickets," she said. "His family's lawyer sent me all sorts of these, you know, to pay off loose ends."

She held the envelope out. "So, here."

"I don't want that."

She pressed it into my hand. "Take it."

"I really don't want that."

"He was your friend," she said. But she took it back.

We got up to leave. It was late afternoon, and the next morning I was heading back to Los Angeles. Leonard had been working in France and had been unreachable. But he was finally back in LA.

Reina followed me outside. We stood for a long moment.

"Look," I said, "you need to take care of yourself."

She looked down at the pavement. "Is this about that?"

"I don't know," I said. "I have to go."

"Wait," she said. She looked a little confused.

"I have to go. I've got a flight in the morning."

"Are you going back to Los Angeles?"

"Yes," I said.

"Why'd you move out there?"

"Because I was offered a job."

She looked at me.

"Because I had to leave Helen," I said. "Now, I have to leave."

"Let me ask you one more thing."

"All right."

"Did you ever know June? I mean, when Helen knew her?"

"June Foote? I don't know. Not really, I guess."

"Not at all?"

"I'd met her a few times, talked with her a few times once when Helen was ill," I said. "But I already told you, she was a friend of Helen's, not mine. Look, I've got to go." I turned around to leave, then turned back to her. "Wait, what is this about?" I asked. "What . . ." I shook my head.

She seemed to want to say something. She hesitated, looked at me. "June told me not to call you," she blurted out. "I know, I know, I know. And you'd left that message about that stuff in Will's pocket, and I *did* want to call you back. That day, when I came back after driving Will, if I'd talked to you about what you'd told me, I might have insisted on turning around and going back up there and none of this would have happened."

"It's nobody's fault." I was trying to stay indifferent, but I was looking at her.

"But, Hayward," she said. "That same day, over the course of a couple phone calls, your name came up and June said some things. And then I never called you back."

"What did she say?"

"I can't say."

"What can't you say? It's obviously important."

"I promised her," she said faintly.

"Well, then maybe it's not important. Look, whatever June said, you should have just called me back."

I started to walk away down the street.

"She said that you left her—Helen, you know—not in a good place."

I stopped, turned to face her. "What did she say, exactly?"

"I can't, Hay. I promised her."

"Well, if you believe her, you won't need to speak with me again."

"No," she said meekly.

I turned around. Across her flattish face her eyes were wet.

"She said you left Helen while she was in the hospital."

I sat down on the curb, stared at the row of brick buildings. There was a pressure in my chest and I had to catch my breath. Cars and taxis whizzed by close to my feet. I shook my head, talking into the traffic, "She has no idea. If I'd left Helen when she *wasn't* in the hospital, she would have . . . you know? And who would have found her then? *Who* would have fucking found her?"

Reina didn't say anything.

I turned and looked up at her. "Nobody could understand that," I said, trying to calm down. "But I never saw June in the hospital. I never saw anyone in the hospital. How could *June* know? How could anybody know but Helen and me?"

I stood up. "Look, I know things aren't too good for you right now . . ."

"It didn't seem right," she said.

"But I don't deserve this," I said angrily. "Not June's gossip or your insinuations."

She stared at me, her hard, inquisitive stare. "But how do you know?" she said. "How do you really know what you do and don't deserve?"

I shook my head. "You are unbelievable."

But there was also something suggestive about what she'd said, and it scared me. I stepped around her.

"I'm not excusing myself," she said, her voice trailing after me. "What June said seemed odd because I know what happened. I mean, Will told me how long you took care of Helen, how long you were together."

I stopped, turned back to face her. "Wait. When did this happen? When did June tell you all this?"

"I told you. She called me after I got back from driving Will up. It's terrible to admit, but at that point I was so tired of Will's shenanigans, I just wanted to talk about something else. I mentioned your call, and June and I went over you a bunch of times, like girls do."

"Went over me?"

"You. Helen and you. I didn't mention what you'd found. I thought Will was safe by then. I was so tired . . . I should have . . ." She shook her head, caught herself, and changed her tone. "June said you worked in television. She said it like all you did was watch television."

"And that was that?"

"That day, yes. But I spoke to her again, at the service."

"About? Why?"

"Well, you left before I had a chance to talk to you. We watched you leave. I told her I wanted to call you. She said not to. She said what she said then, too."

I looked at her. I kicked a beer bottle. As it skidded across the street it shattered, pieces of glass clanking across the pavement. At the service for Will. This was the hardest thing to take. It made me feel completely hopeless about trying with people.

I stepped around Reina.

She grabbed my arm. "Don't be mad," she pleaded. Her other arm brushed against my waist, and I felt a tiny pull in my coat pocket.

I waited a moment—in some way I knew—and then jerked my arm away and walked down the street.

I walked down Second Avenue. I bought a ginger ale in a deli, went into a liquor store and bought two airplane bottles of Jim Beam. I poured half the ginger ale out and poured in both whiskeys. I walked along Houston, and turned down Crosby Street in the corrupted exhaust of a school bus heading back to the outer boroughs. I followed a girl along Spring Street. Followed her down into the subway and through the turnstile. I'd picked her right out of the crowd and felt a heated, mutinous desire. There was something familiar about her, although I could not see her face and knew she was a stranger. She had medium-length blonde hair curling gently against the collar of her jean jacket. I followed her down the narrow platform. She walked with a lazy hunch, twisting her heels slightly with each step as if gaining a hold in sand. I sped up my pace to pass her, to get a look at her face. But as I came up alongside her I realized what was familiar. I stopped. I did not want to see her face. It was how Helen used to walk. Before. Way before she got sick.

I sat down on a platform bench and let the train come and go.

I finished the drink, and threw the can in the trash. I got up and paced the platform. I thought of Sitting Bull's horse. When Sitting Bull had been shot, his horse had done a strange, mournful dance around his body. They'd taken the horse and put him on show—like Cody had with Sitting

Bull. Sitting Bull's horse became a soldier's horse. Not even a real soldier, but the flag bearer of a touring group re-creating the Rough Riders charge up San Juan Hill. The Sioux and whatever other recruited Indians played the role of the Spanish troops. Sitting Bull's horse, now bearing an actor waving the stars and stripes, had led the charge up San Juan Hill amid fake shots, blown smoke, and mad applause.

They should have just shot it when Sitting Bull lay there. They could have done that, at least.

But I'd also read that the horse was a show horse. Cody had given the horse to Sitting Bull when he'd left the Wild West. When Sitting Bull had been murdered, the horse, spooked by the gunfire, had begun performing circus stunts.

The subway came and I stepped onto the end car feeling dismal and careless and I don't know what. Angry at nothing, needing an enemy at close range. There was loose newspaper at my feet. A piss smell. I watched the tracks recede from the window of the back car. I watched the tracks run through my reflection. Feeling an emptiness. Not knowing what about those empty rails provoked it. The speed. The speed of things. But the emptiness is also nothing. Or if anything, the invisible lines of current around warm air. And the space inhabited, however interstitial: steam on a shaving mirror, a caring word withheld, the smell of popcorn in airports, a car door slamming on a quiet summer day. The emptiness is the subway-car air itself. Everything and nothing. Silence and clatter. There's no happy roundness and no sad, knowing precision. My life is inventory and can only narrow.

I got off at Thirty-third Street and walked west. I bought a beer in a brown bag and stood outside a T-shirt shop. I bought another beer, walked up Broadway and over to Forty-second Street, through the renovated square. Times Square was an old canyon, old as any other. But it felt hard to keep up the curiosity under the black glass façades, repetitious marquees, ten-story vodka bottles, and humongous faces—like phantom colossi lurking in neon, rising up the buildings. It was a sheen of new wealth saturating the old architecture, and it felt like a permanent Gilded Age.

Finn had commanded his. I was out of work in mine.

Once in the mid-nineties, Will and I had been up all night and had spent the morning into the afternoon with the exquisite kind of hangover, roaming around the now long-gone porn parlors and peep shows, lost in the dizzy uncertainty and worn-out desire of those places. With Will, back then in semi-derelict Times Square, it had felt like action in closed-off places, murmurs and secret meetings, the smell of a river behind a wall, and the feeling of giving up women forever.

I walked along Forty-second Street. Everybody looked well-to-do, from out of town, in for the sights with sure hands full of shopping bags. It was a strange thing to see no marginal fuckups in Times Square. Not the crack heads and asylum refugees, but the bad-luck citizens working the main arteries—Forty-second Street, the Bowery. Out of work and alcoholic, shaking coffee cups in front of electric shops and wholesale kitchen stores, drinking from a water fountain built for horses, fishing the East River and Hudson piers, rolling tires and tuning cars for liquor money under the FDR. Men with pasts so recent they could still feel the warmth of wives and sons and daughters, pasts a street like the Bowery barreled right through. Men gone now from New York, gone just in time for me to believe, to have seen them, like the clichés of the West.

I found myself walking down soot-choked street Fortieth Street, the Port Authority in my sight. As I approached the station, the smells of rot and urine rose up decisively, and I noticed the only people around were lying on the ground. Either out for the count in dark bundles or nowhere to be seen. The squalor was still here; it had simply moved west. But the big neon scale and the dimmest hopes had been sucked out. Only low, sooty blocks remained, with no larger promise of swindle or temporary luck. There was no glow. No tourists. No money. No middlemen. No half-in half-out alkies indifferently begging, porn functioneers pitching, beleaguered luncheonette line cooks casting out glances. Just men so dirty and bombed out they looked like they'd burned for days.

I turned into the dim, yellow mouth of a deli for another beer. There was a greasy smell—pork chops in a metal vat of red oil—and the walls were lined with racks of porn videos. I had to point to the kind of beer I wanted behind the thick plastic divider. I walked back around the block, past dozens of hole-in-the-wall porn parlors and greasy Chinese takeouts. All silent fronts, as if ashamed of what they were—single, dark doors, and paper over the glass, a single light, and crushed vials glinting on the sidewalk.

Ahead, the light rose from Times Square, capped by a prophylactic yellow loam. I walked toward Broadway. The *Annie Get Your Gun* marquee was down the avenue. With Olivia Newton-John as Annie.

I stopped, stood there drinking my beer. The amiable tunes rolled through my head. I'd never heard the whole soundtrack. Irving Berlin (whose second home had been an Addison Mizner castle in Delray Beach) had written it for Ethel Merman, and everybody from Mary Martin to Dale Evans to Jamie Lee Curtis to Barbara Stanwyck to Judy Garland to Susan Lucci to Bette Midler to Bernadette Peters had played Annie. The musical was still around. There had to be something to it. Nostalgia, maybe. An almost religious kind of optimism.

Sitting Bull, in the show, is a simpleton in an opera hat who can't handle money and eats pastries like a greedy child. He winds up funding the cash-strapped Wild West with newfound wealth from the oil-rich lands the government gives his tribe. This was how—with its indefatigable postwar can-doism—the largest-grossing musical of all time ended. *Sitting Bull. He came into our midst, strong as a buffalo bull, and sat down.*

Just a few years after his victory at Big Horn, Sitting Bull, in the comedown days of surrender and just off the flat jail of a reservation, was a celebrity and a captive, promenaded around and gawked at like an astronaut or the pope. One afternoon he was put up in a box with South Dakotan politicians, and glumly watched Buffalo Bill's Wild West Show. Black-eyed and stoic, he suddenly came to life when Annie began to perform. In many ways, she must have been something to see.

She came into the ring standing on the back of her galloping, moon-colored horse, her rifle propped backward over her shoulder. Her manager flicked a blue marble into the air. She rode past him, holding up in her other hand, like a compact mirror, a bowie knife. She sighted the rising marble in the knife blade's reflection, shot backward, and there was a resolute ping.

She turned and faced backward, still standing on the horse as it loped around the ring.

Glass balls rose into the air.

She pocketed the knife, loaded and swung her rifle back up. She shot left-handed, then right-handed. Back and forth, and the glass balls shattered, one after another like splashes in the air.

"Little Straight Shooter," he named her. "Little Sureshot."

And with a vanishing kind of instinct, he adopted her as his daughter. Sitting Bull had been the only possible father to someone like Annie Oakley. If it is a father's will to, whenever possible, give a daughter life, for Annie Oakley it could only be Sitting Bull and not any browbeaten, rigid Quaker farmer ancestor of mine. Only Sitting Bull, Killer of Custer, Buddha of Dakota, only the great last Indian chief could give life to the daughter of the new West. Life, for her, being career. *One morning when we arrived in Pittsburgh a stranger wearing a holster and carrying a wicked-looking six-shooter hurriedly made his way toward the Indian teepees. "Show me the old renegade. He killed my brother in that massacre," he shouted.*

A cowboy pointed out Sitting Bull driving a tent peg. The stranger ran over there and told Sitting Bull what he intended to do to him.

Sitting Bull, to all appearances, never saw or heard this would-be slayer. He drove vigorously at his pegs. He raised his arm for a swing, and like a flash of lightning, the hammer went straight to the mark, dropping the man like a log.

But the cowboy had the stranger covered from the first step toward the teepee.

Sitting Bull lasted only a year with the Wild West. He'd tried to make a case for his tribe amid Cody's traveling hoopla, but it had done no good. He'd retreated to the realigned West, "Sick of the houses and the noise and the multitudes of men."

I'd actually found some truth to Annie's own life in a comic book. On the comic-book cover, Annie stood, a young blonde in white fringe, two pistols blazing and a headline blazing:

Annie Oakley in: **THE STORY OF MY LIFE**

I'd had the comic as a boy. It had been free. A religious publisher based in Dayton had put it out. The story was not an adventure with a dog or a sidekick. It was nothing promised by the cover art, but rather a strange, harrowing story of her youth, narrated in the first person by Annie.

When I was older and back visiting Greenville with my father, I'd sat down one afternoon in the Garst Museum and dug out Annie Oakley's autobiography. Her autobiography, which many claimed was as fabricated as Wyatt Earp's, had been syndicated in a newspaper serial immediately following her death. It had then disappeared into a cabinet in the little Garst Museum.

Most of her autobiography—of Cincinnati, the Wild West, the rest of the world—you could tell by the way she wrote, was just easy reminiscence, riding along, cartoon life. But in an early chapter, she'd told a story from her youth, an American Gothic, Odyssean journey she'd endured. To my astonishment, this had been the story in the comic I'd had as a boy. It had been taken directly from her autobiography. When I read the story in her own handwriting—off a carbon copy of her original draft—the recollection was extremely careful, and I had the feeling it must have been what gave her such a perfect eye.

A blizzard come on and daddy did not come home.

Mary, the eldest, got her feet wet and was soon a tuberculosis victim. In March Mary died. Our cow had to be sold to pay for Mary's funeral.

One day, mother took a short cut through the clover field. As she passed the grave she saw three timber wolves digging. She went two-thirds of the way on her hands and knees for fear the wolves would scent and attack her.

Mother had a hard time before the crops came in. We had nothing.

A dark-eyed stranger showed up one day, took mother away and when they came back she had changed her name to Mrs. Daniel Brumbaugh. Her husband was cousin to Martin Grove Brumbaugh, ex-governor of Pennsylvania. We moved to town where my stepfather's business was. I was deprived of my hunts through the beautiful snow-clad woods.

My stepfather died. He never gave a deed for the grounds we lived on and when he lay ill so long with his bad knee and mother with typhoid, his partner got our pretty home. Mother, with her brand new baby girl, moved back near where my own father had died. Some friends of mother's named Shaw came and got my other sister. I went away to a life long friend of mother's. Her husband was superintendant of the county Infirmary. Their name was Edington. About three weeks later a man came. He looked at all the little girls, and then asked about me. He explained that he wanted a small girl as company for his wife. The girl would have no work, he said, except to watch the baby. When he was told how I loved to trap and shoot, he said, "Why, she should go right home with me. We have quail, partridges, pheasant, and rabbits. She could go after them when she liked."

I donned my homespun linsey dress and knickerbockers and started for the woods.

The work began to stack up. I got up at four o'clock in the morning, got breakfast, milked the cows, fed the calves, the pigs, pumped water for the cattle, fed the chickens, rocked the baby to sleep, weeded the garden, picked wild blackberries, got dinner after digging the potatoes and picking the vegetables.

Mother wrote for me to come home. But they wouldn't let me go. I was held prisoner. They wrote letters to my mother telling her that I was happy and was going to school.

One night I nodded over the big basket of stockings I had to darn. Suddenly she struck me across the ears, pinched my arms, and threw me out of doors into the deep snow and locked the door. I had no shoes on and in a few minutes my feet grew numb.

I was slowly freezing to death. I got down on my little knees, looked toward God's clear sky, and tried to pray. But my lips were frozen stiff and there was no sound.

It was not long before I heard footfalls crunching through the snow and he'd opened the door, commanding me to come in. But I could not move, so he yanked me in, pushing me into a chair by the fire.

My head sank just as he demanded to know what was the matter.

I tried to answer him but my tongue was swollen to the roof of my mouth. He tried to stand me on my feet, but I just went limp. I was dragged up the steps to bed.

I went into delirium, and was left to rest for the first time since I had come there.

But they did not bring me a thing to eat or drink until I could crawl downstairs.

I begged to be sent back to my mother.

Christmas came, blows on the back from Santa.

One fine spring day, the family was gone. I was ironing a large basket of clothes. Suddenly I thought, Run away.

I made a package of my meager belongings, locked the door, and put the key in a tin cup that set in the spring house.

I started. It was many miles through rough roads and night.

The one little coach was almost full as I entered the train. A gentleman moved over and made a place for me. The conductor came along and asked for a ticket. I told him I didn't have any.

The gentleman in the seat took some money from his pocket. He asked me where I was running to. I said, "I think the county seat."

He told the conductor to come back later. Then he had me tell him the whole story. His face was clean shaven and he looked so kind that I did so.

He said, "Why, you would have some twenty miles walk through rough road, and night would come while you were in the deep woods. Where would you sleep?"

He persuaded me to go to the end of the road we were on, have dinner with him at the hotel.

I had my very first hotel dinner with the kind man. He took me to the depot, put me on the train, and gave me the price of my half-fare ticket.

Then he spoke loudly "Is anyone in this car getting off at——?" And an elderly gentleman with St. Jacob's Oil whiskers said that he was. My friend asked him to see that I did not get off the train before that station. And so he passed out of my life.

I got off at the station and flew for home and Mother. When I got to the house, a woman said, "Your mother has not lived here for some time."

She told me I'd better stop at Shaw's and get my bearings before hunting my mother.

I started on, but she made me come in, supper, and stay the night.

I left after breakfast, eaten by lamplight, and was far on my way when the sun was up. I kept saying, "I will see Mother."

I met an ugly tramp who looked at me strangely. I leaped to the left as I passed him and ran like the wind.

I reached the Shaw's. Ms. Shaw took me in. Mother was away. Our house was further on.

There was a tap on the door. It was a loud rap! Ms. Shaw started. Cold beads of perspiration came out on me. The door opened and he came in. A wolf. He had trailed me.

I just screamed "No" when I saw him. Ms. Shaw, sprang between him and me and said, "You cannot take her."

He grabbed her wrist and twisted it until her arm was almost broken. He took me by the arm, twisting it until I almost fainted with pain, and dragged me to the door.

He pushed me up near the horse's head, holding onto me while he untied the team, and was off as Ms. Shaw gave chase with a stove poker.

We rode a long time through Darke County. I kept figuring how to escape. I planned to turn a back somersault, and leap. I saw a six foot two figure in the road. He spoke kindly, started to unbridle the horses and just took for granted we were stopping for dinner. Frank Edington. He sent me in first. Big Henry the farm superintendant was inside. Mrs. Edington had me go upstairs. I told her my story, unbuttoned my dress and she looked at the scars on my back where he'd struck me.

"My God, child," she said, "your back and poor little shoulders are green."

Two doors were locked.

I told her that I could not sit down or sleep on my back.

She went downstairs.

Soon, I heard footsteps on the stairs. She came back in, dressed me, and took me downstairs.

He rose. "Well, we must be going. Come, Annie, we have a long way to go."

"Yes," Mrs. Edington said, "it is time for you to go. But this child remains right here."

He clenched his fists and snarled. "She is not yours."

He turned to spring, but in the door was Big Henry.

That night I slept untroubled for the first time in long months. I was homesick for the fairy places—the green moss, the big toadstools, the wild flowers, the bees. I dreamed of the rough grouse, the rabbits, the squirrels, and quail.

The next morning they planned what to do with me.

In the forties and early-fifties, when my father's family would take him to New York, they would go and eat at Keene's Chop House. *Annie Get Your Gun* was running at the Imperial Theatre in Times Square. After dinner they'd go to the Imperial, be ushered to their front-row seats. A spotlight would drop on them. They would stand and be introduced to the crowd as the "real, true-life Annie Oakley family."

Once at curtain call, Betty Hutton, playing Annie, beckoned my young father to the edge of the stage.

He stood there in his blue blazer, his hair slicked back. Betty Hutton pulled him up onstage, put her arms around my father, and in front of the roaring crowd gave him a big kiss.

I remember being in some Denver Holiday Inn lounge with my father in the late seventies. A blonde woman, her thick face dusted white, was singing "Killing Me Softly."

She sat down in our booth in the middle of the song, next to my father, who, back then with his sunglasses, turned-down mouth, and disheveled tweed jacket, looked a little like Jack Nicholson. She was flirting with him, singing.

Everybody was watching. She leaned over the booth and sang to me:

Strumming my face with his fingers . . .

She did this—ran her fingers down my face. The literalness of the gesture made me sick. Anyway, wasn't it "pain"? Not "face"?

The piano bloomed into a solo and she kissed me on the lips. The crowd laughed. I rubbed my mouth and stared at the red lipstick on my hand. Her mouth had been loose and flabby, and I felt a sadness and a disgust at the fakery in the kiss. I wondered what my father had felt as a boy being kissed on the lips by a woman playing his grandfather's lover and cousin. I wondered if it was anything like that.

She stood up with her microphone.

My father sat there in the booth, staring at me. My father stared at me a lot when I was young and I grew to understand I haunted him. But I also understood my father and I had come to share a deep-down sense of isolation we kept furnished with long-gone images of car windows streaked with snow, of square brick houses with the shutters drawn tight as if binding a silence inside. Of someone you love fading out without seeing you. Of getting drunk alone in some odd search for bloodline, for the old-folk memory, a sad, dry American feeling.

Sitting Bull disappearing into trees on his horse.

It felt so controlled here now in this square, so enforced with safety. A warm, brassy yellow all over everything, and no grime on the windows to hide behind.

Annie Oakley went out with the Wild West and never roped a calf or shot a wolf or anything necessary. But she traveled tirelessly and lived with conviction. The forces moving her around had been, like for Finn, necessary and economic, outside of her. With me, they seemed random and to have come from within.

I passed under the flashing *Annie Get Your Gun* marquee. It felt as far away from me as men dressed up as cats. I scanned between the marquees for a bar. I wanted to get away from this friendly finger fuck of reenactments, from this square cemented in self-consciousness. I had a tinny taste in my mouth for another bourbon, Leonard was in Los Angeles, and I could not stay in New York.

17

Down the slant of steps, I could see the legs and waist of a man. His back was to me, his torso and head cut off by the loft stairs. He wore jeans, work boots, and a yellow tool belt on his waist. A green Pellegrino bottle was perched on the top stair of the loft. I reached out and snatched it back.

The man began to slowly move around. I could hear him checking the windows from the inside, and the fuse box in the pantry. He'd been humming, and he stopped.

There was a long silence.

He walked around the room, checking windows one more time. He paused at the steps up to the loft. I was shrunk back enough so he could not see me. For some reason, maybe because there were no openable windows, he did not come up.

I heard the beeps as he reactivated the alarm. The door slammed shut and I heard footsteps in the driveway.

I jumped up, and ran down the stairs to the window overlooking the driveway. There was a red pickup, and he sat a few yards below with the driver-side door open. It gave me a huge shock. He had a beakish nose and thick blond hair. He could not see through the black glass, but I flattened myself against the wall.

I waited a minute or so, heard an engine start, and glanced back out the window. The truck was gone.

At the end of the driveway, a few construction workers milled about. They were accessing the scaffolding from this driveway, not next door. Suddenly the red pickup reappeared, reversing past the men and parking across the mouth of the driveway. The blond man got out and slowly approached the circle of men, shaking his head, and looking up to the house and talking. The construction wasn't starting next door; it was here.

I turned and rushed downstairs for my stuff. I remembered the conch shell, resting on top of the loft's bookshelf. I went back up the loft steps. I had just gotten my hand around the shell when I heard a noise again at the door.

I turned and swung down the steps three at a time, my free hand on the rail. As I came to the bottom, the door opened.

The man stepped in.

I froze.

The alarm box began to beep.

Without looking up the stairs, he crossed the entrance hall to punch in the code.

I jumped off to the side, and had just slipped into the pantry as footsteps started up the stairs. I could hear him walking around the big living room, creaking open floor vents, and the snap reversal of a tape measure.

He walked up the steps to the loft, his footsteps going silent on the carpet, and after a few moments came back down.

He came into the kitchen. I pressed myself back deep in the pantry. I could hear him circling the chef's island. The fuse box, I realized, was right by my head.

The footsteps stopped in front of the stove.

I heard a small clang. He'd picked up a pan. The saucepan of tea from the morning, I'd left it out.

There was a long silence.

"Oh," he said.

I heard him move quickly out of the kitchen and down the steps. He closed the door behind him without bothering to stop and reset the alarm.

I rushed over to the window and saw him standing in the driveway, on his cell phone. He was shaking his head and talking.

The colony had security. I only had a few seconds.

I hurried downstairs, locking the door of the teenager's room behind me.

I grabbed the packed Gucci bag.

Before I stepped into the closet, I paused.

I dropped the bag, knelt down, and zipped it open. I dug through the side pocket. There it was, the folded-up bank envelope. I wanted to be sure.

I heard the front door swing open, voices in the hallway just outside the teenager's door.

I jammed the envelope back into the bag and zipped it up.

There were sounds of heavy boots on the steps, and I heard someone try the door. I watched the doorknob swivel and shake, as if on its own volition.

I grabbed the Gucci bag, slipped into the closet, and pulled shut the closet door behind me. I opened the trap door and slipped through. I crawled under the house, stood up, and moved quickly down the shaded alley. I jumped over the glass fence and stepped onto the beach.

18

The motel was in Santa Monica. The room was carpeted and clean, with a fake-wood television and plastic-wrapped cups. Through the sliding doors was a view of a brightly lit, green patch of park, and beyond the park the dark ocean. I put my bag down, cleaned up. I lay on the bed and called Leonard. I left a message.

I showered, dressed, and went out. It was a cool evening. I walked down Main Street, past dolled-up shops and a modern building shaped like a giant car tire. Main Street's air was full of the chemical, bready steam of restaurants. I walked into a bar called the Galley. It was an old bar, but renovated in such a way to make its age obvious, an exaggerated sort of self-mockery obviously appreciated by the young, well-heeled crowd. But its old neon sign had drawn me right in.

I had a drink. The plan was to confront Leonard about Will. The rest had to be worked out. It was a plan at arm's length, anyway.

I kept getting up and going over to the pay phone. I got Leonard on the sixth try.

"I've left an awful lot of messages," I said.

"I know," he said. "We need to talk. I have some work for you. Come out. Tonight's good. Tomorrow not so . . .

leaving on the red-eye for Paris and I've got a party with the French money people before I go . . ."

"I'll come tonight," I said.

"Good," he said. He gave me the address. "It's the beach house the company rented. There's a gate. I'll put your name down."

I sat back down, ordered another drink. But after talking to Leonard, I felt a wave of leadenness come over me. I really didn't know what I was doing out here. I looked at the clock. The time change was fucking me. I'd come here too early, had too much time to kill. The drinks were strong, and I was drinking fast. The next drink came, and I gave it a stir. Will could have cleaned up, come off the booze and everything else, and had another round. Another five or ten clear and good years before it all started to wear him down again. But what wore him down? He worked hard. He was doing well. I knew his problems, but I'd never known him well enough to understand what was beneath them. Even when I was with him, he seemed to be moving past me. Not that he was elusive, he just had this simmering internal momentum, this bristling spirit of forward motion and the bad things he did to himself he did to slow himself down. I'd only see him a few times a year, but it was just at the end when it seemed we were really becoming friends, when something was gaining a foothold between us. I held my glass. Leonard could never have had much effect on Will. It had to have been an accident. I thought of Will in his zipped-up college crew jacket, sitting next to me in a London grill, one of those bean and egg places full of steam. Grabbing my elbow with the sudden realization he was late. "Oh, man," he'd said, getting up and swinging his duffle bag behind him, knocking over a glass and not noticing as he rushed out the door.

But the memory, the wholeness of him, was gone. The dead do disappear. Make no mistake about it.

I signaled for another. I felt dizzy again. I'd drunk too much bourbon on the flight, staring down at the empty deserts of the West, my forehead pressed against the little oval window, looking down over hours of motionless expanse, horizon after horizon of useless plains. High, dry, plateau country—just desert. So many people must have been tempted and then lost it all down there. Nothing growing. Nothing staying. No structures except oil probes and highway shacks for subsidized cowboys, tourists, and truckers laying over amid the arid plains, canyons, and the yellow, rippled crusts of lakebeds. The bartender set my drink in front of me.

I dug out eight more dollars, laid it on the bar, and asked him for a pen.

I took a napkin from the holder. I made a list.

The yellow of the West:
1. *spurred columbines*
2. *the fingernails of the pharmacist*
3. *pyramids of shucked corn*
4. *cheddar cheese on tacos*
5. *John Denver's greatest-hits hair*
6. *dust on my father's boots*
7. *light rising across my jeans, my face*

I must have been ten—it had to have been 1976 because there were little American flags in the Colorado dirt, poking up all over town like red, white, and blue flowers. My father and I were heading out from Crested Butte up to a lake north of Florissant. We were going fishing and camping overnight. He was telling me about all the people he knew who'd died driving their jeeps off mountains. One of them was his sister's ex-husband. He'd been a pool player, an Aspen playboy. He'd designed pool cues, and when he'd died earlier that summer, he had been ranked the fourth best eight-ball player in the country. He'd once let me win, and for a thrilling day I'd walked the dirt streets of Crested Butte as the fourth best eight-ball player in the country.

"It's the Aspenites who are always going off the cliffs," my father said, looking at me. "They're sniffers."

Something past me caught his eye. He braked suddenly, pulled the jeep half off the empty two-lane highway. A sunny dust rose up around the jeep as he was looking back over his shoulder at a dilapidated old house. "God," he said with a reflective gloom, "look at that."

I turned. There was a golden retriever sleeping in the sun on the porch's warped boards. His head on his paws, his black flanks rising through chewed-up yellow as he breathed.

"This decade," he said, shaking his head.

He bumped the gear, and I felt the jeep accelerating.

We wound up along the gold-speckled Gunnison, toward a white-crowned cluster of mountains. The houses began to disappear between a gaining relief of yellow hills. As we drove through the dynamited cuts in the hills, diamond light from the exposed mica skitted across the windshield. He asked for his sunglasses. I dug the steel-rim glasses out of the glove compartment and held them out. The road suddenly leveled off, straightened as the hills broke up, and gave way to a barbwire–fenced high plain. The light on the plain became gold and muted and my father relaxed his squint and did not take the glasses.

He sped up on the straightaway, turned on the radio. Only two stations came through. He flipped back and forth between Paul McCartney's "My Love" and Rod Stewart's "Tonight's the Night."

I still held out the glasses, but he was deep in thought and did not notice. I laid them on the dashboard where he could see.

"But don't worry," he said to me as if we'd been talking, "everybody back home will say the sadness is social, but it's really economical."

"What sadness?" I asked. I could see antelope running way out in the distance.

"You'll find out."

"Like eating too much candy?"

He'd flipped back to "My Love." "No," he said, his hand hovering over the dial. "Like choking to death in a sugar storm."

He snapped off the radio, and I felt him staring at me while the jeep barreled ahead. A woman had come out and stayed with us. The only woman I'd ever seen him with. She had brown hair and a soft southern voice. But then, after a few days, she'd left.

We tried to camp, but neither of us were handy. My father could not even really fish, even though he'd grown up on a farm. He didn't have the patience. He was scatter-brained, in a way. He never used his wallet. Bills were always loose everywhere in our house in Washington and I could take what I wanted. When he'd leave, there'd be a clump of assorted bills jammed under the stone Sioux ax on the hall table. He was always disappearing with little notice, and although when he was around I never had more than a few dollars, when he'd leave, I always had much more money than other kids my age.

We didn't catch anything and ate freeze-dried beef stroganoff for dinner. It felt consequential, sitting around a fire in the cool, wilderness air, noises in the dark and the slow resilience of the night.

After dinner he buried the fire and went down to the lake, disappeared at its black edge to drink the six-pack of beer he had cooling there.

I got my canteen, brushed my teeth out of my sierra cup, and went to sleep.

Later, the tent door flapped open and my father came in. I could smell beer and the mineral depth of the lake. He said my name.

I pretended to sleep.

He said my name again. I sat up and rubbed my eyes.

He crouched at the tent's mouth in his hiking boots, jeans, and down vest. He asked me two questions:

Did I want to move to a New Zealand farm?

Did I want to take a six-month trip around the world?

I thought he was in trouble. I thought we were out of money. I thought he was leaving again.

I stared at him. My father had a round and weathered, handsome face. His eyes were permanently crinkled with wariness, and he had a cool hard-to-read smile. But lit from behind by the bright moon, he looked dead serious and he looked at a loss.

"The farm," I finally said. Both seemed far away and unknowable, but the farm seemed more secure for us. It was the last year of my life I would have answered that way.

We left in the morning, and didn't bother to fish again, although we could see the green heads of trout poking up out of the milky blue water. On the way down the mountain, a tree had fallen across the road. He stopped the jeep, turned off the engine. He got out, crossed his arms, and leaned against the hood. There were patches of wildflowers all along the edges of the road. Up a nearby hill, there was a rusting yellow propeller plane. I climbed up the hill, crawled around in the wreckage while we waited for somebody to drive up on the other side. Then there was nothing to do.

Instead of New Zealand or circumnavigating the globe, my father and I spent another summer in Crested Butte. His relatives had sold the last of Finn's gravel company to a South American diamond conglomerate, and my father and Ray—stone faced behind mirrored Ray Ban's—were looking into companies out West. A uranium mine, an anarchic herbal-tea company. They were always gunning off somewhere, disappearing for days in their Land Rover. A pilot's wife lived next door and would check in on me. The pharmacy on Main Street had a pinball machine, hamburgers, and good malts. The pharmacist would give me quarters for the machine when I ran out. It was still a faded mining town—there was no real ski resort or mountain biking yet—and the wilderness came right up to the back of our house. I found there were deep dark hills and golden fields in the world. Found the forests are not ancient, or even old, but that they are mostly pine. I found a scythe and flower on the same stalk, and, like my father, I had a taste for solitude. Walking on a seemingly endless parched plain, I saw a cabin, a woman on a ladder cutting off the highest fruit from a tree, a man hunched over below her, beating the dust out of dried-up stalks. I found the bare, wooden planks of a church out of service, a piece of turquoise in icy water, and what looks like lights from a distance is never easy to say.

I looked down into the shellacked grain of the bar. The clarity of the memory left me strangely elated. There had to be others like it—a forgotten contentment in youth—and even the bar air suddenly hinted at fresh possibility. There was a past to understand about my father. And my own life, if I could start again from memories like that.

Then the feeling faded, and I was left with the list I'd made. I crumpled up the list and laid the pen back on the bar.

I took up my drink and stared up at the tiny square of television. Baseball highlights, a portrait of the previous season's all-star. I watched a ground ball to short and the all-star's smooth, elastic pickup and throw out. How quickly, in that exact, sudden-burst landscape of good touch, you have to stop and turn, curb your momentum, and throw. In the hit and the response, the time frame was similar to the chance you got with someone and the time you had to respond honestly. Which was only as long as the impulse, and not the thought, was there. A few seconds was all and if your impulse was right, honesty was an instinct-finding gold. But if you missed your chance, if the thoughts and defenses and second-guessing caved in, you could waste your life trying to find one honest moment again.

Back in New York, I'd walked away from Reina. But it'd been too soon. Way too soon. But that didn't make it inevitable. I needed to find some distance. But not too much. I needed to stop and think. To just stop. I finished my drink, waved a wobbly goodbye to nobody, and walked out of the bar.

I walked toward downtown, past the white Civic Center and the white town hall. I entered a boxy building and crossed an air-conditioned concourse. I came onto the Third Street promenade. A few places on the promenade were still open. I drifted into a vintage clothing store. I stared into a glass case of Goth jewelry, smoked crystal skulls, and iron crosses.

I went into a big Mexican restaurant, sat down, and had two tequilas.

I found myself standing in a bookstore, holding a brand-new, red Webster's dictionary. I flipped to the OA page.

Annie Oakley. To my astonishment, there was my father's photograph of Annie Oakley. From 1877, taken in Cincinnati when she'd been with Finn. My father must have finally capitulated to one of those feminist historical societies. They'd been clamoring for years for him to donate the photo. It was the earliest of her in existence.

Under the photo, the dictionary listed her birthplace.

North Star, Ohio.

Finn, I suddenly remembered, had torn down the North Star cabin where she'd been born. One of his big, early road contracts was from Cincinnati up to Lake Erie. A vital road, the Dutch and German farmers relied on it to transport their produce up to the lake barges and on to Chicago. At North Star, the dirt road, amazingly, had turned to wood. Oak and maple beams sturdily corduroyed for miles north through the swamps of Cranberry Prairie. Finn had ripped up the rare old wooden road, and laid down a new wide road of pressed gravel dust. Annie's North Star cabin was right on the road. It was the 1880s and Annie was world-famous by then, but Finn tore her cabin down without a moment's pause.

Finn had started out with ballast. Broken, jagged gravel. His eyes were so hard in 1877. But sixty some years later, with his hard rapping cane and desperate ideas about vertical harbors, he'd ended up in a North Carolina rest home, putting his faith in creased napkin blueprints of piers shooting out causeways, carrying trains across the bay to glass arenas. And as a moldy, mediocre Sea World rose up on the avocado grove north of Miami, his eyes had taken on a soft, caramel sadness. Only at the end did they mellow, like rye into bourbon.

Looking at Annie's eyes in the dictionary, I had a startling feeling. It was as if I'd rummaged through some complete stranger's desk, and found a picture of myself with different parents, with different clothes and countenance. I'd never fully comprehended the young girl in my father's photograph as Annie Oakley. I'd maintained a childlike pre-occupation with the innocent, anonymity of the girl, with her faraway gaze as if she were caught in a strange, idyllic dream between childhood and growing old.

But now, in those same eyes, I only saw incest, mistrust, and betrayal. I stared into the long-dead promise of her eyes and I understood there were no brakes left in me, but I still had this terrible instinct to run. I closed the book.

I drifted out of the store and down the increasingly deserted promenade. I floated in the burnt-sugar air. My ears were clogged and I kept my eyes down. I turned down an alley, and opened a steel service door. I walked down metal stairs. I came to a gray corridor, turned left down a low-ceilinged hall. The hall narrowed into a duct walkway. The walls were a steel mesh. I walked along pipes and socket holes. I heard a strain of music and it somehow reminded me of a soldier dying. I sat down for a while and listened, felt myself drifting off in the direction of the music, toward a light behind a distant grate, as if the music were growing louder. Through the grate I could see the back of a man sitting at a white-clothed table, a napkin tucked in at his neck. The back of his head was familiar. There was a setting: cutlery, a plate, a candle, and a bottle of wine. But it was just a single table in an empty basement, the floor painted a gummy steel color. He held up his wineglass and he was looking at me in its reflection. I opened my eyes. I was sitting on the wide metal service steps, leaning against the whitewashed wall. The white blazed under the florescence. Rust from red spigot handles dripped down in craggy streams. There was a strong smell of paint and chemicals. My back ached. My mouth was dry. I had been sitting there for a long time. I stood up, leaned against the wall, and got my breath. Hollow sounds rung out from somewhere down the steps, and there was the faint layering of noise from machines. I walked back up the steps and out of the building.

I sat down on one of the promenade benches. Helen was always quiet, moved without noise. She spoke little and when she did, carefully. I'd been following her all my adult life. I'd come to a stop behind her as she disappeared into a house. I'd stood outside. Nothing had happened. No lights came on, and there was no movement or noise. The stillness and dark inside was unchanged. But there was something teasing about the windows—as if the windows, darker than the house itself, vibrated with a soft, drawing melody.

I sat with my head in my hands on the promenade bench. Tears rolled down my cheeks and I did not know exactly why. Missing, probably, what was there and is now gone. The way children cry when something is there and then they see it's gone. They are crying because they expect it to return. The feeling is the premonition of loss, not of loss itself.

And it is a child's feeling of displacement. Things suddenly disappearing all the time and what does that mean for me? I wiped my eyes with my shirtsleeves. There were fancy stores around, and it did not seem an appropriate place to cry.

The last time Helen was really with me, we were on a North Carolina beach. The beach had still been crowded, and we'd laid our towels down close to the water where it was cooler and where there weren't so many people. Helen took off her hat and sundress and sandals. I watched her slip into the water. She swam assured and slow, all but submerged except for a swan neck of an arm looping down and disappearing as the other arm rose.

We lay quietly for a while, but neither of us could relax on a beach for too long. I stood, looked around, and then down at Helen in her black bathing suit. Her blonde hair was pulled back and shiny with conditioner.

"When did we last sleep together?" I asked.

She looked up at me, shielding her eyes with her hand. She answered without embarrassment, a medicated distance in her voice.

"Did it feel good?" I asked.

"No."

"Did it feel right?"

"I don't know," she said. "No."

She closed her eyes. Sunlight and shadows reeled across her body. She opened her eyes and in the sun, black trails slicked out the corners of her eyelids. Her eyes were like a burnt-out fire, busted black along the rims. Nothing would settle on her, not even sunlight. Deep under the medications, I realized, she was still wobbling inside with a broken-legged, antique sadness.

I looked past her, down the beach. It was getting late in the day and there were fruit peels and trash on the brown sand where a family had been. Nearby, two fat men sat on canvas chairs, legs spread, and their Speedo-bound crotches open to the ocean. Everybody on the beach had the sadness, her kind was just more devouring.

I stood and slowly began to get our things together. The beach had made me so tired, and I stopped for a moment and stared out at the deadening tarp of gray sea. The tide rolled up at my feet and retreated, leaving an arc of dirty foam on the wet sand.

A few hours later, Helen overdosed in the shower stall of our beachfront motel. After a night coming in and out of consciousness between the starched sheets of the Wrightsville Beach emergency ward, there was still sand on her ankles and feet.

In the morning, I walked back to Main Street and had breakfast.

I walked around town.

I went back to my motel room. I called Leonard, and without explaining my no-show the night before, left a message I'd be out there around six. I lay down. I'd barely slept, and could not sleep. I lay awake for hours with the blinds closed, until I grew too uneasy to stave off having the first drink.

I went to the Galley around four. I ordered a Jim Beam and asked for a pen.

Reina,
On the street in New York,
I was talking to you one way,
and thinking about you another . . .

My glass was empty. With the one drink in me I felt a hollow, scary vacancy. I was waiting to do this one last thing, and then I had nothing to do. I ordered another. Drank it down. With the second drink down, I felt all right for a few minutes, did not feel disappointment. The old guy next to me drank gin and orange juice and twitched like a curtain. He kept glancing at me with this look, as if to make sure I didn't say anything to him.

I told him I had nothing to say to him. I did not realize I'd actually said it out loud until I was done and there was silence and he was looking at me.

I turned the other way. I was beginning to sweat. My arms hurt, my veins compressing with a hard, unpleasant pressure. I needed to take it easy, to switch to beer, to walk. I had one thing left to do and then nowhere to go. Nowhere I wanted to go.

Then again, I could *not* do the last thing, and I would have somewhere to go. A job here at least—Leonard was offering that much. Since I'd landed, I had a strange, stalling ambivalence about confronting Leonard. Not out of fear, but because it would mark an end to so many things. And what I'd decided about Leonard, more and more, felt like nothing. What had Leonard done, exactly?

I asked myself this, but I did not have the patience to sift through the answers.

I had one more drink. Drank it quickly, and I finally felt a gliding sensation and in the glide was a renewal of anger and purpose. It was past five o'clock. Before I paid and got up to leave, I crumpled up the note to Reina and threw it in the trash behind the bar.

I walked back to my motel room.

I lay down. The sun was melting into the sea and the white ash of dusk filled out the air. Instances of dreams came, moments of strange clarity in a jumbled alcoholic slumber. Explosions. A charge. A man spitting out the dust to loutish applause.

I was circling in a plane, in a holding pattern. A car was circling below, in a holding pattern, coming for me. There was a series of soft pings and then an announcement. Clouds gave way to an endless field of densely chipped light. The plane righted itself, and as the wings smoothed over the lights of the city, the world leveled itself off for our landing.

The car slowly turned, coming back around to meet me.

There were eyes close to mine. Lashes flickering. Opening.

An upset woman at the curb, her red dress soaked with rain and hitched up at the thigh.

The sound of car tires on gravel.

A red brick building in the sun, and with the red bricks came fear. The fear settled in the back of my throat with a clogging residue.

I sat bolt upright. I could not remember the dream.

I lay back down in the sticky sheets, drifted back into a nervous, light sleep. Engine sounds, like water boiling into screeching tires, came from outside. From between the cracked, sliding doors a green, phosphorescent warmth rose off the stalks and palm fronds splayed like dug-out canoes beneath the concrete patio. The air in the room felt compressed with thick heat. Again and again my throat went dry and I gulped, struggled with myself in the tight net of a hangover. My insides felt like metal hangers rattling, metal hangers unraveling and twisting down my arms. The pressure in my veins was getting unbearable. Alcohol worming itself out of me.

I sat up.

The moon is down. The sun is wheeling freely. I am not sleeping right.

I could not bring myself to remember things the way things were actually happening. I simply could not face it.

The engines resumed their noise. The curtains swayed and moonlight fell in like old, stacked papers. I pulled the pillow tight over my head. I thought of cleaner landscapes: a field of snow, stark gray trees, a few poisonous red berries.

Of driving with my father under the Colorado sun. Bare brown hills, clumps of white birch, and the shallow Gunnison flecked with light. The day stretching out like caramel, and it is like driving around in someone else's dream.

I had a sense of something lost around the memory greater than the memory itself.

Cool alleys between the neat, red brick town houses of Georgetown, the shiny, cobblestone streets and Will's youthful, unerring decisiveness.

Will rowing a single scull at a reservoir in England. Digging the oars, gritting his teeth. All the solitary work he'd put into that moment. His scrappy, staccato groans echoing over the water with each pull, like an engine not quite turning over as he broke the line first.

And then I felt a strange movement, a lightness of body, a cleanness of feeling and a narrowing of purpose. My life was—untranslatable to all others—still mine to deal with. And lightness and hope were still just symptoms of a hang-over I'd kill soon enough with some beer.

There was a beeping, a truck reversing, and then the phone began to ring and between the rings, the noise of engines echoed in my head.

The phone was ringing.

I opened my eyes. It was a black receiver and seemed to try to jar itself loose as it rang.

I picked it up.

It was Leonard.

"Where the fuck are you?"

"Oh," I said. "No."

Leonard saw me right when I came into the house. He rushed up, took me by the arm, and hustled me straight through the party and out the back door. "It's almost *nine*," he said. "You said six. I have a plane to catch."

He took a quick look back through the glass doors. He glanced at his watch, and then up at me. "You look like shit," he said.

The ocean spread out flat and dull in front of me, and the air smelled like seaweed. I was thinking hard about what to say, but bleariness had settled over me, and I could not speak.

He led me down steps, around a fence, and along a sea wall to the black glass beach house next door. He took another look around, and then we ducked into a narrow, dark alley along the house. He crouched down between the stilts and told me to follow him. We crawled underneath the house on soft, cool sand. We came up through a hole in the floor and stood up in a closet. He opened the closet door and we stepped into a bedroom. He flicked on the light. I looked around. We'd come up into what looked like a teenager's room. The room was windowless except for a skylight.

He went into the bathroom. He turned to me, held up a tiny Ziploc bag of white powder. He gave it a little shake. "Speed, Hay. California turnaround and the only thing that is gonna get you back to Santa Monica."

He turned and shook most of the speed onto the counter. "These people are long gone for the season," Leonard said as he divided the powder into lines. "Back to Hamburg or wherever the fuck. Their kid, he was always sneaking in and out this way. I could see him from the kitchen. A real dipshit metalhead."

He pulled up with a snort. He glanced back at me with a grin. He shook his head, "Jesus, Hay, I'm amazed you made it out here."

"Well, to tell you the truth, I stopped for beer. And then I don't remember much of the drive."

He gave me a bump on the edge of his Fred Segal card.

I felt a sudden brightness behind my eyes and forehead. I felt, for an instant, grateful.

We did a few lines. He pinched the top of the bag shut, and tucked it into his coat pocket. He unwrapped a pack of cigarettes, shook one out. He looked around. "Fuck, better wait."

He looked at me. "Oh, okay, look, I have two people for you. I'm leaving in an hour, so here."

He handed me two opalescent cards with production logos.

"There are gigs for you at either of those places. Fairly low level. Call them, talk to them, and see what you think." He grinned. "Both are mobile—one's nature, one's reality."

He did a last line, jerked his head up, and looked around.

I stared at him. I was at all different speeds inside and couldn't say what I was thinking. I held the cards in my hand.

"Isn't that what you wanted to talk to me about?" He brushed the counter with his hand without looking up. "Oh fuck, the service. This new project's been a clusterfuck. The French, you know?" He glanced up at me. "I know, Hay, I hardly knew the guy but I probably should have come. But I couldn't. I've been back and forth so many times—do you know how far Paris is from Los Angeles?"

He shook his head. "Anyway, I sent flowers."

He stepped around me.

"Leonard," I said.

He crossed the room to the closet, pulled up the hatch. "No time now. Can't smoke in here. Gotta have a smoke and gotta get back over. I'm juggling, you know?"

I came up behind him and put a hand on his shoulder. "It's about Will."

He turned back to me, "Not now."

"What did you give Will?" I asked.

He looked surprised.

I stared at him. "I found, you know, a bag. It was in the pocket of one of the shirts he had out here. But it wasn't speed."

"Give Will?" His eyes narrowed and he stepped up into the space between us.

"What did you give him?" I said. "Before I took him to the airport? Before he went in?"

"Jesus, Hay? You're serious." He arched his eyebrows. "Not now, all right? I can't talk about this now. My bags are packed and the finance people are over there."

"When, then?"

"I really don't have time. I thought you wanted a job. I'm trying to help you out here . . ."

"When!" I cut him off. He was suddenly being elusive, and I surprised myself by yelling.

He put up his hands. "All right Hay," he said sharply. "But not here."

I did not want to wait—his defensiveness had made me even more suspicious. But my head was so light with the speed, I had no gravity.

"Where?" I said.

"Where are you again?"

"Santa Monica."

He looked at his watch. "That's on the way, I guess. Ivy, by the shore? If you leave now, I'll be a half an hour behind you. But just a drink, I have a red-eye."

I nodded.

We crawled back out.

We stood up in the narrow alley between the houses. We could hear the party. "Those people," he said, brushing the sand off his knees and reaching over and brushing the sand off mine, "they have a wholesome vibe." He touched a finger to his nose. "They don't like me doing that."

He felt around in his pockets for his cigarettes.

I drove back down the Pacific Coast Highway. I drove up and down Ocean Boulevard, back and forth by the Ivy. I eventually parked along the green ledge of park, sat in the car drinking beer and watching the bums camped along the benches, camped on the lawn along the adult recreation center, tucked away in rotting sleeping bags, brown and crusted by sea spray. My knee bounced up and down and I spun the radio dial ceaselessly through snatches of songs and echo-laden voices. At some point, I turned and looked across the street.

Leonard stood in front of the restaurant. He wore a red shirt and glanced impatiently at his watch. Bad air suddenly corkscrewed up through me, a hothouse anger dormant for so long, rusting my insides with indifference just like those wretched whiskey bums sleeping there. I turned the key, U-turned, pulled up in front of the restaurant, the air in my throat blooming up, as the valet opened the car door. I stepped out swept up in a dreamy, chilly furor.

I was yelling.

I don't know what I was yelling but I was moving fast, as if already determined by a momentum out of the past rather than any way I could have acted. Leonard was backing up. He wore his moccasins and his red shirt was strewn with mermaids. His hands were out and he was hunched slightly, his lips pursed, and his face dumbfounded.

And then I could hear myself again. "You are a liar," I was yelling. "A liar."

We were in a blue-tiled, pink-walled entrance way. Potted plants lined the walls and an ocean breeze swept through the shadows. I stood up close to him, my hands up. But I did not hit him. I could see he thought I was going to, and he'd backed up against the glass doors of the restaurant.

When he felt the door behind him, he evened his shoulders, regained his composure, and finally spoke. "What the fuck, Hay, is all this about?"

"What happened? What did you do?"

"What did I do? I didn't do anything. What the fuck is the matter with you? I'm here at ten the fuck for what the fuck ever. I'm here because I'm wondering how you are, because you don't seem so good."

"What did you give to him?"

"Jesus, Hay. Easy buddy. I heard what happened. I was in France."

"On the flight back, he had heroin in his shirt pocket . . ."

"I thought it was a car accident."

"C'mon, Leonard. You set him up with that stuff. I mean, why do you think he was in the car?"

He took a step forward. "Easy, Hay. You should be careful . . ."

He took a deep breath. He seemed to shake off something. "Look, I didn't *give* him anything." He looked at me with unflinching eyes. "When you came and got him from the Wilshire, that guy, that friend of yours, had just left. That musician kid. He'd been around for days. We were getting it from him."

I stared at him. "Wait . . ."

"That's why Will went with you so easily. His source was gone. He only had what he took from me to get back east on."

"What guy?"

"You know him. They were talking about you, so fuck off."

"There was no other guy," I said. But I'd lowered my voice. I remembered the guitar pick on the television.

He shook his head. "You know, this whole deal, coming at me like this . . ."

"Wait," I interrupted, "what did Will take from you?"

"I don't know."

"What, exactly?"

"From me? Not much. A little bit of this, a little bit of that," he said.

"What, exactly?"

"Couple bags of heroin, couple pills."

"That's all?"

"Yes. Look, Hay, after you two left, when I found what was missing, I called and told him to throw it out. That stuff, anyway, I repeat, was brought to us by your friend. Will was a big boy. He knew he needed to straighten up and get back to work. I called him, I *told* him to throw it out."

"When did you talk to him?"

"Well, it was on the machine, you know. I left it on the machine, in a kind of veiled way."

"The machine? Wait, when I called you from the airport with Will, why didn't you tell me he had it?"

He looked confused for a second. "I'll tell you Hay, it just didn't cross my mind."

"You never called him," I said.

He rubbed the side of his face with his palm. "But it wasn't anything. C'mon, two bags. That's nothing."

"You didn't go there? You didn't bring him anything?"

He took a step forward. "Now why the fuck would I do that?"

He looked at me, his eyes angry. "I didn't give him *anything*. And he didn't take enough with him to do any harm. He probably got it there. The guy that met him had it. You should find *that guy*."

"*You* got him going back on it."

"Fuck you." He tried to step around me. "I have a flight."

I stayed in front of him, poked a finger into his chest. "Don't you even understand what you did?"

He grabbed my finger. "What I did? *Your* friend," he said, "died alone."

I swung at him but my feet slipped and it was a windmill shot landing on his back as he ducked. I fell forward with the momentum. He lunged at my waist, pushed me back against the pink wall. The stucco ridges cut into my back. I got my feet, grabbed his shirt at the shoulders, and we wobbled back and forth. We fell over. I got up on him, and with a knee over his shoulder, pinned his arm down. I hit him in the face. An electric jolt shot down my arm. My fist felt broken, throbbed listlessly as I dropped my arm. His legs thrashed but he lay dazed and slow moving. I stood and I began to kick him. In the stomach, in the chest. Gritting my teeth and kicking as hard as I could. He was soft, and I kicked harder and harder. His arms flayed out. Moaning, he finally managed to get an arm around both my legs. He began to pull me down. I kicked free of his arms, turned, and ran out of the red alley.

The valet stood in his green vest, open mouthed, the car door still open.

I jumped in the car. I zoomed out onto Ocean Boulevard. My eyes rose to the lights of the houses in the dark hills ahead. They were like the stars in the sky. I looked up into their promise. Fake stars, fixed on me. I had it all wrong. I was all turned around, going the wrong way. I swung the wheel.

Approaching lights came on huge and blinding and in an instant, caved in on me.

I stood in the low, skittering neon of the avenue, blood dripping down my face in the warm air. I felt eyes on me from the Ivy, from the porch of the Georgian Hotel, and the blinding headlights of every oncoming car was a new interrogation. A green car was jammed up against mine. The driver-side door was open and I could see a silent profile of a man sitting there, his head in his hands and blood on his shoes. It was like a still life, a still life with car crash.

I turned and walked trancelike into the narrow park overlooking the Pacific. I crossed the lawn, the turf springy under my feet. I could sense the shadows of men lying on the grass, at the base of royal palm trunks thick as elephant feet.

I came to a concrete fence. Coconut palms curved away like kites toward the night sky. A cliff dropped at a sharp angle down to the highway. I heard sirens. I climbed the fence, looked down the gully. Orange peels and pieces of Styrofoam were scattered at the lip. To my left was a canon, and past the canon an arched concrete overpass. I heard voices behind me, shouts.

I turned. Beams of light caught the white, peeling trunks of the cedar trees.

I eased down the steep, eroded slope. Directly across the highway stood a gingerbread-brown beach house, still lit up with Christmas lights. At the bottom, cars flew by. I began to slide, grabbing for roots and rocks as dried-out palm fronds, newspapers, cans, purple flowers, and a shopping basket shifted and began to tumble by. My shoes dug hard against the drop and I began sliding faster, hands grasping for a hold.

I lost my feet.

I reached out desperately but could not find anything grounded. I slipped and half-rolled down the weedy, trashed slope. I gained momentum and in the moment I lost control, I thought, there are only days and nights, and then last days and last nights, and if you have been thrown through the glass and lay hurt, the headlights coming are angels on light coming to pick you up and shoot you in. I tumbled head over heels. I scraped and clawed the earth to slow myself down, did a half spin off a rooted shrub and my forehead hit rock. There was a loud crack, a hollow ringing silence where my jaw went numb. Everything went black.

19

I walked straight down the beach. It was a bright, wind-less afternoon, the sea as calmly rippled as the back of a shell. I did not look back at the house, and had no idea if anybody had seen me.

I ducked under the fence, came out of the colony.

I crossed the wood bridges of the marsh, the parking lot, and turned and walked between the fence and the highway toward the mall. Across the highway, on the field, was a fair of some sort. It looked crowded, and instead of continuing on to the mall, I stopped at the light and crossed the highway.

I walked around in the dusty, subdued buzz of the carnival. I bought a Coke and a hot dog, bought tokens. I asked the token clerk what day it was.

"Friday," she said.

I watched kids shoot squirt guns and lean determinedly over spin art. One of the booths had pellet pistols mounted onto a wooden counter. I gave the guy a token and took up one of the guns. The pellets were attached by fishing line so they would just reach the target and nothing else. There was absolutely no chance of an accidental thrill, the whole point of it when you are a kid. But this was the way the world was narrowing.

I missed four out of five.

The guy behind the booth barely gave me a look. "Try again?"

"Sure," I nodded.

I jammed the pistol into its makeshift holster, dug in my pocket for tokens, and looked back up at the targets. I never believed much in signs. But the more you look around, the better. Particularly as you grow older and look at the mistakes you've made, look at the signs around the mistakes versus the signs around the things working out. When Custer rode out to explore the Black Hills for the first time, a brass band on white horses accompanied them. They rode out across valleys of flowers—fields thick with wildflowers so strange and fragrant, the whole of both columns, cavalry men down to mule skinners, threaded their hats, bridles, and the manes of their horses with bouquets.

When Custer set off to the Black Hills for the last time, for Sitting Bull, it hailed.

I gave the guy token after token, shot until I finally hit five out of five. He offered a prize from the top tier.

I looked at the toy prizes. Giant stuffed squirrels and stuffed brown trout.

I looked at him.

"Well," he said apologetically. "It's a missed shipment. I can, if you really want, reimburse your tokens."

I took the tokens, walked back to the change booth and exchanged them for quarters.

I found a pay phone in the cool, marble-floored hall of a government building. I dug the check out of the Gucci bag, loaded the phone with the quarters and dialed Reina's number in Massachusetts. The coins rushed down with a clang.

"You have one . . . and one half . . . minutes," the robot voice said.

Reina answered. "Hello."

"Hello."

"Oh. You."

"It's Hay."

"I know," she laughed. "Where are you?"

"West Coast."

"Are you all right? Where have you been all this time? I got a few calls, people are looking for you."

"I'm fine. I wanted to come and visit you."

"That'd be nice. When?"

"Well, soon," I said. "A few days, maybe. What's today?"

"Oh, today is Friday."

"No, the date?"

"I don't know offhand."

"Tomorrow. I'll be there tomorrow. Is that all right?"

I remembered the accident. "No. Wait. I need a few days. Wednesday. Is Wednesday all right?"

"I'm here. Wednesday would be fine."

And then, after finally speaking with someone after so long, I suddenly let myself understand something about Will's death. "Or wait. Sorry. I need one more day out here. Is Thursday all right?"

"Do you have a pen? I'll give you directions."

I took the bus to Santa Monica. I got a little room at a Santa Monica youth hostel. I sat around catching up on the television news with a group of young Germans in black Gore-Tex pants. They'd come to LA, they said, to buy sneakers. They'd laughed when I'd called them tennis shoes. I did too. It sounded wrong.

Saturday I walked around alone and had dinner alone in the Jade Chalet.

Sunday was a big football game. I watched the game with the Germans and a lone Japanese girl. During one commercial break, they talked about the various times they'd wound up on television. In crowds, on a dating show, interviewed for local news. They all had. I'd never been on television. I felt like a pilgrim that way.

The game was good, a thriller and a great upset. We'd all rooted for the same team. "Okay, go," the Japanese girl said at the end, jumping up as the game ended and even the Germans got excited and stiffly high-fived me.

Monday morning I sent a postcard to my father saying I was all right and would call soon. I bought jeans, three Arrow button-down shirts, a sweater, and new shoes. I threw away the teenager's high-tops and Hilfiger sweatshirt. I went to the bank, cashed the check from Will's estate, and withdrew most of the last of my money. I bought a plane ticket, stuffed three thousand into my pocket to live on for the next few months, put the remainder of the money in the Gucci bag, and went to find a lawyer.

After a few calls, I took the bus to an office in the warehouse part of Santa Monica and told the lawyer my story. He was a middle-aged white guy, balding with nervous, monkey-like eyebrows.

He asked me how much money I had. I pointed to the bag and told him.

He said it just might be enough. He outlined my options. I told him what I wanted to do.

Tuesday morning I took a bus to Encinitas. I got a cab at the station and gave the driver the address. The cab stopped at a white, prefab apartment complex. It hung on a small ridge across from the oceanfront condos. I crossed a narrow, monoxide-stained patio. The air had a push of coolness to it, of eucalyptus and raw cement. A sprinkler arced gray sheets of water onto the side of the building. The stucco on the lower wall was cracked where the water had lost its course and had pooled between the path and the wall. Mosquitoes wavered listlessly.

I knocked. I stood at the door, my shoes shaking the brown water, stirring the bits of singed, transient algae, dead semen, drunken mosquitoes, and shadows. It was a stab in the dark trying to find Kimmel here, even assuming I'd remembered the address correctly. But I had a feeling.

I could hear someone inside. The faint drone of a television.

Kimmel opened the door and looked at me with the beginnings of a smile, as if he couldn't help himself. Then his expression went blank. He had swollen up a little, his jowls like a donkey. He wore glasses and his receding hair was black and thick on the sides.

He smiled again, but in a fraction of a second the creases around his mouth tightened. He wore plaid flip-flops, gray sweatpants, and a blue sweatshirt. He'd drawn up the hood but it kept falling back.

I stepped inside and asked him for a glass of water.

He pointed to the little alley of the kitchen. In the refrigerator was a Brita. As I reached in, I noticed the lower shelves were full of cellophane packages of meat.

He saw me looking.

"I've been eating a lot of pork chops," he said, "and getting sort of fat."

Everything in the apartment, from the appliances to the lamps, was nailed down. The walls were bare and the table and counter surfaces were empty except for what was on the stand beside Kimmel's isometric leather chair: pills and herbal potions, various new-age and alternative-medicine pamphlets, teas and balms. A guitar case leaned against the closet door.

The television was still on, and he'd sat back down and was flipping between sports and religious shows. A humidifier gurgled in the corner. The blinds were drawn, and I could smell the ocean but not see it. I brought a foldout chair from the kitchen and sat down across from Kimmel. He muted the television with the remote, but he didn't ask me anything. Didn't say anything about Will. He'd always had a Bostonian, unforgiving resiliency about the past. But that was fine. I wasn't there to talk about myself. This was probably clear to him. Kimmel was no fool.

Kimmel seemed to be ailing, as if a long sickness had dulled him. It was as if he had run out of characters to assume, to invent for himself, and had simply exhaled much of his personality. I looked at the bolted-down telephone.

He asked if I wanted to go to the beach. He'd seen the way I was studying him, and I got the sense the beach offer was his general exit strategy with guests.

On the way out I noticed, touchingly, the cover of his one record was framed on the wall over the entrance. So you only noticed it going out.

At the beach, he sat in the car with the air-conditioning on, stiff and disinterested. I took off my shoes and walked to the water's edge.

I came back and sat down in the passenger seat, my sandy feet on the car frame, the door open to the beach and sea. "I knew I was mistaken about Leonard," I said immediately. "I knew that whole pursuit was irrational. But it didn't matter. I had no other answers for Will, and I had to do something."

I looked at Kimmel. "I was wrong but I stuck by being wrong," I said. "It's a modern kind of loyalty, I guess."

"That kind of loyalty," he said, "is highly acceptable these days."

"Way back in college," I said, "you guys were scoring."

Kimmel looked straight ahead.

"That's why you got kicked out. You got busted, right?"

His eyelids flitted and he looked down at himself. "Will would come down and visit and we wouldn't tell you . . . we did it a few times. They caught some dealer, but I was on the list, not Will."

"You started him on it?"

"It was a kind of test at first. Between us. We were scared of it, so . . . and then it became something else. I've always been so bored, underneath it all. It comes very natural to me. Not a lot else does. So what else should I do?"

He looked at me. "I mean, why *not*?"

"But why did you keep on doing it?"

"Well, Hay, I don't know if anyone's let you in on the little secret . . ."

"What secret?"

"The stuff's addictive." He shifted, gave me an oddly resigned look. "Look, you are making way too much of this."

"I am? Look at you now, look at your apartment."

"With Will, I mean. Or Will and me. We never did it together much. It was more like a resilient bad joke. It was really never Will's desire. He just wanted a pause once in a while. A bit of the rarefied world, like back in boarding school. But I've kept my distance with Will. I started in with him early on. Later, I kept my distance."

I looked at him. "Are you sure about that?"

"I kept my distance."

"No, you didn't. You were up in LA, at his hotel. You were doing it with him up to the very end. You were bringing it to him."

"No, that's not true."

"No, sorry you're right. You were selling it to him."

His hands hung off the rim of the wheel.

"Your guitar pick," I said, "it was on top of the television in Will's hotel room."

Kimmel shrugged with what seemed to be relief. "I was getting him down off all that speed Leonard was feeding him. Anyway, I knew you hated that stuff. Will did too."

"But neither of you ever told anyone. I knew it was something. Something was always . . . I'd always thought it was some boarding school pretension I didn't understand . . ."

Kimmel looked at me. There was maybe a kind of tenderness around his eyes. It was hard to tell.

"I thought I knew, but I only knew for sure," I said, "just now, at your apartment."

"But you have to understand, Hayward, whatever it has become for me, Will just dropped in once in a while, you know, to make things stop. He wasn't built for that sort of stuff. He had too much flying around in him, too much motion inside."

Kimmel looked down. "Youth, you know, is mostly an extremely misconceived race," he said. "You go so hard, you don't realize you have all this time at the end."

"You're still talking about Will?"

"Will took on too much. He was vulnerable, sometimes he'd just collapse inside."

"That's where you'd come in?"

"He didn't want one feeling like this." Kimmel looked around, as if what he was describing was all around us.

"You went there, to the center, and picked him up. It was you."

Kimmel grimaced.

"Fuck, Kimmel." I shook my head. "Why?"

"He asked."

We were silent for a while. The sun burned through the white commotion of waves hitting the beach.

Kimmel began to shake his head. "I *know* what those places are like," he said. "But I didn't go there, you understand. I wasn't really directly involved. Will called. And then I called a friend in Boston, and he went and picked him up. I didn't go."

"What's the difference? I mean, that's even worse."

Kimmel shrugged.

"What did your friend bring Will?"

He stared straight ahead. "What do you think?"

"You know," I said, "it's funny, because looking at you, I don't care about what it's done to you. I don't care in the least. But with Will—if it's like you say, then you should have cared too."

He looked at me. "He didn't want it."

"What do you mean?"

"There was a service entrance, a big steel door. He came out through there and then climbed the fence. He came down on the other side and got in the car and they drove off. They went to a bar. They ordered drinks and Will, you know, went to the bathroom with my friend's shoulder bag. Only Will didn't go to the bathroom. He took out the keys, dropped the bag, and walked right out the back door."

Kimmel stared through the windshield, his hands buried in his sweatshirt pockets. "But the car," he said, "it was a big old square sedan. The car didn't maneuver well, you see."

We sat there in silence.

I looked out over the ocean, then back at Kimmel. He was a deeper kind of impenetrable, his last permutation a sad-sack Brian Wilson.

The sound of the ocean loomed, and I was suddenly sick of the sounds of the ocean.

"Kimmel," I said, "there's one more thing."

He stared out the car window, across the parking lot to the sand cliffs veined with pipes and vines.

"I'm going back east to visit with Reina. It's only, you know, a few months since Will died."

He did not react.

"I don't know. Things have not been going well in my life," I said. "I was in an accident. I might have to go to fucking *jail*. And I hit my ex-boss recently. I still can feel the vibration up my arm. But maybe I need more of that sort of thing."

"Are you going to hit me?"

"No. I hit *him*. I had to hit somebody, what else could I do?"

"Because I really would prefer not to be hit."

"All I'm saying, I just need a place to go for a while. To get it together. But not alone, I can't get it together alone anymore."

"You want me to say it's all right to go and see her?" he said flatly.

"I don't know."

"And then all you know about me, and all you know about Will and me will be disposable?" He looked at me. "Is that the deal?"

Wednesday morning the lawyer picked me up at the hostel. He'd looked into my case. He told me, as we drove in his big black Mercedes to the Santa Monica police station, between the fees, the bail, and the damages, it would probably take the rest of my money.

He did all the talking. I was put in a cell, and five hours later made bail with part of the money I'd left with him.

"Six months tops," he said as we walked down the station steps, "or nothing but a fine. It depends entirely on the mercy of whoever turns out to have been in the other car."

The court date was set for a month later.

Thursday I boarded an early morning plane bound east to see Reina. I rented a car in Boston. It was a long drive

272

without many turns, and it was late when I pulled into the driveway. The porch went ablaze with lights and Reina stepped out.

I stood by the car as dogs ran in excited circles around me. I breathed in the clean, piney air, looked up at the old farmhouse. The night sky was a mailbox blue, stars everywhere, and the cold air on my skin felt wet with the chill of the moon.

I came up onto the porch. She opened the screen door for me. I put down the worn-out Gucci bag, saw the clock. It was past midnight.

"Do you want anything?"

"One drink," I said.

She brought me a large whiskey on ice and sat down across from me. It smelled like hay and cedar. I took a long sip.

She studied me. "You look tired."

"I'll tell you about it tomorrow."

"I've only known you when you are tired."

I nodded.

"Look, I'm sorry," she said. "I don't know exactly what for, but I am."

I opened my palm. "For you."

She looked at the tiny conch shell, took it in her hand.

I looked at her. I remembered going home with Helen on a rainy night, groceries in the back, on one of the first nights we'd ever been up in Maine. The car had been tight and warm, the radio low, and she'd clung to my arm.

Reina had gotten up and was stirring a pot of something on the stove.

"This is the first drink I've had in long time," I said.

"How's it taste?"

"Good." I laughed.

She'd made a big vegetable stew, and without a word, she put a cracked and yellowed china bowl of it in front of me.

I looked up at her. "Reina, there's something you should know about Will."

"Yes."

"When he took off out of that place, it wasn't about what you think. It was to see you. That was the only reason."

She lingered for a moment, looking at me.

She went to the sink, began cleaning and straightening up.

I stared down into my drink.

After a long moment, she shut off the tap, and turned back to me. "There are small things," she said, "deep in the past you've done, that even if you've forgotten about, people still love you for."

Then she turned to finish the dishes.

As I ate, I stared up at a gray cat on top of the fridge. It stared back at me with glazed, fierce eyes.

Reina was stacking plates onto a shelf. "What are you going to do now?" She asked.

"I have to go back to Los Angeles."

"Oh. For how long?"

"Maybe a while. Maybe just a few days."

"And after?"

"I don't know."

"You could rent a room here."

I looked up at her.

She did a little turn and put the kettle on. "Do you want some tea?"

"No, thanks."

"I'll make you some. It's herbal. It'll help you sleep."

"All right."

After a few minutes, she set a mug down.

I drank the tea. I began to sweat. My eyes got heavy.

"Do you want to go to sleep?" she said.

"Yes."

At the top of the stairs, I put my arms around her and tried to press her back into her room. She slid out from under me, pushed her forearms against my chest. "You are in that room."

She walked me down the hall and kissed me goodnight on the cheek. She went back to her room and shut the door behind her.

The bed was made tight, the lamplight reddish, and on the nightstand was a glass of water. There was a line of books on the shelf. Eastern and Hindu stuff, a few old cloth novels. *Emma*.

I lay back in my clothes with *Emma*. But I could not take off with that happy first paragraph. I pulled out a biography of Bruce Chatwin. On a trip to England, in the fall of our last year in college, Kimmel and I had gone up to a reservoir near Oxford to see Will row. Will had said we could ride up from London in the crew van, but then of course we weren't allowed. We'd had to get a bus and then hitchhiked in the rain. We arrived at the reservoir freezing and starving. We were standing and watching Will drag the scull off the rack and toward the dock when a little Renault pulled up with a big windsurfing board strapped to the roof. A thin, fair-haired man in a black wet suit got out and began to help Will. His eyes darted back to Kimmel and me. It was a joke that we were not helping Will, but the man could not have understood. He seemed intense and preoccupied, his blond hair blowing in all directions. They got the scull in the water. The man came back, unhitched the board, and went down to the edge of the water. He made some adjustments, plunged in, and disappeared into a speck.

It was windy and raining. Will was out in his scull warming up. The crew van was locked. The races weren't for an hour and there was no shelter. The man had left his keys in his Renault. Kimmel saw me looking, and suddenly we were in the car and I was turning on the ignition and Kimmel the heat and we were heading toward a pub we'd seen on the way in.

The police brought us back.

Will's crew coach dressed us down, and then the fair-haired man stepped forward, still in his wet suit.

Kimmel looked right at him and explained we'd taken his car because we were hungry.

He looked surprised, a smile setting off a slow cascade of wrinkles around his mouth. And then under the wrinkles I could see pockmarks. He motioned for us to follow him around to the trunk. He opened the trunk, bent over, and reached into a big canvas bag. He rummaged around, came back up with a makeshift newspaper bundle of cold chicken, radishes, a big wedge of cheese and bread.

The policemen shook their heads.

Grinning, he held the food out to Kimmel.

He shrugged off the policemen's request to press charges. "They're just kids," he said.

He fixed the Windsurfer back onto the roof, got into his car and drove off. The police took off after him as if in pursuit.

I looked at Bruce Chatwin's photo, and sure enough, there was the windsurfer. In the biography, he called it his "dismal reservoir." He'd known he was dying.

I remembered reading one of his books. I thought it was a cold, terse, somewhat baffling book. I liked the odd structure, but you felt his sentences for a pulse and they seemed to break apart in your hands. I'd once met a man at a party who had known him in London. I don't remember how Bruce Chatwin had come up, but this man had said he had a baby face and these lovely, chilling blue eyes always gleaming for the best bits of things. But for all his roaming and knowledge and success, it seemed as if he hadn't grown. Hadn't found new depth.

In the biography, a friend of his said, "He knew the mystery was there but he didn't understand it. You have to earn mystery. It's only lovers who get there."

I closed the book, undressed, and turned out the light. I didn't know anything about Bruce Chatwin.

When I woke up and looked out the window, the air looked cold and the trees aglow. I was thirsty, and drank the glass of water. The dogs were sitting on the lawn, their heads resting on their paws. The bare maples and oaks were fringed with orange light, and past the silver slope of a barn were pine-green hills, the wind orchestrating giant shadows on the hills as if pterodactyls were passing below the sun.

Sam Brumbaugh has worked in the music industry for two decades, touring with bands such as Pavement, Cat Power, and Mogwai, producing music specials for PBS, and, most recently, a documentary on the great Texas musician Townes Van Zandt. His fiction has been published in *Open City* magazine and *The Southwest Review*. A relative of Annie Oakley himself, he lives in New York City.

Author photograph by Roe Ethridge

Also available from **OPEN CITY** . . .

OPEN CITY Magazine

"An athletic balance of hipster glamour and highbrow esoterica."
—*The Village Voice*

actual air Poems by David Berman

"One of the funniest, smartest, and sweetest books of the year."
—*GQ*

Venus Drive Stories by Sam Lipsyte

"A wickedly gifted writer."
—Robert Stone

SOME HOPE A Trilogy by Edward St. Aubyn

"A masterpiece . . . fiction of a truly rare and extraordinary quality."
—Patrick McGrath

MY MISSPENT YOUTH Essays by MEGHAN DAUM

"Pretty damn irresistible."
—*Newsday*